For Sam

PROLOGUE

Somerset, England 1810

ANNA COLBROOK WATCHED FROM THE sitting room window as Mr. George Harley's carriage left Wareton Manor. The sound of the wheels crunching against the gravel drive faded along with her dreams—dreams of finally having a home of her own and a husband she might grow to love.

From the moment they'd met, Anna had been attracted to Mr. Harley's gentle smile and wry humor. Other gentlemen had quickly lost interest in her when they learned of her modest inheritance, but not him. And though they'd known each other only a few weeks, she hadn't been surprised when he'd proposed. Finally, she would have a chance at happiness. She could experience the joy of affection deepening into love.

And she could escape the despair of Wareton Manor.

But after speaking with the earl for only a few minutes, Mr. Harley had stormed out of the manor without a word.

After watching his carriage leave, Anna forced back·tears and strode into the study.

Within, Alfred Sinclair, fifth Earl of Wareton, hunched behind his enormous desk. The candles in the room were unlit, the curtains drawn, and the coal fire glowed feebly. The dim light deepened the shadows on his ashen face.

"Your Mr. Harley was most displeased with my refusal," Lord Wareton rasped. "And most surprised." His dark eyes, sunken beneath bushy gray brows, looked almost cheerful.

Anna marched to the desk. Her stomach rolled at the

stench that surrounded him: stale perspiration mixed with the sharp, alcohol scent of laudanum.

"Why did you refuse him?" she demanded, forcing herself to speak calmly.

Her mother had been the earl's daughter-in-law, his son Gerard's second wife. In the years since her mother and stepfather's deaths, the earl had rarely let a day pass without reminding Anna how much he resented her presence in his home. She had believed that he would welcome her marrying. And when he unexpectedly allowed her a season in London—at last—she had hoped he might care just a bit for her after all.

The glee in his eyes now made it clear that she'd been a fool.

"You assumed I would agree," he said, "but you should know better." The high-backed chair creaked as he leaned forward. He'd grown so stooped over the past several years that the worn spot in the wood where he'd rested his head for decades was now several inches above his bent head.

She gripped the edge of the desk. "Why?"

"Because I am old. And ill. While you have been off enjoying yourself these past weeks, I have been considering what will happen after my death." He straightened as much as his crooked back would allow. "I want you to care for your stepsister."

"You know I would never abandon Madeline! She could come live with me—"

"She is the granddaughter of an earl. She belongs here, not in some pitiful manor no bigger than my stables." He began to cough, a dry hacking that made him tremble. He still managed to choke out, "Mr. Harley's home would have been well enough for you, but not for Madeline."

Of what use was a huge manor when it was so cold and so lacking in love? Mr. Harley's home would have been the warmest home Madeline had ever known. But Anna knew better than to speak such thoughts aloud.

Instead, she forced herself to say calmly, "I am old enough to marry without your permission."

"You are." His coughing subsided, and he wiped spittle from his mouth with the sleeve of his black coat. "If you can find a gentleman who will have you now."

Her mouth went dry. "What do you mean?"

"I have settled the terms of your inheritance," he said. "Now, if you marry before your stepsister, you forfeit everything. I've also ensured that when I die, Horace or—God forbid something befalls Horace, if that wastrel Adrian should inherit—neither of my nephews can undo it."

She gripped the desk tighter, ignoring the pain in her fingers. "That was my mother's money," she said, "intended for me."

"Yes, and she gave me the care of it. We both know your inheritance is all you have to bring to a marriage. You have no rank, no great connections." He leaned back in his chair and tapped his gaunt fingers together. "So you will stay here, unless you can find a man who will marry you with nothing."

A man who would marry her with no money?

Even her mother, beautiful as she was, was married for her money. Twice.

Finding Mr. Harley, a gentleman who wanted her despite her modest dowry, was a miracle enough. But he could not likely afford to marry her with nothing. If she were forced to wait until Madeline married, she'd be at least twenty-seven—hopelessly on the shelf.

Her face grew hot. "But Madeline is only twelve—"

"It is only six years until she is out. Not likely much longer until she marries." He spoke with the same cold, bored tone he used when he ordered her to change the dinner menu or have a carriage brought round. "You have enjoyed many advantages living here, advantages far above your birth. Is it so unreasonable that you stay to care for her?"

"I shall always care for her," she said, "as long as she needs me, whether I am married or not. I only want a home of my own!"

His pale lips twitched into a horrible smile. "My dear, your home is here."

For years, she'd longed to hear those words from him. Now he had finally spoken them, but to imprison her.

Suddenly, she wanted to scream at him all the things she never dared, and to lift the heavy paperweight close to her hand and hurl it at his miserable face. Years ago, she'd given up hope of ever winning his affection. But she never thought that he despised her enough to crush all her dreams.

From the hallway behind her Anna heard sounds of arguing and the scuffing of feet on the floor.

"Anna!" a girl's voice called out. "Sophie will not let me come in—" More muffled arguing followed.

Madeline.

Fresh anger surged through Anna. If not for Madeline, she'd be free to marry—

She forced the thought away. No, Madeline was only a child. It was not her fault. Only Lord Wareton's.

And if Madeline learned what had happened, if she knew why her grandfather was forcing Anna to stay, it would break Madeline's heart. Madeline had already known far too much sorrow in her short lifetime.

And now, Madeline was all Anna had left.

Anna glared at Lord Wareton. The miserable wretch had won. And he knew it. She couldn't bear to look at him a moment longer.

She turned and strode from the study, nearly running into Madeline waiting outside the door. Madeline's black braids were mussed and one of the snowy ribbons undone. Sophie, her white cap and apron crooked, held Madeline by one arm.

"I tried to keep her away, miss," Sophie whispered.

"Why did Mr. Harley leave?" Madeline pulled free from Sophie and grasped Anna's sleeve. "Will there not be a wedding?"

"No," Anna said, "there will be no wedding."

Sophie shook her head and turned away. She stood with her back to them, her apron raised to her face.

"Why not?" Madeline frowned. "Does Grandfather not like him?"

Anna reached out and began retying the satin ribbon in Madeline's hair. Her hands trembled, and it took her two tries to make a proper bow.

"Is it because I was not friendlier when he first arrived?" Madeline lowered her gaze. "It was just... He was going to take you away and it was so sudden. But it was wrong of me. I like him, truly I do."

She is just a child, Anna reminded herself, a child who needed her desperately.

"It has nothing to do with you," Anna said.

"Do you not like Mr. Harley?"

"I do." Anna smoothed Madeline's braid. "But I will stay here with you."

Madeline frowned. "But when will you marry?"

"I do not know." Anna forced a smile. "Perhaps not until you are married first."

Sophie, her back still turned, sniffled loudly.

"Truly?" Madeline's face brightened and she threw her arms around Anna. "Then we could have a season together! I wish I were eighteen now. I wish it were not so far away."

Once again, Anna fought back tears, and she forced herself to hug Madeline back.

Soon Lord Wareton would be gone. No matter how old she was, no matter how difficult he'd made it for her, Anna vowed that one day she would marry.

The miserable old wretch wouldn't win in the end.

CHAPTER ONE

Somerset, England 1816

ADRIAN SINCLAIR, SEVENTH EARL OF Wareton, had enjoyed more pleasant meals while camped in a muddy battlefield with rain battering his leaky tent and a bayonet wound throbbing in his side. The bread had been stale and the cheese moldy, but at least the company had been warm. Here at Wareton Manor, it was quite the opposite.

He savored a mouthful of exceptionally good red wine as he looked across the linen-draped table.

"Improvements?" Miss Anna Colbrook lowered her fork to her plate, a bite of roasted pheasant untouched on the end. "What do you mean?" It was the most she'd said to him since his arrival that afternoon.

"The design of the orchards is outdated," he said, setting down his wineglass, "and while the grounds are well kept, some areas need enhancements."

"Enhancements?" She frowned at him as if he were saying something impossible. Was that to be the extent of her conversation, to repeat everything he said back to him?

"How do you find your dinner, Lord Wareton?" Madeline said quickly.

Adrian turned his gaze to his cousin. At least she was friendly. He'd been worried about meeting his new ward, but he was relieved to discover she was sweet-tempered and diplomatic—nothing at all like her stepsister.

"Everything is delicious," he said. As he enjoyed a bite of pheasant, he was forced to admit that the food was far

better than at his home at Eastgate. Even so, he looked
around the table at the members of his new household and
wished he were back at Eastgate, lounging in his study with
a good book and a mediocre dinner in peaceful solitude.

He hadn't lived with a female since he was orphaned
at thirteen. His sister, Cecelia, had been put in the care
of their aunt, while he and his brother, Edmund, had
gone to live with an elderly uncle. Boarding school and
a bachelor's existence in London had taken up much of
his life before the military, and since returning home, he'd
lived alone except for the intermittent company of his
brother. Suddenly, along with unexpectedly inheriting an
earldom, he was the head of a household of four female
relations. A disorienting situation to say the least.

"Adrian," his aunt, Lady Carlton, said, "your sister, cousin,
and her stepsister require new wardrobes."

"Of course," he said.

"We must get started immediately," Lady Carlton said.

"Whatever you wish," he said. He was depending on his
aunt to manage such matters.

"I shall have new ball gowns made," his sister Cecelia said,
smiling across the table at Madeline. "One in burgundy
with satin—"

"Burgundy?" Lady Carlton said from beside Cecelia. "I
think not."

"But why?" Cecelia's pale blue eyes narrowed, and she
fidgeted with her fork.

"You are only nineteen," Lady Carlton said. "You will
look like a jezebel."

Adrian sighed. Cecelia and Lady Carlton had grown so
alike that they now looked more like daughter and mother
than niece and aunt. They had always resembled each other
in their fair coloring, but now they also shared mannerisms.
When annoyed, Cecelia mimicked his aunt's hair toss, the
arrogant tilting of her head that practically pointed her
nose to the ceiling, and even the way her nostrils flared

when she felt truly put out. She hadn't yet developed Lady Carlton's terrifying scowl—Cecelia still pouted petulantly instead—but he feared it was only a matter of time.

Poor Cecelia. He blamed himself as much as his aunt. After observing his sister and Lady Carlton together for the past few days on the journey to Wareton, it had become clear that leaving Cecelia in their aunt's care for so long had been a mistake. An enormous mistake.

Yet another failure to add to the horribly long list he'd accumulated during years wasted in selfish indulgence.

But no more. All that would—had already—changed. He was an earl now, and he had great responsibilities that he had every intention of living up to.

He would see the estate prosper. And fulfill his family duty by seeing Cecelia, Madeline—and even Miss Colbrook, if he could—married off. As soon as possible. He would then be able to manage his new estate without distraction.

His aunt inspected Madeline and Miss Colbrook from across the table. Madeline glanced at Lady Carlton nervously, but Miss Colbrook ignored her and continued to eat.

"You, Miss Colbrook," Lady Carlton said, "need the most improvement. To begin with, we must lower your necklines. I will select new styles—"

"Thank you, but I can choose my own gowns," Miss Colbrook said.

Lady Carlton frowned. "Nonsense. You need my help. Far more than the others." She eyed Miss Colbrook's gown critically. In his aunt's view, anything but the latest fashions and one might as well be wearing sackcloth.

The offending gown was plain, high-necked, and a pale blue—several years out of fashion but still quite acceptable. It was the type of gown a woman wore when she didn't wish to draw attention to herself, neither too shabby nor too stylish. Miss Colbrook's chestnut-red hair was likewise pulled back into a simple, unadorned knot, except for a few loose strands that she was constantly tucking behind her ears.

But the simplicity of her dress did nothing to disguise her beauty. Indeed, if she had been wearing sackcloth, he'd still know she had a stunning figure. He recalled her curves quite well from her time in London years earlier. Likely because her appearance was usually the only pleasant thing about her.

"Miss Colbrook," Lady Carlton said, "I must insist. We must improve your wardrobe if we are to find you a husband. Do you not agree, Adrian?"

Four sets of female eyes looked to him.

He glanced from his aunt's stern face to Miss Colbrook's even graver one and quickly took an enormous bite of herbed potatoes. He chewed slowly, shrugging noncommittally. As he'd hoped, his aunt continued

"I shall brook no refusal," Lady Carlton said, turning back to Miss Colbrook. "You must allow me to help you."

"You are too kind," Miss Colbrook said, "but surely your efforts would be better spent on Madeline and Miss Cecelia."

"Adrian," Lady Carlton said, "do you not agree that Miss Colbrook needs my guidance?" Unfortunately, this time his aunt waited for him to finish his bite of food.

"Not if she does not want it," he said.

Miss Colbrook's eyes widened, as if she'd not expected him to defend her. Madeline and Cecelia stopped eating, both watching the exchange with great interest.

"She is of an age that she can make her own decisions," he added.

A sudden pain shot through his temple, likely the beginning of another headache. He'd never suffered from headaches until a few days ago. He was weary from traveling and had no wish to be caught in the middle of their argument. Miss Colbrook's appearance was certainly not the reason she remained unmarried. More likely it was her icy personality.

"Miss Colbrook," Cecelia said softly, "I think your dress is quite lovely. The color suits—"

"Do not lie, Cecelia." Lady Carlton said, scowling. "And stop fidgeting like a child. Your manners this evening are disgraceful. I can only imagine what your cousins think."

"Surely, none of us could claim perfection," Madeline said, forcing a smile.

Lady Carlton sniffed. "I am always most exacting about such matters."

"Of course, Lady Carlton," Miss Colbrook said, "some of us come far closer to perfection in manners than others."

"Indeed." Lady Carlton nodded curtly, clearly taking her words as a compliment. Adrian had no doubt that Miss Colbrook meant quite the opposite. Foxed as he'd often been when he'd encountered Miss Colbrook in the past, he could still clearly recall many of her put-downs.

Miss Colbrook met his stare. "Lord Wareton," she said, "will you be replacing any of the staff?"

In contrast to her sharp gaze, her voice was soft, with a hint of huskiness he might find pleasing—if she would only say something pleasant.

"I cannot be certain until I've had a chance to look over the entire estate," he said, "but if everything is as well run as the kitchen, perhaps not."

She seemed relieved by his answer; the furrow in her brow disappeared.

"The past few years while the last earl remained abroad," Madeline said, "Anna was quite involved in caring for the estate."

"Indeed." He took a sip of wine and gazed at Miss Colbrook. If she had been helping his cousin Horace manage things from overseas, that could account for some of her behavior since his arrival. Her dislike of him likely explained the rest.

"Anna," Madeline said, "perhaps you should accompany

Lord Wareton when he tours the estate tomorrow?"

"Mr. Evans will be here," Miss Colbrook said, frowning. "He is planning on escorting Lord Wareton."

"But you know the manor as well as Mr. Evans," Madeline said.

"I am certain that Lord Wareton would prefer the steward's company." Miss Colbrook gave her stepsister a hard look. Everyone else at the table watched him, waiting for his response. He wasn't eager to spend much time with her, but if she'd been involved in managing the estate for his cousin, it made sense for her to go with him.

"I can meet with the steward at another time," he said. "I would be pleased if you would accompany me, Miss Colbrook."

Her full mouth thinned into a familiar frown. Although she'd barely known him before they encountered each other in London six years ago, from the start she'd seemed offended by his reputation alone and had treated him with a chilly reserve. If he hadn't deserved her contempt at first, he'd soon earned it with his rudeness. While he'd offended many people during his years in London, she'd been especially satisfying to unnerve. He suspected now it was partly because he found her gaze particularly piercing, her blue eyes reflecting too well the truth of what a wastrel he'd been.

He didn't blame her for her past contempt. For years, he'd done his best to unnerve many attractive young women, including her. He'd looked at the world with disdain, and when he lost himself in drink or gaming or women, he'd been skilled at denying any sense of guilt or responsibility. For too long, he'd behaved without a thought for anyone else. But that was when he was a different man, before everything changed.

Well, maybe not everything.

As he gazed at Miss Colbrook, an old but familiar desire to annoy her overtook him. He couldn't resist adding,

"A ride together will allow me to tell you about all the improvements I have planned. If that is agreeable to you?"

"As you wish," she said. Her tiny gold earbobs—the only jewelry she wore—flashed in the candlelight as she dropped her gaze to her plate. She began cutting up her asparagus, allowing her knife to squeak repeatedly against the china.

"Tell me, Miss Colbrook," Lady Carlton said later that evening, "is it true you've received no offers of marriage these past six years?"

The sitting room was suddenly so quiet that Anna could hear the fire hiss in the hearth behind her. On the sofa across from her, Cecelia and Madeline turned towards Lady Carlton. Madeline's mouth had fallen open in shock. Even Cecelia looked embarrassed. And Lord Wareton at least had the decency to cringe. The chair he sat in on the opposite side of the hearth—Anna's favorite chair— creaked as he leaned back, closed his eyes, and began rubbing his temples.

He looked as if he wished he were anywhere else. One thing they could agree on, Anna thought.

She folded her hands in her lap and forced what she hoped was a serene smile. Meanwhile she silently wished the ground would open and swallow the new arrivals to Wareton Manor, leaving her and Madeline in peace.

Well, maybe not Cecelia. The earl's sister might be quite tolerable away from her overbearing aunt. And Lord Wareton, unpleasant as some of his comments at dinner had been, was still vastly improved from years before. He was sober anyway.

He certainly looked healthier. He'd always been handsome, but now there was no hint of dissipation in him. His hazel eyes were unclouded by drink. His legs were more muscular than she recalled, and his shoulders broader.

Not that she cared one bit about his impressive physique. Other than her fear that after a few more evenings, his large frame might break her favorite chair.

"Do not look so shocked," Lady Carlton said, glancing around. "I only raise the most important issue, one that is on everyone's mind." She returned her gaze to Anna. "After all, you are the one we shall likely have the most trouble finding a husband for." Lady Carlton pointed an embroidery needle in Anna's direction. "You lack the direct connections or fortune of Cecelia and Madeline. And your age presents a challenge. However, I was married for the second time at your age, and I refuse to give up on anyone, no matter how old."

"You are too kind," Anna said, unable to keep her tone even.

It was their first night at the manor. She must try to be polite, no matter how much she had been dreading the new earl's arrival, and no matter how rude his aunt was. And she knew the topic of marriage would be unavoidable. Which was fine, so long as no one pried too much.

"Who was the gentleman who offered for you?" Lady Carlton asked.

"Mr. George Harley," Anna said.

"Yes, I recall now," Lady Carlton said. "I heard you turned him down."

Anna said nothing. Let her believe that. She'd allowed so many people to believe it for so long, she'd almost convinced herself. The truth would have been far too painful for Madeline as a child. Perhaps now that Madeline was old enough to not necessarily blame herself, Anna would finally tell her stepsister what had really happened. But not yet. And certainly not here, in front of people who were practically strangers.

"And is it true your parents left you only four thousand pounds?" Lady Carlton asked.

"Yes," Anna said.

"A modest sum," Lady Carlton said, "but enough to attract a suitable gentleman for you, I would think." She pointed the needle at her again. "If you would only make it clear that you would welcome an offer, you might manage to find a suitor."

"Anna remains unmarried because she chooses to," Madeline said, "not for lack of a suitor."

Wonderful. Anna glared at Madeline, adding her stepsister to the list of people she wished the earth would swallow.

"Indeed, Miss Madeline." Lady Carlton jabbed her needle into her embroidery, leaving it there. "And what gentleman has expressed interest in your stepsister?"

"I am…" Madeline glanced at Anna and looked quickly away. "Not at liberty to say." Madeline grabbed her own needlework from the table beside her and hunched over it until her dark curls hid her eyes.

Lady Carlton leaned forward. "I shall learn soon enough, so you may as well tell me now—"

"I have no suitors," Anna said, "because I have made it known that I wish to remain here with Madeline until she marries."

"An older sister waiting for a younger to marry?" Lady Carlton scowled. "*Nine* years younger? Ridiculous!"

Madeline's fingers stilled on her embroidery. She lifted her head and glanced toward Anna.

Anna pushed away a familiar stab of annoyance. It was not Madeline's fault that her grandfather had been so cruel. She never wanted Madeline to feel guilty for what had happened. She met Madeline's gaze and smiled.

Madeline quickly returned the smile and resumed her needlework, her head held higher.

Anna leaned back in her chair. She met Lady Carlton's sharp gaze and smiled again. Lady Carlton's frown grew.

Horrid woman. And yet, she should still probably welcome her arrival. And Lord Wareton's.

Madeline was eighteen now, at last old enough to marry,

and Lady Carlton and Lord Wareton would help secure her future. Anna wanted more than anything to see Madeline happily settled. And once Madeline wed, Anna would finally be free to do so as well.

But she'd be damned if Lady Carlton would choose one gown for her, let alone a husband. She refused to be manipulated into marriage and to be used as a commodity like her mother was. When she married, it would be on her own terms.

The truth was, although once she'd been desperate to escape Wareton Manor, everything had changed when the old earl, Alfred Sinclair, had died.

His heir, Horace Sinclair, the sixth earl, had been in no hurry to leave his beloved home in the West Indies. Anna had boldly written to him and offered to manage things in his absence. Miraculously, he'd agreed.

So after years of being a poor relation relegated to the shadows, she had become caretaker of a vast estate. She'd immersed herself in improving Wareton, challenging herself to see how quickly and how thoroughly she could banish the dismal atmosphere that had hung over the estate for so long. She'd fallen deeply in love with Wareton, and at last it had felt like her home.

But she'd been deceiving herself.

She never truly belonged here, as the new earl's presence demonstrated. His aunt had already returned her to her proper place as a step-relation, fortunate to be permitted to live in a household so far above her birth. Undoubtedly, she should be grateful for the past few years of happiness. At the moment, she just couldn't bring herself to feel thankful.

"Now that we are living with Madeline," Lady Carlton said, "there is certainly no reason to continue to deny yourself opportunities. I shall help—"

"Lady Carlton," Anna said, rising, "it is kind of you to concern yourself with my happiness, but you must excuse me. I have a book I am eager to finish."

"Books," Lady Carlton murmured, frowning. "No wonder."

That comment snuffed out any guilt Anna felt about not remaining by the fire. She snatched a book from a nearby shelf and marched to the window seat at the far side of the room.

A person could only endure so much in one day.

Adrian envied Miss Colbrook's escape.

As his aunt began to interrogate Madeline about local bachelors, Adrian stood. He took a turn about the room, wandering from painting to painting. He only half-listened to the ladies' conversation about potential husbands, though he knew he should probably pay close attention. Marrying them off was of primary importance.

Unquestionably, Miss Colbrook would be the most difficult to find a match for. Her decision to remain with her stepsister had undoubtedly cost her any chance of marrying. In spite of his aunt's determination, Miss Colbrook would probably end up a spinster, likely living with Madeline when she married.

Yet if Miss Colbrook already had a suitor, as her stepsister implied, perhaps there was still hope. Then again, she might have little interest in the gentleman or in marrying at all. Remaining at Wareton to care for her stepsister might simply be an excuse to avoid marriage altogether.

As he neared her, he paused. "What are you reading?" he asked.

"A book." She didn't glance up, but briskly turned a page and kept reading.

She hadn't changed much. She was still an extremely irritating woman. And now she was snubbing him on his first night at his new home. After nearly a week of traveling, three days under constant barrage from Lady Carlton's prattle, and now faced with Miss Colbrook's rudeness, he found his patience was wearing thin.

He crossed his arms. "What is the title?"

"*A Guide to Game Keeping.*" She kept her eyes on the book.

"Game keeping." Leave it to her to be reading something so unconventional for a woman.

"Yes." She finally looked up from the book. "Have you not read it?"

"No."

"Ah." The look she gave him implied that she'd expected as much. "You really should read it. It is considered the best—"

"I am familiar with it." Arrogant woman. Did she believe he was that ignorant?

"Then why have you not read it?" She drew a bookmark from her lap and dropped it between the pages. She gently closed the cover and gazed up at him. "Do you not keep game at Eastgate?"

Her eyes were a lovely deep blue, and so deceptively sweet-looking.

"I do," he said, irritated at himself for noticing her eyes. "My steward has read it."

She straightened and frowned. "Ah." And there it was again, that look both disapproving and yet not surprised. "Of course."

She might have time to sit about reading every detail of estate management, even those best left to the staff, but he had more pressing matters to see to.

"Is the steward here not competent?" he asked.

Her eyes widened and then narrowed. "Mr. Evans is quite competent. I hired him myself."

"And the gamekeeper as well?"

"Of course."

"And yet you still feel that you must read this?" he asked.

She scowled. "One cannot judge competence from a

position of ignorance." She flipped the book open again.

A blatant insult now. He felt a jolt of anger that energized him; for the first time in days, he realized that he didn't feel tired and bored. Annoyed, but at least not bored.

"Indeed," he said. "But the care of the estate is no longer your concern."

She flinched, and he pushed away a twinge of guilt. He only spoke the truth, a truth she obviously needed to be reminded of. Besides, she'd been rude to him since his arrival.

She kept her eyes on the book, frowning. But she was only pretending to read; he could tell that her eyes were moving over the same lines again and again.

"I also have no need of a book on the subject," he added, "as I am quite knowledgeable from firsthand experience. But I am not surprised you require such a book, you likely have no personal experience with—"

She abruptly raised her head. "You know almost nothing about me." She dropped her gaze back to the page.

He knew one thing about her—she wasn't hampered by an overabundance of good manners. He found it both irritating and refreshing.

"Adrian!" Lady Carlton called out. "I must speak with you." He turned away, but as he crossed the room, he glanced back at Miss Colbrook.

She was right—he didn't know her at all. He had the sudden disturbing notion that he wanted to know more about her, much more. Purely to find a way to convince her to marry, of course.

The sooner she left his home, the better.

CHAPTER TWO

W HILE WAITING FOR LORD WARETON outside the stables the next morning, Anna discovered a thick smudge of chocolate on the sleeve of her riding habit. Last night it had taken her hours to fall asleep and then she'd overslept. She'd been forced to eat a hasty breakfast in her room while she dressed, which explained the chocolate. As if she weren't already mussed enough, she thought.

In addition to the stain, her left boot was noticeably scuffed, and her hair was already falling from beneath her hat. Those annoyances only added to her already dark mood, brought on by the fact that the entire household was treating Lord Wareton's arrival with as much enthusiasm as if he were the Prince Regent himself. Even Madeline seemed completely taken in by him.

"Good morning, Miss Colbrook."

She turned to see Lord Wareton emerging from the stable entrance. She nodded, unable to force a smile. "Lord Wareton."

His dark green double-breasted coat, black breeches, and striped cravat were spotless. He looked as if he never went out with one thread out of place, let alone a stained coat.

He smelled good too. As he strode past her, she inhaled the scent of his shaving soap, a clean, masculine aroma that was startlingly unfamiliar.

It had been a long time since a gentleman had resided at Wareton, and at thirty, he was far younger than any in her memory. He mounted his horse in one graceful motion. Like the previous evening, he seemed restless, as if he might easily ride all day—so different from the lazy, alcohol-influenced manner he'd possessed in the past.

Yet he wasn't completely changed. He was still rude, and his comments last night about her book had been particularly obnoxious. Perhaps she hadn't been completely well-mannered either, but he'd been worse. He'd made it clear that her help with the estate was no longer needed, yet he still expected her to accompany him today.

She mounted her chestnut mare and declined the groom's offer to accompany them. She nudged her horse onto a path that ran to the north, towards the woods and the tenant farms. The day was warm and breezy with only a scattering of puffy clouds. Yet the perfect weather only made her feel worse; she wished it were gloomy out, like her mood.

As Lord Wareton rode alongside her, looking much too pleased with his new inheritance, her mood dropped even further. As much as she'd braced herself for his arrival, his presence was affecting her even more intensely than she'd expected.

She knew she must pull herself together. But each time she glanced at him, her heart ached more.

She should at least be grateful that he was improved from the wastrel she'd encountered occasionally in London and at family funerals. Apparently, the war had changed him dramatically, and he had even been honored for bravery, though she knew little of the details. But the experience had seemingly so altered him that since his return, he'd behaved irreproachably for over a year now. Or so went the gossip.

Still, for all his improved behavior, she'd heard that his estate at Eastgate was deeply in debt. Would he manage Wareton any better? Most likely he would have little involvement in the details—his attitude towards reading about game keeping certainly suggested as much. He was probably a gentleman who would enjoy shooting but think little of the work that made it possible.

He slowed his horse and gestured towards a small hill crowned with a Grecian-style temple. "A lovely spot to construct a terrace," he said. "The view would be wonderful."

Her mother had designed the site soon after arriving at Wareton, but it had fallen into disrepair after her mother's death because the old earl had refused to pay for its maintenance. This past spring, Anna had spent several weeks repairing and updating the temple with new plants and statuary.

"You are not fond of the temple?" she asked.

"Not especially." He shrugged. "The design is outdated."

Outdated? She bit back an angrier retort and said instead, "To tear down recent improvements seems wasteful." Not that she was surprised, knowing the financial state of Eastgate.

He gave her a sharp glance. "The materials might be used elsewhere."

"I suppose." She tightened her grip on the reins and nudged her mare faster, until they were out of sight of the hill.

The estate was his now, she reminded herself, feeling even more out of sorts. He could be as impractical or foolish with his property as he wished. She only hoped that she wouldn't have to see all of her hard work undone.

Soon they reached a fork in the path and went left. The air felt cooler as they moved into the shade of an apple orchard. He slowed his horse.

"If this grove was cleared," he said, "the view from the manor to the wood would be improved." He looked closely at the trees. "And many of these are old and unhealthy. Why haven't they been removed?"

She straightened on her horse. "They have been deliberately left. They provide cover to watch for poachers." Which he might have realized, if he had read *A Guide to Game Keeping*.

He frowned, as if he could read her thoughts. "They should at least be pruned more carefully," he said stiffly. "I shall speak to the steward."

The small bit of satisfaction she felt from that exchange soon faded.

Over the next two hours, they toured the woods, fields, and many tenant properties. He questioned her relentlessly about everything from the quantity of game in the forest to the tiniest detail of haymaking.

At first, she responded to his questions easily, and he was clearly surprised at the extent of her knowledge. But to her embarrassment, after a while she couldn't answer more and more of his questions. Much of what she couldn't tell him were details that the steward or others kept track of. Other things likely no one knew, such as the year certain old tenant homes were built or what crops had been grown over a decade ago.

Clearly, she'd been wrong in believing that he left all the work to his staff and knew little of running an estate. He was extremely knowledgeable—and enthusiastic. She should be pleased, or at least relieved. Yet each question he asked irritated her more.

"When was this built?" he asked as they rode over a small stone bridge.

"I do not know," she said. "It was well before I arrived." The bridge was in good condition, so what else mattered?

He pointed beside the road. "And this stone wall?"

"I could not tell you." Again, unless it needed repairs, why should he concern himself with its age?

They rode on, his inquiries seemingly endless. As they neared the southern orchards and the small lake that marked the estate border, he finally fell silent. She breathed a sigh of relief that he seemed to have at last exhausted his questions.

But the silence was brief.

As he reined in his horse at the edge of the water he

asked, "Are there any fish in here?"

"None that I know of."

"Frogs?"

"No. There are fish and frogs in the natural lake to the west." She couldn't keep the irritation from creeping into her voice. He didn't seem to notice.

"Another question, Miss Colbrook."

No, she thought, she couldn't endure any more.

"This water," he asked, "how deep is it?"

She scowled at him. How should she know the answer to such a question? Did he think she went swimming in the lake? Or regularly ventured into it with a measuring stick?

"I do not know," she said, letting out a long sigh. "Perhaps you should ride into it and find out."

For a moment it was so quiet that she could hear the faint calling of birds at the far side of the lake. He moved nearer and reined to a halt facing her. The sun glinted off the small gold and pearl pin in his cravat as he stared at her.

"Miss Colbrook," he finally said, his voice unexpectedly soft. "It is clear from your extensive knowledge of the estate that you have done far more for Wareton than merely see the last earl's wishes implemented. You have done an excellent job managing the estate," he added, "and for that, I am most grateful."

She only stared at him, too stunned to speak. Had he not only admitted her knowledge was extensive but was also expressing his gratitude? She hadn't expected him, of all people, to be at all gracious.

"But tell me," he continued, the gentleness leaving his voice, "for how long will you punish me for the crime of inheriting Wareton? Or is it my past behavior that continues to earn your contempt?"

She suddenly felt hot, and she knew she was likely blushing. With embarrassment.

He was right. She was behaving badly and treating him

unfairly.

The truth was that part of her didn't want to see that the estate was now in good hands. She loved Wareton and wanted it to continue to prosper, truly, but knowing it would go on without her... Her chest felt tight and tears threatened, but she forced them back.

She realized her fingers hurt from clutching the reins too tightly. She relaxed her grip as she struggled to respond.

"I am sorry for any offense I caused you in the past," he added. "But it was six years ago. May we have a truce?"

"Yes," she finally managed. She knew that she should apologize as well, but she was still too shocked to say anything more.

"Good," he said. "Perhaps it would be easier if you would stop judging me by my past behavior?" His somber expression gave way to a smile. "At the least, perhaps you can find new reasons to dislike me?"

She meant to smile in response, but her words came out seriously. "No doubt I can."

He laughed—not the dry, sarcastic laugh she recalled from the past, but a deep, resonating laugh. As he gazed at her, his eyes suddenly seem disturbingly warm. "No doubt," he said, grinning.

Then something beyond her caught his eye, and his smile faded. Anna turned to see a rider moving slowly down the hill on the far side of the lake. After a few seconds the man raised his arm in greeting, and he turned his dappled gelding toward them, onto the path by the water.

"Sir Neville Kent," she said. "His estate borders Wareton. Are you acquainted with him?"

"We have met," Lord Wareton said, not meeting her gaze.

Had they? She didn't recall Sir Neville mentioning they knew each other.

"Did you know that he was knighted and granted his estate by the Prince Regent?" she said as they rode slowly towards Sir Neville. "He rescued several gentlemen who were being attacked by robbers. Though he was wounded in the leg, he still saved everyone."

"I believe all of England knows the tale," Lord Wareton said, sounding bored.

So much for his improved manners. "But did you know that two of the gentlemen he saved are from Somerset?" she said. "Lord Harwick and Mr. Roland, the old earl's solicitor."

"Indeed." He sounded no less bored; in fact, he appeared to be stifling a yawn.

They stopped their horses and waited in silence as Sir Neville approached.

"Miss Colbrook." Sir Neville halted his horse close to her and tipped his dark hat, briefly revealing the peppering of gray at his temples. He was only thirty, the same age as Lord Wareton, but he looked much older. The past year had been especially hard on him.

She smiled. "Good day, Sir Neville. I believe you are already acquainted with Lord Wareton?"

Lord Wareton inclined his head. "Sir Neville."

"It has been some time, Lord Wareton." Sir Neville's usually mild brown eyes narrowed.

"It has." Lord Wareton's tone was amiable, but his shoulders seemed to stiffen.

"Sir Neville," she said, "you never told me you were acquainted with Lord Wareton."

"Didn't I?" Sir Neville said.

"No," she said, "I am certain of it."

"It must have slipped my mind." Sir Neville's voice was clipped.

She didn't believe him for an instant. Clearly Sir Neville thought little of Lord Wareton, reformed or not.

After a few moments of awkward conversation about their estates, Sir Neville excused himself, citing a meeting with his steward.

"I shall be away the next week," Sir Neville said, "but

I look forward to seeing you at the Dunbury's ball, Miss Colbrook." A smile briefly softened his handsome face. "Lord Wareton," he added curtly, his smile vanishing.

Sir Neville turned and rode back toward his estate. Did she imagine it, or did he push his horse faster than usual?

At least she wasn't the only person who didn't believe Lord Wareton's arrival was the greatest event of the year. But why they were so cold to each other?

"Where did you first meet Sir Neville?" she asked.

"In London, I believe." Lord Wareton offered no more details and turned his horse back the way they had come.

"Where in London?" she asked, catching up to him.

"I do not recall," he said.

He remembered, he just didn't wish to tell her. Perhaps they'd met at a gaming hell or other place unsuitable to discuss with a female, although Sir Neville had a reputation for strictly avoiding anything improper. More likely, during his wild years Lord Wareton had offended Sir Neville somehow. There were few respectable people whom he hadn't offended back then.

He might not wish to tell her how he knew Sir Neville, but she would probably learn eventually. And in the meantime, she would keep talking. Tight-lipped as Lord Wareton seemed, he still might reveal something interesting.

"Were you acquainted with Sir Neville's wife?"

"No."

"He was widowed only last year," she said.

"I have heard." He kept his gaze on the path.

"Lady Mary was ill for many years. They never had children. And Sir Neville's ward, who was like a daughter to them, went to Scotland to stay with relatives. So now he is all alone."

"How unfortunate," he said, again sounding bored. Clearly, he wanted her to drop the matter.

"So it was over a year ago," she said, "that you first met him?"

He abruptly stopped his horse. "I could not say," he answered curtly. "But perhaps you would assist me with something else, Miss Colbrook." He met her gaze. "I began to look into the financial accounts last night, and I discovered a few issues that the steward could not help me with."

She tightened her grip on the reins. He'd already looked into the finances on his very first night here? Surely, he wouldn't have concerned himself with the marriage settlements so soon? No, it was unlikely such affairs would be a priority. She should still have more time, hopefully much more, before he began prying into those details.

But it was all the more reason to help him with the accounts. She might be able to steer his interest away from such matters, at least for the time being.

"I should be glad to help," she said. "When?"

"Tonight, after dinner?"

"Tonight?" She imagined them in the study going over the books together, late into the night. Alone.

She felt a strange flutter in her stomach. Hunger, she decided quickly. She'd eaten barely any breakfast.

"Unless another time would be more convenient?" he said.

She shook her head. "Tonight would be fine." She was still shocked that he had thanked her for caring for the estate, and now he had even asked for her help with the accounts. And he was an earl while she was only a step-relation, and—as his aunt had so enjoyed pointing out—the daughter of a merchant, closer in status to his servants than to him.

The gossip seemed to be true. He'd indeed changed dramatically from the man she'd known before. Why was that idea so. . .unsettling?

"Good," he said. "Also, perhaps I might ask you now about some documents that are missing—"

"Surely that can wait until later?" she said. She quickly

turned her mare towards the manor. "Should we give the horses some proper exercise on our way back?"

"Are you proposing a race?" he said from behind her.

She glanced back at him and nodded. Anything to distract him from asking too many questions. And if she were to win, it would definitely improve her mood.

A moment later, they were racing towards the manor. He passed her, fell behind, and then caught up again. He rode close to her—almost dangerously close. As she briefly met his gaze, a wicked, challenging smile lit up his rugged face.

Again, she felt the strange flutter in her stomach. Her pulse sped up even faster. Only because of the race, she quickly told herself.

She pushed her mare even harder, but she still couldn't pass him. She resisted the urge to glance at him again. Instead, she kept her sights on the manor in the distance.

No matter how improved his character, no matter how charming he was, she mustn't let down her guard. With his keen interest in finances and his aunt's desire to marry her off quickly, concealing certain matters wouldn't be easy. Yet she would find a way.

Wareton might be his estate now, but there were still some secrets she must keep from him.

CHAPTER THREE

A S THE TIME NEARED WHEN Miss Colbrook had agreed to meet him in the study, Adrian found it increasingly difficult to concentrate on his work. The financial ledgers that had engrossed him for the past two days now only made him restless. He closed up the books before him on the table, and he glanced once again at the clock. She should arrive shortly and, in the meantime, he would examine the nearby storage room. Perhaps some of the documents that he'd been unable to locate were there.

The scent of dust filled his nostrils as he opened the heavy door. Stepping inside, he raised a lamp to dispel the shadows. There were no books or documents within the small chamber, only portraits—dozens of them, leaning upright against the walls.

He shifted the lamp closer and scanned the paintings. And burst out laughing.

All the portraits of his granduncle Alfred that had once hung throughout the manor now collected dust in this storeroom. Adrian had already noticed that some portraits he recalled from years ago were gone, but he'd not realized the full extent of the changes.

Miss Colbrook's doing, no doubt.

Well, she'd saved him the trouble of ordering them removed.

He scanned the portraits again, stopping as the light fell on the largest depiction of Alfred Sinclair, one that must have been painted within the last decade of his life. The artist had captured the old man eerily well.

Adrian's smile faded. He set the lamp on the floor and

crouched before the painting. He studied the old earl's countenance—the dark eyes sunken beneath bushy brows, the pallid skin, and the perpetual scowl. The depiction was so accurate that he even felt a chill, just as he had on the few occasions when he'd been forced to interact with his late granduncle.

The old earl had never shown any interest in him, even after his son Gerard had died and Adrian became second in line to inherit the earldom. The day of Gerard's funeral was the only time Alfred ever spoke to Adrian about the possibility of inheriting. When Adrian had stammered out his condolences on Gerard's death, Alfred had stared at him in silence, his eyes full of malice. *You must be pleased,* he'd finally said, *as this puts you one step closer to becoming earl.*

But Adrian never wished for his cousins to die, strangers that they were, and he never wanted to be earl. At that time, he could barely live up to being simply Mr. Adrian Sinclair, master of Eastgate Manor.

Alfred had added, *Should something befall your cousin Horace, it would not be the first time that a wastrel has inherited Wareton. Hopefully, it will survive even you. And at least neither your father nor I will be alive to witness it.*

That had been the extent of the old earl's remarks on the subject. Adrian had soon laughed off the comments, as he had nearly everything important in his life at that time. But every so often he would allow himself to remember the old earl's words, and he would imagine what his father would think of the man he'd become. It would then take a great deal of drink to drive away those depressing thoughts.

"He was…a very unpleasant man." Miss Colbrook's soft voice jarred him from his reverie.

She stood in the doorway, gazing down at him with a sympathetic frown on her face. How long had she been watching?

"Indeed," he said, "the old monster was kind to no one." He grasped the lamp and rose. "You least of all."

He immediately regretted his words. Though her face was in shadow, he saw her flinch. A floorboard creaked beneath him as he stepped closer to her.

He raised the light until he could see her face clearly.

Pain shone in her eyes, though she quickly concealed it. She tilted her head to meet his stare, her face composed. Only her hands, now curled into fists at her side, gave away her emotions.

"I always considered his dislike of me a compliment," she said.

He smiled.

She might hide any bitterness she felt about her inferior station, but he had no doubt that her situation had often been painful. Outside of Madeline, who clearly adored her, he knew that Miss Colbrook had never been embraced by her stepfamily, merely tolerated. The old earl, as he recalled, had barely even done that. The past six years, without anyone at Wareton to remind her that she was but a poor relation, must have been delightful for her.

Until his arrival had changed everything.

She looked away, and he realized he'd been staring. Staring at her while standing only an arm's length apart in the shadowy room.

"I was just noticing how much you resemble your mother," he said quickly. He turned and gestured to one of the few paintings not of the old earl. It appeared to be a wedding portrait of her mother, Victoria, and the old earl's son, Gerard, Madeline's father.

Miss Colbrook did indeed look a great deal like her mother. Both were striking women, with the same large eyes, dramatically arched brows, coppery hair, and full mouths. But Victoria's face was softer, round in contrast to her daughter's high cheekbones and proud chin.

In the portrait Victoria looked happy, sitting beside her second husband. Likely it was a wedding portrait. According to Lady Carlton, the marriage had soured after only a few months. Apparently, Victoria had never been happy at Wareton, and her despondency led to her decline and eventual death.

"Why was your mother so unhappy here?" he asked.

Miss Colbrook's eyes widened and she blinked, clearly startled by his blunt question.

"Because," she said, "she quickly realized she'd been married only for her fortune."

She glanced at the portrait and pain flashed in her eyes. Then she clasped her hands together and stared up at him again, her face composed.

"You asked for my help with the accounts," she said. Then she turned and retreated from the storeroom.

Adrian followed her back to the study, her last words about her mother repeating in his head.

Did Miss Colbrook fear a miserable marriage like her mother's? Was that why she remained unmarried?

A short time later Adrian watched as Miss Colbrook sat across from him in the study, hunched over a ledger, frowning in concentration while she rapidly scanned and flipped pages. Every so often she paused to tuck a strand of auburn hair back behind her ear.

Over a dozen leather-bound books lay scattered atop the table between them, some new, some cracked and faded with thread unraveling from the spines. Half a dozen additional ledgers that he'd brought from Eastgate were stacked in front of him.

"I know it is here somewhere," she muttered without looking up. Again, a lock of hair slipped down, obscuring one sea-blue eye.

"Here it is." She lifted her head and pushed the book across the table.

He caught the scent of her perfume. Roses. Soft as it was, he'd noticed the aroma lingered in a room for a time after she'd gone—

"This page," she added, pointing to the ledger.

He frowned and forced himself to focus. Usually he wasn't so easily distracted.

He glanced over the entry about the old earl's purchase of land outside of London, one the estate manager had been unable to locate.

"You know as much as Mr. Evans," he said.

"More," she said, matter-of-factly.

He held back a smile. At first her proud manner had irritated him, but now he admired it. She was pleased with her knowledge and accomplishments regarding the estate, and her pride was, he now acknowledged, well deserved.

But that pride also presented a problem. While she seemed to reluctantly accept the estate was now his, it was clear she couldn't completely let go. He'd also learned that she had been quietly looking over changes he'd made. That afternoon alone she'd apparently questioned the groom about two new horses brought from Eastgate, and she'd also asked the housekeeper about his instructions regarding the kitchen.

All the more reason to have her go as soon as possible. He would not have anyone scrutinizing his affairs.

Yet he felt a twinge of guilt when he thought of all she'd done for the estate. He was in her debt. The best way to repay her would be to secure her future through a good marriage. He could even add to her inheritance to help her make the best possible match. Perhaps now she could be persuaded to marry before Madeline who, despite his aunt's best efforts to search here in the country, might very well not find a suitable match until she'd had at least one season in London, perhaps more. The longer Miss Colbrook waited, the smaller her own chances for a match.

If indeed she wished to marry. From the way she'd rebuffed his aunt's discussion of her prospects the night before, marriage was clearly a sensitive subject. Yet if he treaded carefully, in time he was certain he would learn what she wanted for her future.

He would risk raising the subject—indirectly. He'd not yet located inheritance documents for her or Madeline, documents apparently drawn up separately from the old earl's will. This afternoon he'd asked the steward about the papers, but Mr. Evans had claimed no knowledge of them. Perhaps Miss Colbrook would know.

"There are a few other documents I've been unable to locate," he said. She tensed at his words, her shoulders drawing closer together, her expression suddenly grave. As if she knew what he would ask about. "Ones regarding what arrangements Alfred made for Madeline and—"

"Some papers are in the care of the solicitor," she said quickly. "But surely you do not require them at present?" She began organizing the ledgers nearest her, piling them neatly and lining them up in an unnecessarily exact manner, all the while avoiding his gaze.

"No, I suppose not." She clearly knew what he was interested in, and once again, resisted discussing marriage. Did she simply not wish to marry? Or was she really so dedicated to seeing Madeline wed first?

He would let the matter drop—for now. He would learn soon enough.

"I have one other question for you, Miss Colbrook. The cottage off the road from the mill, near the river…" Her hands stilled on the ledgers. "The rent recorded in the books seems too low. I almost thought it an error."

He expected she would welcome the change of subject. Instead, she seemed even more nervous. She sat up straighter and folded her hands in her lap.

"It is not an error," she said quietly, meeting his gaze. Something flashed in her eyes—worry and a hint of defiance?

"Who lives there?" he asked.

"A widow and her five children." She spoke

uncharacteristically fast. "They cannot afford any more."

"I see." Did she fear he would raise the rent? "This widow, she is not a relation?"

"No, but..." She looked him the eye and spoke softly. "She is a friend. And," she said, her voice fast once again, "she does a great deal of sewing for us to make up for the low rent. She is a talented seamstress."

"It would appear to be an acceptable arrangement," he said, nodding. Her shoulders relaxed and her expression softened.

Allowing her friend lower rent was a small thing he could do to repay her for her care of the estate. He wasn't in the habit of tossing impoverished widows out into the cold anyway. For some reason, the thought that she worried he might bothered him. More than it should.

Her opinion of him should not matter. Yet he was forced to admit that he might learn from her. Her skill in managing the estate was impressive and, in some aspects, he reluctantly admitted, better than his own. He'd already concluded her method for organizing the accounts was an improvement.

"I am considering modeling my books after these in the future," he said, gesturing to a ledger. "The structure seems better."

"May I see one?" She pointed to the books he'd brought with him from Eastgate.

"Certainly." He handed her the top black ledger and watched her flip slowly through the book.

"Is this your accountant's handwriting?" She pushed the book closer to him. As she leaned across the table, the bodice of her dress drew tightly against her chest. Beneath the taut fabric, her corset did little to hide the shape of her delightfully full breasts—

"Atrocious," she said. "Truly atrocious." He snapped his gaze away. Had she caught him staring at her chest? But she was looking down at the ledger between them and shaking her head. "You should let him go for that reason alone," she added.

What the devil had they been discussing before he'd become so foolishly distracted? Ah, yes, the accountant's handwriting.

He looked more carefully at the page and frowned.

"That is my writing," he said.

"Oh." She quickly looked back to the book. Was she hiding a smile? He had the sudden desire to see her truly smile, not the fleeting glimpses he'd caught so far.

"What are these entries for Miss Carpenter and Mrs. Jameson?" she added, apparently trying to change the subject. "Are they relatives you support?"

He instantly forgot all about wanting to see her smile.

"They are servants at Eastgate." He tried to keep his voice casual. Damn, why had he let her look at that particular book? He wasn't normally so careless.

"Then why are they not listed with the other servants?" she asked.

"They are. . . former servants."

"Of course." She shut the ledger and pushed it back towards him. She looked away, her face impassive, but she wasn't likely fooled. She would know the amount was far too generous for servants. But to claim they were relatives was out of the question, as she could too easily learn he was lying.

"Did you require my assistance any longer?" She clasped her hands in her lap and continued to avoid his gaze. Obviously, she suspected something improper, but there was nothing to be done about it. She wasn't exactly predisposed to think well of him, anyway. But she would never guess the truth, and that was all that mattered.

"No," he said, a bit too harshly. "Thank you for your help."

They both rose. As she said goodnight, he met her gaze. Her blue eyes flashed a clear message, and for an instant she looked at him much as she had years ago. She obviously thought him a libertine and a scoundrel, but this time her expression held a hint of disappointment as well—as if she'd expected more of him.

Let her think what she wished, what did he care?

She turned away. Scowling, he listened to her footfalls fade in the hall outside.

To hell with what she thought of him—and anyone else who continued to make assumptions about him based on his past.

He strode toward his desk, trying to ignore the lingering scent of roses. He paused near the fireplace. The hunting scene that had been above the hearth when the old earl was alive had been replaced with a painting of two women walking along a beach. Both had reddish-brown hair poking out from beneath their hats, hair a similar shade to Miss Colbrook's.

He frowned.

There was hardly a room in the manor that she hadn't altered, hadn't made her own in some small way. Here was one change he didn't find agreeable. In the morning, he would order the portrait removed.

Then he'd set about getting the vexatious woman out of his home as well.

CHAPTER FOUR

SERVANTS INDEED, ANNA THOUGHT AS Lord Wareton entered the breakfast room the next morning. She, Madeline, Cecelia, and Lady Carlton had already taken their seats around the table.

He returned from the sideboard with an astounding amount of food—three crumpets, three pieces of fruit, four slices of ham, a large serving of baked eggs, and half a dozen sausages. It was proving to be his usual-sized breakfast, along with half a dozen cups of tea, which he nearly overflowed with cream and sugar.

He glanced across the table as if he felt her gaze. She looked quickly away, sipping her chocolate.

Despite trying not to think of the account entries that she'd stumbled upon yesterday, she kept conjuring up possible identities for the two mysterious women. There was only one likely explanation, and it was hardly surprising given a man of his charm and past reputation. Apparently, he wasn't as reformed as he wished people to believe, but at least he'd learned to value discretion. He'd seemed embarrassed at her discovery, even if he'd hidden it quickly.

She glanced at him again, watching his hands as he ate. They were large and strong, looking as if they should hold a blacksmith's hammer rather than a teacup. Yet his long fingers curved around the china handle with surprising refinement. Despite his ruggedness, there was an intriguing gentleness about him. She found herself wondering whether he showed much tenderness to the women he kept. And what type of women did he like, anyway?

She quickly berated herself for such thoughts. Why should she care about his promiscuous tastes? She took a large gulp of chocolate, savoring the sweet warmth as she tried to distract herself from thinking of him. The diversion worked for a moment—until he ruined it by speaking to her.

"Miss Colbrook," he said, "I have a question regarding an expense I came upon last night."

"What expense?" She stirred the remnants of her chocolate.

"An annual listing for 'the Forlorn Females Home.'"

This morning he was dressed simply, in a dark coat and waistcoat and a plain white cravat, his usual gold and pearl pin missing. Even so, he looked every inch an earl. It was his bearing, perhaps, or the confident tilt to his head that made him always look aristocratic. It was certainly not the way he ate, she thought, as she watched him pour yet another cup of tea.

"If you feel it is too much of an expense," Anna said, "I can make do other ways."

"Out of your own pocket?" he said. "That will not be necessary. But what is it?"

"A charitable organization," Anna said.

"They take in fallen women," Madeline whispered loudly, leaning so close to Cecelia that her napkin slipped to the floor.

He smiled. "Indeed? You will have to give me the address."

"Adrian!" Cecelia tried to look offended before she burst out laughing. Straightening from having retrieved her napkin, Madeline laughed as well. Lady Carlton narrowed her eyes at Lord Wareton, likely remaining quiet only because she had a mouthful of chocolate.

Anna looked him in the eye. "It is for those unfortunate women who have been ruined and abandoned."

He stared back at her. "A worthy cause."

There was certainly no hint of embarrassment in him this morning.

Lady Carlton plunked her now empty cup onto the saucer. "Enough jabbering! We have important matters to discuss." She leveled her gaze at Anna. "Miss Colbrook, it is no wonder you remain unmarried if you waste time involving yourself with charities. Such activities are unlikely to attract a husband." She didn't wait for Anna to reply.

"Tomorrow," she continued, "we shall all be fitted for new clothing. Something to keep us presentable until we can have proper attire made in London. Then we shall begin searching for potential suitors."

"I cannot wait to meet the local gentlemen," Cecelia said, sighing. "Perhaps I shall fall in love with one of them on sight."

"You will do no such thing," Lady Carlton said. "Not unless he is of high rank, excellent connections, and meets with the approval of your brother and myself first."

Cecelia frowned. "How unromantic."

"Only commoners marry for romance," Lady Carlton said. "You are now the sister of an earl."

Cecelia pouted, her pale eyes flashing, but she said nothing. Apparently satisfied at having cowed her, Lady Carlton returned her attention to the entire table.

"I am quite determined that I shall have made four matches within the next year," she announced.

"Four?" Madeline asked, glancing at Lord Wareton.

"Of course," Lady Carlton said.

"Did you mean to find yourself another husband?" Lord Wareton said, resuming his breakfast. Lady Carlton had been widowed three times, all within a few years of being married. Anna suspected Lady Carlton had nagged her poor husbands to death.

"You know perfectly well I speak of you, Adrian," Lady Carlton said. "You are an earl now, you have a title to pass on, and a responsibility to make a match that will add to our family's influence. And you are thirty. Why, if you wait much longer, Wareton might end up in Edmund's hands. That would be disastrous."

Lord Wareton frowned at the mention of his brother.

"Adrian," Cecelia said, "When will Edmund visit?"

"If we are fortunate," he said, "never."

"You will invite him?" Cecelia pouted. "Please? He's not visited me in almost a year."

"I do not know where he is, Cecelia," Lord Wareton said as he stabbed at his ham, "even if I wished to invite him. Other than receiving some monstrous bills, I've had no word of him in weeks."

Anna recalled meeting Edmund Sinclair long ago, when they were both little more than children. Mr. Sinclair had seemed a pleasant, agreeable young man. She had trouble imagining him as the troublemaker that Lord Wareton described. Despite Lord Wareton's complaints about his brother's current behavior, Anna had heard little of him here in Somerset.

Cecelia smiled sweetly. "You could find him—"

"If he wishes to visit," Lord Wareton said, "he will not wait for an invitation. He will almost certainly appear to bother us eventually."

"Adrian," Lady Carlton said, "back to your obligation to pass on your title—"

"Aunt," he said, "you will help Cecelia and my cousins to find matches but leave me out of it." He gripped his teacup as if he might crush it.

He looked so disturbed at his aunt's mention of finding him a wife, Anna almost pitied him. Yet Lady Carlton was correct; marriage was his duty. At least he would have no shortage of women to choose from. His title and wealth all but assured a spectacular match with a high-ranking heiress, and his youth and good looks guaranteed it. Most likely he would bring a bride home within a few years, perhaps much sooner if his aunt had her way.

A new Countess of Wareton.

Anna's throat tightened. The last woman who arrived here expecting to one day have that title was her mother. She'd come here so full of hope for her new marriage, only to quickly learn of the mistress who had long ago claimed her new husband's heart. The realization that she'd again been married only for her fortune had broken her mother's spirit.

Within a year she'd died from a pneumonia that normally killed only the very old, leaving Anna with an indifferent stepfather, ailing himself, and his father, the old earl. After her stepfather's death, his father had made clear to Anna how much he resented her presence in his home. Caring for Madeline had been the one bright spot in Anna's life— yet even that had been used against her. She pushed away the unpleasant memories.

Her gaze was drawn again to Lord Wareton, who was starting on yet another cup of tea.

What type of woman would become his countess? Someone well born, certainly, and rich, and likely as handsome as he was. The sort of woman who would probably look the other way should she discover he had a mistress or two, quite possibly a woman who would even expect as much.

She thought once again of the mysterious account entries. Inexplicably, her mood sank even lower.

Lord Wareton's secrets were none of her affair, she reminded herself. The only thing she must concern herself with was keeping him from discovering her own.

Later that morning Adrian checked on some repairs he'd ordered. In a field not far from the manor, he assisted the workers in clearing some brush that had overgrown a gate. When the breeze suddenly picked up, he paused and loosened his cravat, letting the air cool the sweat on his neck. He breathed deeply, and along with the scent of brush came another scent, one that was increasingly familiar.

Roses.

Was he imagining it or—

He spun toward the road. Miss Colbrook stood several paces away, staring at him.

"Lord Wareton?" she said, her eyes wide. Her gaze lingered on his bare neck.

"Miss Colbrook." He wiped the sweat from his brow with one gloved hand and strolled towards her. "You are surprised to see me here?"

"I...no," she lied. He had learned that she really was a poor liar. Her blue eyes were simply too honest, and her full mouth too expressive, so quick to frown or—though rarely at him—to smile.

"You are visiting a neighbor?" he asked.

"Yes."

"Which neighbor?"

Annoyance flashed across her face. And something else. Evasiveness?

"Mrs. Hunter," she said.

"Mrs. Hunter? Where does she live? I don't recall hearing her name when we toured the estate."

"She lives to the east, not far from the river," she said vaguely. "If you will excuse me, I am in haste." She curtsied and turned away.

In haste? He'd heard her discuss her plans for the day with the other ladies at breakfast, and he knew it was unlikely. Did she dislike his company so much that she wished to escape quickly, or was it something else? Did she have some other secret she didn't wish him to discover?

"Wait a moment," he said.

Her shoulders stiffened as she turned back to face him.

"Does Mrs. Hunter live in the cottage by the river?" he

asked.

"Yes." She fidgeted nervously with her skirt.

Yet they had settled the matter of the low rent. Had she misled him about the situation? There was one way to find out.

"It is quite fine weather," he said. "Perhaps I shall accompany you." She gave him a look as if he'd just asked to splatter her with mud.

"Accompany me? But surely you are too busy—"

"I am not." He straightened his cravat. "I could use the walk. And I'd be pleased to meet another tenant." He wanted to learn what she might be hiding, but he also realized that he enjoyed her irritation. What was it about her that made him wish to bedevil her?

He smiled. "Wait a moment."

He arranged for one of the workers to return his horse to the manor, and then he strolled to her side.

She continued to frown at him. Even so, she looked especially attractive today. The sunlight favored her, bringing out the brilliant blue of her eyes and the red in her hair that peeked out from beneath her bonnet.

They walked in silence for a few moments, leaving the fields behind and passing through a small wood of ash and birch trees.

He watched as she lifted her skirt slightly while stepping over a puddle left by the heavy rains overnight. The plain white muslin gown fitted her curves well. He found the way that her skirt shifted as she walked, revealing and then concealing the shape of her thighs, or permitting a glimpse of her ankle, oddly distracting for such a modest dress. He dragged his gaze away from her legs.

He really needed to get out more.

"How old were you when you came to Wareton?" he asked, trying to distract himself.

"Ten."

"You lived in Lyme before then?" He'd heard that her

father's shipping business had been in Lyme.

"My father did, but my mother and I moved to Portsmouth when I was five." She dropped her head, the bonnet now concealing most of her face.

"You did not live with your father after that?" This was news to him. Even Lady Carlton had never mentioned this bit of her past. Had both her mother's marriages been unhappy? Was this somehow behind her own reluctance to marry?

"Not until right before he died," she said, her voice suddenly flat. "But I never expected to end up at Wareton," she added, her tone lighter, "and to gain a stepsister. I've been very fortunate."

Perhaps in some ways she was fortunate, but he still felt a surge of empathy for her. Her parents had lived apart, and her father had died when she was eight. Then her mother had died when she was twelve, leaving her with a stepfamily that, except for Madeline, he knew only tolerated her, never loved her. Many people wouldn't view such a life, no matter how materially comfortable, as advantageous. Yet she seemed quite sincere in focusing on the positive.

Unlike him.

At that moment he felt a flare of shame for all his wasted years.

He'd failed his brother and sister miserably.

When his younger brother had been home visiting from school, Edmund had followed him about incessantly, wearing him down with questions, wishing to do everything his elder brother did. Each time Edmund returned to Eton, Adrian always needed a great many drinks to forget the sadness in his brother's face when he wished him farewell. And Adrian needed a great many more drinks to stop reliving the moments he'd lost his patience with Edmund during his visit.

Visiting his sister had been equally agonizing. Afterwards, as he left their aunt's house, he often watched Cecelia peer out the window after him, her pale hands curled into small fists against the glass. Looking back at her from the window of the carriage, he would count the short number of days of his visit and the total days he'd seen her that past year, and always find it a terribly small number. He could bring her to Eastgate to live with him, and hire the best governess to care for her, but what would she see?

Her oldest brother living like a wastrel.

At least, during his short visits with Cecelia at their aunt's home, he had been able to pretend to be someone else, someone he wasn't ashamed for Cecelia to know. And guilty as he felt for leaving her each time, he knew she was better off in the company of their respectable aunt than with a disreputable brother.

Thanks to a bottle kept stashed in the carriage, he would usually be well on his way to a stupor after only a few miles, and able to bury his guilt once again.

Years of drunkenness and rowdy behavior passed before he'd finally realized he was selfishly lamenting his parents' deaths, and that he'd shamefully neglected his responsibilities to his siblings.

Miss Colbrook had been orphaned at about the same age he had been, and she had far fewer advantages afterwards, yet she dealt with tragedy far better. While he had indulged in self-pity far too long, such wallowing apparently wasn't for her.

"Here we are," she said. They reached the top of a small hill, and a small stone cottage set back from the road came into view.

Moments later, they were welcomed by Mrs. Hunter, a thin, chestnut-haired woman, and seated at a small table in the front sitting room. Toys were scattered about and two young girls, about six and eight years of age, stood near the doorway at the back of the room, eyeing Adrian warily.

"Where are the other children?" Miss Colbrook asked as Mrs. Hunter set down saucers and teacups. Out of the corner of her eye, Miss Colbrook glanced towards him, so quickly that he would have missed it if he hadn't been staring at her.

"Emma is sleeping," Mrs. Hunter said, "and my sister has taken the other two to town, thankfully." She disappeared into the back of the house.

The younger of the two children ventured near and tugged on Miss Colbrook's skirt. "Will you sing the fish song with me?"

"Do not bother Miss Colbrook," Mrs. Hunter said as she returned and set a plate of biscuits on the table. "Let her have her tea." From a backroom, an infant began to cry.

Miss Colbrook immediately tensed, glancing at him.

"The baby again," Mrs. Hunter said. "Emma just needs a good burp, and she'll go back down. Excuse me." Mrs. Hunter hurried away and a moment later the crying stopped.

The girl continued to tug at Miss Colbrook's skirt. "The fish song, please?"

"I would be glad to, Meg," Miss Colbrook said, turning to the girl. "Come sit beside me."

Meg climbed onto the chair beside her, and they turned to face each other. They began to sing a rhyming song about a fish swimming in a brook. The song involved a complicated patty cake technique they both had mastered. Miss Colbrook glanced at him nervously at first, but she seemed to quickly forget about him and sang louder. Unfortunately.

She sang terribly. For a well-bred young lady to sound as if she'd never had a single voice lesson was quite startling. But Meg seemed not to care at all, and the girl smiled broadly as she sang–only slightly better than Miss Colbrook did. Usually poor singing grated on Adrian's nerves, but as he watched Meg glowing from the attention, he found that he didn't mind.

Miss Colbrook clearly had a soft spot for children. But

did that mean she wanted to marry and have her own?

Soon after, Mrs. Hunter joined them. She and Miss Colbrook exchanged gossip about some of the neighbors, many of whom Adrian was still unfamiliar with. While they chatted, he talked with the girls, who introduced him to their calico kitten, Lady Havoc, named for her ability to knock over objects. The girls were thrilled when, against the advice of their mother, he took the cat in his lap and scratched its head until it purred.

"Are you really an earl?" the older girl, Diana, asked, watching him with the kitten.

He laughed. "Should earls not hold cats?"

The girl frowned, pondering the question for a moment. "I think they *should*," she said, her face grave, "every day."

Adrian laughed and his gaze wandered to Miss Colbrook. She was staring at the little girl with unconcealed amusement and affection, her face lit up with happiness. She caught his gaze and for a moment, she was smiling at *him*.

As he stared back at her, the room grew suddenly quiet.

"You are dropping Lady Havoc!" Diana scolded, snatching the cat from him. He glanced back at Miss Colbrook. She quickly looked away and fumbled for the teapot.

"Please, let me," Mrs. Hunter said. She poured Miss Colbrook a fresh cup, glancing at Adrian with an odd expression.

He frowned. What was wrong with him, becoming so distracted? Enjoying the visit was well enough, but he must not forget his purpose. Yet it appeared Miss Colbrook had told him the truth about Mrs. Hunter and her children. So why did it still seem as if she were hiding something? She'd tensed when the baby cried. What was it about the infant that had her worried?

Mrs. Hunter served them each another biscuit, pausing to brush some stray crumbs from her gown before she sat down again. Her *white* gown.

A sudden suspicion hit him. Followed quickly by irritation that Miss Colbrook thought to conceal such a thing from him. He stifled his annoyance for the time being.

As soon as they were alone, he would get the truth from her.

Lord Wareton was angry.

Anna was certain of it, though he had done his best to conceal it from Mrs. Hunter and the children as they said goodbye. They'd been getting on so well, too, having a surprisingly pleasant time together. And when Diana had instructed him to hold kittens every day, the way he'd laughed and the startling way he'd looked at her had made her wonder if they might even become friends. But soon after, the warmth had vanished from his eyes.

Had he guessed the truth about Mrs. Hunter?

"Lovely children," he said as they walked away from the house.

"You are fortunate the other two were not here or you might not think so," Anna said. "Meg and Diana are the best behaved."

He said nothing for a moment, until they were back on the road and had rounded a corner, out of view and earshot of the cottage.

"How long ago was Mrs. Hunter widowed?" He clasped his hands behind his back, keeping his gaze on the road.

She should have guessed that he would ask. He was not a man of few questions, as she had learned all too well.

"Not long ago," she replied, trying to keep the worry from her voice.

"But she does not wear mourning clothes," he said. "More than a year, then?"

"I do not recall the exact date." With his attention to detail, she should have known he'd put things together quickly.

He abruptly stopped walking. "How odd. Such a vague answer from a usually so precise woman."

She knew she was caught. She would not lie outright, and he could easily learn the truth from someone else anyway. But that didn't mean she wouldn't put up a fight if necessary to protect her friend.

She lifted her head and met his stare. "Two years ago."

"And she has not remarried?" He glared down at her. "No."

"But the baby is hers?"

Her throat tightened. "Yes."

"I see." He took a step closer and raised his voice. "And you thought it best to conceal this from me?"

She wasn't accustomed to men towering over her, particularly angry ones. She resisted the urge to step back.

"Her old landlord was unkind to her and her children," she said. "He wanted her gone." As most landlords would, unkind as it was. "That is why I offered her the cottage—"

"And you assumed that I would want her gone as well? That I would send a widow and her children off into the streets?" He straightened and looked away, as if he'd just realized he was losing his temper. After a moment he gazed at her again, his expression composed, and he added quietly, "Miss Colbrook, exactly what kind of monster do you think I am?"

"No, I…" Her face felt hot. She clenched her hands together, tugging at her gloves.

He was not a monster at all. In fact, to her surprise, she was beginning to believe quite the opposite. Mistresses or not.

"I am sorry," she said, meeting his gaze. "I was wrong."

His eyes widened. Clearly, he hadn't been expecting an apology, at least not so quickly. The anger left his expression, but he continued to stare at her.

Say something, she thought. *Anything.*

"It would seem your charity towards fallen women extends to your own neighborhood," he finally said. "Tell me, are dozens of such women living throughout the estate?" A hint of a smile softened his face.

He was angry only a moment ago, and now he was teasing her? She might have been annoyed if she wasn't so relieved.

She lifted her chin higher. "Just Mrs. Hunter."

He smiled. "She is fortunate to have you for a friend."

"Thank you," she said softly, gazing up into his hazel eyes. She'd noticed they changed with the light, sometimes an emerald green, and sometimes a paler green, like summer grass.

She realized she'd been holding his gaze too long. Quickly, she turned away and began walking again.

He fell into step beside her in silence. The open sky, stone walls, and hedgerows gave way to the cover of tall trees as the path turned away from the fields and into the woods.

No, she thought, he was certainly not a monster. Unpleasant as he could be at times, more and more he seemed to be quite an agreeable gentleman. Nothing like what she'd expected.

When she'd first encountered him during her walk, his cravat loose and sweat glistening on his neck and forehead, her first thought had been disbelief that he was laboring along with the workers. Her second thought, and even more surprising, was how utterly handsome he looked.

And still looked.

As they walked, the filtered sunlight dappled his dark coat and made patches of gold in his hair. And she would have to be blind not to notice his broad shoulders and muscular legs. He didn't wear the skintight fashions that many dandies preferred, but his clothes were well-fitted and did little to hide his fine form.

She forced herself to keep her eyes on the path. Most of

the time. What on earth was wrong with her? For years, she'd kept herself from liking any gentleman. Even with Mr. Harley, she'd never felt anything like the awareness she felt for Lord Wareton. It was only natural that she would notice him, she supposed, sharing a house with him and seeing him so often. He was turning out to be such an interesting gentleman.

His manner with their tenants was especially remarkable. She never would have predicted finding him working alongside them. Most men of his rank would be uncomfortable socializing with those so beneath him in status, but there was nothing snobbish about him. And while many landowners would refuse to rent to someone in Mrs. Hunter's situation, he didn't seem the least concerned other than being angry that she had tried to conceal it from him.

Nothing in his past suggested such good qualities. His parents had been lost at sea while traveling back from France when he was thirteen. He'd been left in the guardianship of an elderly uncle, a senile man who had allowed him to become spoiled and wild, setting him on the path to the wastrel he became later. Yet despite his wild behavior, somehow during that time he'd clearly learned a great deal about how to manage an estate.

Still, she couldn't rest all her fears about him inheriting Wareton. There was the matter of Eastgate being indebted.

"Did you manage Eastgate yourself all these years?" she asked. Her worry must have shown on her face.

"You have heard Eastgate is in debt."

"I heard you'd had some difficulties," she said hesitantly, surprised by his candor.

"It is true that some of the debt is my own doing, from my gaming days, but while I was in France it became far worse. I left the management in less than capable hands, although I did not realize the magnitude of my error until my return."

He paused to kick a small pebble out before him. She was unaccountably pleased that he bothered to explain himself to her. And since he was being so candid, she wondered if she might learn the one thing about him that most perplexed her.

Everyone who knew him had been astonished when he abruptly joined the army over three years ago. Eldest sons in line to inherit large estates rarely purchased military commissions. His reputation as a wastrel made it even more of a shock and his reasons a mystery.

"Why did you purchase a commission?" she asked. "Patriotic duty?"

"In part."

In part?

"It is said you acted heroically," she said, hoping he would tell her more. So far, he'd revealed little of his time in the military and when he did, it was never about battles, only of his friends or local civilians he'd encountered. He'd related only light stories, suitable for dinner conversation.

"No more than many soldiers," he said, his face somber. "And far less than others."

"You are modest."

"No." He sighed, his eyes flashing with anxiety. "But I shall not speak of killing as if it were a glorious thing and as if I were brave for merely surviving."

"Forgive me," she said, immediately regretting raising the subject.

"No." He glanced at her and his face softened. "It is all right. It is just...I joined the army for selfish reasons. I was running away." He frowned. She thought he might regret even that small revelation but surprisingly, he continued.

"I realized I was nearing thirty with no accomplishments to speak of." The hesitation in his voice made her suspect there was more to his decision than he was telling her.

"I became an officer to remove myself from many of my old friends and former habits," he said after a moment.

"Since I've been home, I find I miss very little of them. I have quit gambling, I have no desire to go to London and live in the clubs or drive carriages about at breakneck speeds or any such nonsense. It all seems quite tiresome now. I wish to be productive."

"You sound as if you have become a veritable saint," she said. She thought again of the account entries. Reformed as he seemed, he certainly still had secrets.

"Not quite. There is one vice I shall never give up entirely. A man must have some indulgences." He smiled mysteriously.

One vice? What did he mean? Was he actually referring to his mistresses?

He glanced at her and laughed. "Drinking, Miss Colbrook," he said, grinning. "*Drinking.* Although only in moderation now."

Drinking indeed, she thought, stifling her annoyance that he'd read her thoughts so easily. Two vices then.

They walked in silence for a time, the path sloping gently downward as it wound through the trees. The rushing of a brook grew louder, competing with the calls of birds and the scuffing of his boots on the path.

Her irritation with him faded as she thought of all he'd just shared with her. Remembering the questions he'd asked about her childhood, she suddenly wanted to tell him about her own past. Of how her mother had said that her father had only pretended to love her in order to marry her for her inheritance. How over the years her mother had grown to despise him for being below her own class, for tricking her into sacrificing the chance to marry a gentleman by making her believe she was marrying for love. Anna wanted to speak of the anguish it had caused her to be separated from her father. Perhaps because of his own troubled childhood, he would understand.

The strength of her desire to talk to him surprised her. Yet she held back from revealing anything. As pleased as she was that they were becoming better acquainted, it also made her uneasy. Why exactly she couldn't say.

They rounded the final bend in the path before the water.

She frowned. "The bridge is gone." Where the trail met the wide brook, only the splintered remnants of a small wooden footbridge were left.

"The heavy rains last night must have taken it," he said. "Is there a narrower spot nearby?"

"No. We shall be forced to go back."

"Why? It looks shallow, and only a few strides across. I can carry you."

"Carry me?" She looked at his hands and thought of them touching her, imagined his strong arms holding her body. Despite the cool air emanating from the water, she suddenly felt warm.

"No," she said quickly, "I do not think so."

He raised one eyebrow. "Why not?" Would he guess she was having improper thoughts if she refused? Carrying her across made perfect sense. It was the practical thing to do, and if he were almost any other man, she would likely have thought little of it.

"You. . .will get wet," she stammered.

"Barely. It looks no more than a foot deep."

"It is really not a long walk back the way we came—"

"Don't be silly." Then he was at her side, towering over her. He lifted her off her feet and held her against his chest. His arms were warm and strong around her. Disturbingly so.

"No, I am too heavy," she said. "Put me down." It was a feeble excuse. Tall as she was, he was clearly very capable of carrying her.

"You are not. Keep hold of me."

She had no choice but to slip her arms over his shoulders. He smelled delicious. Not of cologne, but something subtler. The scent of soap and something else clung to his clothes. Wood, that was it. He smelled like the forest, probably from his work earlier.

He held her beneath her knees and at her back. The soft fabric of his coat tickled her through the thin sleeves of her dress. He waded into the brook as if she weighed little. It was slightly deeper than he'd guessed, and he lifted her legs higher to keep her feet from touching the water. Her skirt slid back, revealing her ankles and white stockings.

He suddenly looked strained. Perhaps she was too heavy after all.

She stared up at him as he took several careful steps. "I am too heavy."

He stopped in the center of the brook, the water flowing around him to almost his knees. He held her high against his chest, his arms steady, and looked down at her. He smiled mischievously, his expression similar to the one he wore when teasing his sister or Madeline, playful and gentle.

"Perhaps you are right," he said. "Shall I put you down here?" He lowered her nearer to the water, until the heels of her shoes skimmed the flowing surface.

She laughed and held him tighter. "You wouldn't! Even for you, that is..." She gazed up into his green eyes and instantly forgot what she was about to say.

His smile faded. He looked down at her strangely, his eyes wide, as if he just realized that he held a woman in his arms, and their faces were only inches apart. His breath caressed her face as his gaze slid from her eyes to her lips.

She stopped breathing. *Surely, he wasn't considering...?*

For an instant she was uncertain what he would do next: kiss her or drop her in the brook like a hot coal. Or perhaps, she thought as she felt him sway slightly, he would lose his footing, and they would both fall into the cold water.

But he quickly steadied himself. Then he drew his head up and strode to the shore, splashing her skirt with each stride. He deposited her abruptly on the other side and began marching down the path, leaving her standing there, dazed. Finally, he paused and looked back.

"Are you coming, Miss Colbrook?" He turned fully around. His face was sober and restrained.

She hurried to catch up with him.

"You are in a hurry?" She spoke as if nothing unusual just happened. Did something unusual just happen, or almost happen?

"I am traveling to Eastgate today." He walked more quickly than he had before they crossed the brook. He may not have wanted to kiss her—no of course he hadn't wanted to—but he'd suddenly become aware of the potential impropriety of the situation, probably from the foolish way she'd been gazing at him. It was the obvious explanation for his sudden reserve.

"Business at your estate?" she asked.

"Yes."

She'd learned that he planned to visit Eastgate once every week and to stay overnight despite the relatively short journey from Wareton. She wondered if he planned to visit either of the women listed in his account books during his time there. It didn't take much imagination to guess that they might be the reason for the overnight stay.

That unspoken suspicion seemed to hang in the air between them. He glanced at her and, almost as if he could read her thoughts, his eyes went cold.

The amiable man she'd spent the morning with was gone.

CHAPTER FIVE

A WEEK LATER ADRIAN SAT IN the study, contemplating how to best avoid his aunt, when he heard her determined footfalls growing louder in the hall. Damn. He thought that he'd have more time to make himself scarce, given the debate that had been raging in the sitting room only a short time ago over what the ladies would wear to that evening's ball. He briefly considered climbing out the open window into the garden. If only there were fewer shrubs, it could be done without too much noise or difficulty...

Lady Carlton marched into the room and cornered him at his desk.

"You have been avoiding me, Adrian." She wore a yellow and black striped afternoon dress that made her resemble a bumblebee.

"My dear aunt," he said, "you are imagining things. I've been extremely busy." He gestured to the ledgers scattered across his desk. "These books are still quite disordered—"

"Rubbish! Nothing about this estate is disordered." She lifted a paperweight from the desk, a miniature swan carved from limestone, and frowned at it.

"Several eligible gentlemen will be attending the ball tonight," she said. "You must make their acquaintance as they may be potential suitors for your sister and cousin, and perhaps even Miss Colbrook." She placed the swan back on the desk with a thud. "Have you spoken to her yet about the subject of marriage?"

He sighed. "No, not yet."

"You must encourage her to invite suitors."

Lady Carlton had repeated the same words every day since their arrival at Wareton, but he had avoided raising the subject with Miss Colbrook. And after what had almost occurred a week ago, he avoided speaking to her as much as possible.

What had possessed him to ramble on as he had, to tell her his reasons for joining the army? He rarely spoke of it to anyone, yet he had confessed his epiphany as if he wanted her understanding or even her approval. The idea was preposterous. Even if he'd stopped short of telling her everything, it still irritated him that he'd shared so much.

Even worse, when he'd carried her across the brook and she gazed up at him, her face bright with laughter, she'd looked so attractive that he'd almost forgotten himself completely. The flush of excitement on her face and her delightful warmth against him had caused him to actually contemplate kissing her. He'd been angry with himself ever since. Four years ago, he would have kissed her and never considered the consequences, but not now. There was no longer room in his life for selfish indulgences. Yet it frightened him that he'd come so close to behaving recklessly again. If he'd kissed her, he would have invited a tempest of problems that he had no wish to even consider.

Even if she weren't unsuited to him in nearly every way —situation, connections, and temperament—and even if she had any interest in him, which she almost certainly didn't, their unequal positions made even a kiss unthinkable. He wasn't legally her guardian, but as her only male relative, however distant, he was still in a sense her protector. To even think about her in such a way was not only foolish, it was also dishonorable. Yet for the past week, even while trying to avoid her, he'd found himself distracted by her.

And it was growing worse.

Since returning from Eastgate, he'd tried his best to ignore her. When he couldn't avoid her company, he acted as reserved as possible, and if that failed, he resorted to deliberately irritating her. She'd quickly responded in kind, much to his relief. Still, he noticed things about her that he had no wish to, such as the way her hair changed color in candlelight and sunlight or the distinctive rhythm of her shoes brushing against the carpet or the subjects of the books she read.

His aunt was right; encouraging Miss Colbrook to marry was the best course of action for many reasons. He shouldn't delay any longer. It was time to learn why she remained unwed.

"You must attend the ball tonight," his aunt continued. "Not only will your presence likely hasten a match for one of them, but also..." She smiled and he knew something bad would follow. "A lady will be there who is of particular interest to you."

"No such lady exists." What on earth was she up to?

"Is that so? Forget I mentioned it then. You have always liked surprises." She turned away.

He sighed. "What lady?"

She faced him again, smiling smugly. "Lady Jane Stratford."

"Why should she be of interest to me?" He rose, strolled to the window, and pulled the heavy glass shut. The scent of flowers dissipated and the study suddenly seemed oppressively quiet.

"Perhaps you have not heard the most recent news?"

"No, I have not." He turned back towards his aunt. Her smile had become a smirk. She remained uncharacteristically silent, apparently savoring the suspense.

"I thought not," she finally said, "for it seems you two have been completely out of touch the past few years. She was not even aware of your elevation to earl. When I wrote to her—"

"You wrote to her?" He tried to keep his voice calm.

Lady Carlton sniffed. "Why should I not?"

"You always ridiculed Miss Farth—Lady Stratford.

Claimed she wasn't good enough to associate with, even when I was of no rank." He turned and gazed out the window again.

"That was before she became a baroness and inherited a fortune. That is the news. Lady Stratford is now a widow, and she is just out of mourning."

Widowed? Oh hell.

"She wrote that she was looking forward to leaving York and returning to civilization," his aunt continued. "She has family here, and she is to visit Somerset indefinitely."

"Why are you telling me this?" he asked, no longer bothering to hide his irritation.

At that moment Miss Colbrook strolled into the garden. She was close to the manor, examining some plants that had been added only the day before. She wore a wide-brimmed bonnet and the same white muslin dress from their visit to Mrs. Hunter. She seemed oblivious to his presence at the window as she stopped to inspect a fledging juniper bush. She bent forward to touch the plant, presenting him with a clear view of her shapely backside. He momentarily forgot all about his aunt and Jane Stratford.

The sun shining through her skirt made the outline of her legs quite—

"Because..." Lady Carlton was suddenly beside him. She glared at Miss Colbrook. "It is my duty to help you find a lady *worthy* of your interest."

"Indeed." He turned away from the window. Was his notice of Miss Colbrook so obvious? He thought he hid it well. He didn't even wish to notice her. In fact, he resented it profoundly.

He walked as far away from the window as he could, stopping at the hearth. He came face to face with the painting, the one of the auburn-haired women that he'd intended to order removed but for some reason hadn't gotten around to yet. He scowled at the picture, then leaned against the mantel and crossed his arms.

What the devil had his aunt been talking about? Ah yes, finding him a wife.

"So poor Miss Farthington is suddenly worthy?" he said. "Of an earl, even?"

Lady Carlton strode away from the window. "*Lady Stratford* is now one of the wealthiest women in England. She may have been born to a family of modest means, but her parentage is quite respectable. Her father was a gentleman, and now she has many new, high connections." Lady Carlton glanced back toward the window. "There are certainly no merchants in her family."

Adrian sighed. "It is an unpardonable sin to have relatives in commerce."

"I am in no mood for your sarcasm," Lady Carlton said. "You will speak to Miss Colbrook tonight and encourage her to accept suitors?"

"It seems I have little choice."

She nodded. "That is correct."

Out of the corner of his eye he glanced toward the garden again. Miss Colbrook had straightened and was strolling beneath the rose arbor, away from the manor.

"The Duke of Dulverton is expected to make an appearance tonight," Lady Carlton said. "I shall see that he is introduced to Cecelia. Apparently, he is a man of great fortune and respectability. He is not yet thirty and said to be quite handsome."

"Most men with huge fortunes are said to be handsome," Adrian said. But the idea of Cecelia becoming a duchess pleased him. What better way to fulfill his duty to her? A grand marriage was the least he owed her after leaving her in the care of his aunt for so many years. Yes, he vowed, Cecelia would marry well. If not the duke, then another gentleman of high rank and fortune. Perhaps a match for her would be one thing he and his aunt could agree on.

"I must go help Cecelia prepare," Lady Carlton said. With one final look of disapproval, she swept from the study.

Miss Colbrook had vanished. Adrian returned to his desk and leaned back in his chair. He stared at the books before him without seeing them. He had no desire to go to the ball, but of course he must.

And as for the news Jane Stratford would be in attendance... He sat up and opened the second desk drawer. He rummaged through it, then opened the third drawer. Finally, in the bottom one, far in the back, he found the box. It was small, of battered wood, and engraved with the initials *AWS*. He'd brought it with him from Eastgate but hadn't looked through it in some time. Inside were a few keepsakes—his father's favorite pipe, a picture Cecelia had drawn of him when she was ten, his baby cup—but mostly there were old letters, their broken seals crumbling.

He dug beneath the letters and took out a small burgundy velvet pouch, the fibers crushed in spots. A gilt-framed portrait slid free, a miniature of a striking young woman with fair hair and a beautiful smile—Miss Jane Farthington at age twenty.

For a time four years ago, they had a flirtation. She was the first woman he'd paid close attention to and people began to speculate that Mr. Adrian Sinclair, the hellion of the ton, might have finally met the woman who would tame him. She was uncommonly attractive and far more interesting than the typical debutantes he encountered. She wasn't offended by his behavior or reputation, and he'd enjoyed her company immensely, comfortable in the knowledge that his lack of a title meant she'd never seriously consider marrying him. Their relationship had ended when the destitute Miss Farthington became engaged to the exceedingly old and rich Lord Stratford, a betrothal that was considered the matrimonial coup of the decade.

And now the Baroness Stratford was a widow with a fortune. Clearly, his aunt believed Lady Stratford was now the perfect match for him. She had money and he had an even higher rank to offer her. Lady Carlton was hoping Lady Stratford would draw his interest once again, and it was quite possible Lady Stratford was hoping so as well.

He smiled at the picture. Jane looked so sweet, so demure. So utterly unlike the reality.

He slid the picture back into the pouch. One thing was for certain, it wouldn't be a boring evening.

An hour before the carriage was due to leave for the ball, Adrian strolled into the sitting room and found Miss Colbrook alone, reading in the far window seat. She reclined against a pile of white velvet cushions, her legs tucked under her. Her blue and silver shoes rested on the floor beside her, and her stockinged toes peeked out from beneath the hem of her gown.

As he approached, she briefly lifted her head from her book.

"Where are the other ladies?" he asked.

"Still dressing, I imagine." She didn't glance up again. "They may be quite a while. Madeline is always late for outings." She had already changed into her evening clothes: a plain, dark blue gown and only the barest jewelry—tiny gold ear bobs and a thin necklace that fell almost to her waist. Still, she looked far more ravishing than most women did in much finer clothes.

"What are you reading now?" He stepped close and bent to scan the cover of her book.

A Gentleman's Guide to Prudent Investment.

"Investment?" Good Lord. Next she'd be reading about fencing or how to tie a cravat.

She glanced up only to frown at him. "It's fascinating."

"I'm sure," he said. "Do you mind if I sit?" He didn't wait for a reply but dropped onto the cushions at the other end of the window seat. He leaned back, facing her, his knees a few feet from hers. She shifted the book so it blocked him from view.

"I need to speak with you," he said. He began tracing the edge of the windowpane with one finger.

"About what?" she asked from behind the book.

"Marriage." He watched the volume slide from her fingers and land beside her shoes with a soft thud. She quickly bent over to retrieve it. Despite the conservative cut of her gown, he was afforded a brief, tantalizing view of her breasts. His body reacted instantly, far too strongly for a mere glimpse of cleavage, however voluptuous.

This was what happened when a man behaved like a monk for too long.

She frowned. "Marriage?"

"Yes. I am offering my assistance."

"Thank you, but I am in no need of help." She opened her book and reclined against the cushions again, pretending to read. A lock of hair fell in front of her eyes. He resisted the impulse to lean forward and tuck it behind her ear. What on earth was wrong with him, to be thinking such things?

"It is true, then," he said, "that you have no desire to marry?"

She snapped the book shut and dropped it in her lap. "I shall not be pressured into a match." She tucked her hair back into place and shifted, sitting up straighter. Oddly, her necklace was suddenly shorter, falling only to the top of her bodice.

"Then you might marry someday?" He restrained himself from asking about the suitor Madeline had mentioned. Miss Colbrook had already denied his existence. If she did have a serious admirer, the gentleman would almost certainly make himself known soon, perhaps even tonight.

"I might," she said. "Or I might not."

"But you refused the offer six years ago from Mr. Harley?"

"Is that not common knowledge?" She glanced out the

window.

He frowned. She wasn't actually answering the question. He recalled the anxiety in her eyes when his aunt had raised the subject on his first night at Wareton. Was she hiding something?

"Did you refuse Mr. Harley?" he asked bluntly.

He assumed she would respond as curtly and evasively as before, but she surprised him.

"No," she said softly, meeting his gaze. "The old earl refused him."

"But you did not?"

She slowly shook her head.

Interesting. Perhaps he'd discovered the real reason she remained a spinster. His aunt and apparently everyone else believed that she'd refused Mr. Harley, but this changed everything. Perhaps it wasn't fear of repeating her mother's unhappy marriages that made her reluctant to wed. Was it possible she was still so heartbroken that she simply wasn't interested in other suitors? He felt a stab of annoyance that Mr. Harley might have captured her affections so deeply.

She glanced at him, then down at her hands.

"Why did the old earl refuse him?" he asked.

"He was a miserable old man," she said. She shifted and tugged at her necklace. "That was reason enough."

He wouldn't argue that fact, but she was still being evasive. There was something more, something she didn't wish to tell him.

"Miserable as sin," he said, "but—"

"I am caught on something." She reached awkwardly behind her back, trying to free the chain, but it wouldn't budge.

"May I assist you?" he asked.

"No, I believe I can get it." She struggled for a moment longer. "It is caught on the cushion."

"Let me help. You risk breaking it."

She looked at him gravely. "Very well."

He stood and moved beside her, trying to ignore the disturbing effect she had on him. As usual, she smelled good, like fresh cut roses and linen. He fought the desire to lean closer.

"A link is tangled in the pillow cover," he said. She clasped her hands in her lap as he bent behind her. "Lean back," he said. She did, briefly brushing her back against his arm. She stiffened.

He wondered how she would react if she knew the alarming thoughts running through his mind. No doubt she would be appalled. Perhaps amused, but more likely horrified. He couldn't forget the disappointment in her eyes after her awkward discovery of the account entries. And Mr. Harley, from what little Adrian recalled of the gentleman, was as straight-laced as they came, suggesting her taste in men leaned toward the puritanical. She wasn't likely the type of woman who would find a gentleman with his past at all acceptable, no matter how reformed.

He carefully pulled the white threads out from around the chain. "There. The cushion cover needs mending, but your necklace is undamaged."

"Thank you," she said. As he returned the freed chain to her neck, his fingers touched just below her chignon, brushing the soft, fine hair too short to pin up.

She jerked away.

"Forgive me," he said. "I did not mean to startle you." He straightened, feeling a stab of anger. Was she so repulsed by him that one touch made her draw back so?

Still holding the necklace against her chest, she glanced up at him. In that instant he saw something in her eyes he never expected to see. It wasn't revulsion. It was quite the opposite.

She quickly looked away and a bright flush of red coursed up her neck and onto her cheeks. In all the times he'd encountered her, she'd never once blushed, even under the most obnoxious and improper comments. She'd always been cool and imperturbable.

"You are blushing," he said softly.

She turned and faced the window. In the glass he could see the faint reflection of her eyes, wide and nervous. He had the sudden urge to touch her again, to stroke the soft hair that fell from her chignon and touch the smooth column of her neck. He wanted to turn her to face him, to caress her flushed cheeks, and to see if her mouth tasted as soft and sweet as it looked.

He should step away. He was too near.

"Miss Colbrook," he said. He stepped even closer.

Slowly, she turned her head and met his gaze. Her lips were parted, and she seemed about to say something.

He wanted to hear nothing she could say. More than anything at that moment, he wanted to kiss her.

Footfalls sounded in the hallway, distant but growing louder.

He reluctantly drew away from her, and seconds later Lady Carlton hurried into the sitting room.

His aunt had changed into a burgundy ball gown with black embroidery. Two enormous ebony feathers jutted out from the back of her head like a pair of horns.

"Miss Colbrook," Lady Carlton said, "the carriage will be ready soon. Should you not change?"

Miss Colbrook blinked. "Change?"

"Yes. Surely you will not be wearing that?" Lady Carlton frowned at her plain blue gown.

"Perhaps you are right," Miss Colbrook said softly, rising. Lady Carlton's jaw momentarily dropped, but she recovered quickly.

"Perhaps I am...?" Lady Carlton looked at Miss Colbrook suspiciously. "Are you feeling well? Your face is flushed." Lady Carlton's gaze flew to Adrian. He immediately looked away, carefully adjusting his already perfect cuffs.

"Pray excuse me," Miss Colbrook said a bit too quickly. She stepped into her shoes, took a step forward, and promptly tripped on the edge of the carpet. Adrian caught her. He held her, one hand at her waist, one on her bare arm, until she regained her balance. She felt so good that were his aunt not staring at them, he might not have let her go. Miss Colbrook looked everywhere but at his face, mumbled her thanks, then turned and walked carefully from the room.

Lady Carlton watched her exit and then spun to face him. Her scowl was among the worst he'd ever seen on her.

"That," she said, "was the most pathetic display I have had the misfortune to witness for some time."

He crossed his arms. "I do not know what you mean."

"Poppycock." She stepped closer. "Look at me, Adrian." Her gray eyes were icy. "Remember you are the Earl of Wareton now. And she," his aunt said 'she' as if it were a curse, "is your cousin's stepsister, of common parentage and highly unconventional character. Not to mention she is living here under your protection."

"You are making assumptions—"

"It is fortunate you will be socializing again. I have no doubt you will regain your perspective quickly." She glared at him again before she spun away and marched from the room.

The moment his aunt disappeared, he forgot all about her. Smiling, he recalled how Miss Colbrook had tensed when he drew close to her, how she started from his touch, how she stumbled and blushed. He almost wished she hadn't let him know that she was attracted to him. Now it would be even more difficult to push away such foolish thoughts, and foolish they were, for to act upon them would be madness.

He should be filled with anxiety and foreboding. Instead, he felt happier than he had in a very long time.

CHAPTER SIX

ANNA PACED THE FOYER, HER heels clacking on the floor as she took six slow steps, turned at the fat Grecian vase, took six more steps, and revolved again in front of the portrait of the first Earl of Wareton. He was a squat man with heavy brows and a preposterously long beard. Clearly, over the last several generations the appearance of his family line had dramatically improved. Anna briefly wished it wasn't so, glancing at his descendant who stood not far away, his gloves clutched in one hand, staring up the wide staircase. Lord Wareton looked breathtakingly handsome in his evening clothes, a fact she found quite irritating.

He sighed. "What the deuces can they be doing?"

"Patience, Adrian." Lady Carlton stood beside him, gazing at herself in the small wall mirror and patting the feathers that sprouted from the back of her headdress. "This is a very important night, and naturally, they wish to look their best. Why, even Miss Colbrook has made herself presentable."

Anna ignored her comment and continued to pace. She'd changed into a gown of peach silk, the second nicest of her dresses from their recent visit to the modiste. She tried to convince herself that she had to change after what she'd said to Lady Carlton, and that it had nothing to do with wanting to gain Lord Wareton's attention. Had she not behaved so foolishly earlier, she might have even dared to wear her best gown.

She'd made a spectacle of herself, blushing and stumbling like a debutante simply because he'd caught her in his arms.

Now he could have no doubt that she was attracted to him. Lady Carlton certainly suspected, as she had followed Anna upstairs and made a point of reminding her how out of reach any gentleman of rank was to her. Lady Carlton had also informed her that a former love of Lord Wareton's, a widowed baroness, would be attending the ball, a woman who Lady Carlton implied was all but engaged to him.

The lady was no doubt the reason he was dressed so handsomely this evening, in a black coat and crisp white shirt, and why he seemed to be in an exceptionally good mood. His happiness made him even more attractive, adding to Anna's annoyance.

During their stroll together the week before, she'd believed they might become friends. But after carrying her across the stream he'd withdrawn, and when he returned from Eastgate he continued to act coolly towards her. She'd tried to remain indifferent to his behavior and failed.

Miserably.

She was constantly aware of his presence, and despite her anger, far too often she found herself thinking about him and pondering the few conversations they did have.

He'd all but ignored her for a week, and now he was suddenly being friendly again, and he even had the audacity to ask her personal questions. Not that he really cared about her romantic attachments. She knew that Lady Carlton was pressuring him to help her marry. He likely wanted her gone from Wareton too, especially now that she'd made such a muddle of things.

She glanced at him again. He tapped his gloves impatiently against his thigh as he waited for Madeline and Cecelia to appear. Just the sight of his large, square hands reminded her of his touch, making her feel warm all over once again. She wished she could go back in time and keep herself from acting so foolishly. When he'd leaned close and brushed his fingers against her neck as he freed her necklace, the sensation of his hands on her skin and his breath against her hair had been intoxicating. No man's touch had ever made her heart race so wildly or made her skin shiver so pleasurably.

Madeline and Cecelia finally appeared on the balcony above. They were dressed in nearly identical gowns, Madeline's white and Cecelia's ivory. In her excitement, Madeline moved too quickly down the stairs, catching her foot on her skirt. She might have stumbled had Cecelia not quickly caught her arm.

"There seems to be quite a lot of stumbling going on today," Lady Carlton murmured, glancing from Anna to Lord Wareton. He ignored his aunt as he tugged on his gloves, a hint of a smile on his face. Likely he was thinking of Lady Stratford. And was Anna imagining it, or was he actually *humming*?

Giggling, Madeline and Cecelia pushed past Anna, Lord Wareton, and Lady Carlton, and they hurried out the door, arms locked. Lady Carlton bustled after them, warning them not to dirty their hems.

Lord Wareton offered Anna his arm. Childishly, she wished to refuse, increasingly irked at his good mood. As they stepped towards the door, she rested her hand gently on his arm, touching him as lightly as possible. Still, even through her gloves, she felt the warmth of him intensely. It was a relief to step into the carriage and away from his touch.

A moment later he sat across from her in the coach, his long legs stretched out, nearly brushing hers when the road grew rough and the carriage shook. He laughed with Madeline and Cecelia as they shared gossip about people who would be at the ball. He even drew a rare smile from Lady Carlton, but he seemed quite content to ignore Anna.

Now he would surely keep his distance again. Even as it saddened her, part of her was relieved. As the events earlier made clear, she couldn't be near him any longer and successfully hide the profound effect he had upon her.

Anna wasn't surprised the party was already a crush when they arrived. Mrs. Dunbury welcomed them as they stepped into the ballroom entryway. She was in her mid-forties, with thin lips and glossy, silver-black hair. She spoke briefly with Anna and the other ladies, but she lingered with Lord Wareton, sizing him up as she introduced him to her two unmarried daughters, Agnes and Angeline. The two young women looked especially elegant this evening, their dark hair carefully curled, their silk gowns obviously fresh from the dressmaker. Anna was certain that Lord Wareton's expected presence was a key reason for their meticulous appearance.

He graciously asked both ladies to reserve a dance for him before finally moving on. The wait for the receiving line had grown long behind him, almost every face in it watching the new earl curiously.

As Anna moved into the ballroom, her friend Mrs. Shelby hurried forward to greet her and drew her away from the others. Mrs. Shelby wore a scarlet and gold gown that hugged her plump figure and made her red hair look even redder.

"My dear Miss Colbrook," Mrs. Shelby whispered, glancing at Lord Wareton as he passed nearby with Madeline at his side, "the new earl is simply devastating! It is no wonder there is such gossip about him. What is your impression? Is he improved since you last met him?"

"Tolerably," Anna said. "It is true he is reformed, although perhaps not as entirely as he wishes people to believe."

"Let us hope not." Mrs. Shelby grinned. "That would be quite dull." She glanced about and added quietly, "I have a tidbit of my own to share about him. His old amour, the former Miss Jane Farthington, is here. The now-widowed Lady Stratford. They were apparently quite attached to one another before she married." It was true then—perhaps

Lady Carlton hadn't exaggerated.

"Why is she in Somerset?" Anna asked.

"Supposedly, she came to visit with a cousin. Of course, everyone says it is all an excuse to meet Lord Wareton again." Mrs. Shelby smiled and raised one thin, red brow. "After seeing him myself, I can understand why."

Anna slowly made her way through the ballroom with Mrs. Shelby. Even as she spoke with people, she constantly watched for Lord Wareton, noting where he was in the room and whom he spoke to. She watched as he took to the floor for the first dance with Agnes Dunbury. He was graceful, confident, and so handsome that the eyes of nearly every woman in the ballroom lingered on him. Anna found it difficult not to stare herself.

A short time later Mrs. Shelby was telling her the latest gossip about the Dunburys when she abruptly stopped speaking.

"Here comes Mrs. Lutton," Mrs. Shelby whispered, frowning. "I was hoping she wouldn't attend." At the mention of Mrs. Lutton, Anna's mood dropped even further. There was no time to escape without making a scene, however. She turned, forced a polite smile, and greeted Mrs. Lutton along with Mrs. Shelby.

Mrs. Lutton was small, thin, and at age sixty looked ten years older due to her perpetual scowl. Mrs. Lutton greeted Mrs. Shelby politely, but barely nodded at Anna, never acknowledging her by name. Anna ignored the snub. She'd become accustomed to Mrs. Lutton's rudeness over the past year. She'd resigned herself to being ignored for the remainder of the conversation when she was unexpectedly rescued by, of all people, Lord Wareton.

"Pardon me," he said, "but I simply must ask Miss Colbrook for a dance. Would you honor me?" Astonished, Anna accepted his hand. Even a set with him would be better than Mrs. Lutton's company. She felt slightly dazed as he led her to the center of the ballroom. A moment later she was in his arms, his hand on her back as he guided her across the floor.

"You are surprised," he said. "Miss Madeline implored me to ask you to dance. She believed you desperately needed rescuing from that unpleasant looking old woman. Is it true?"

"Yes. Thank you." She studied his face. He was so handsome tonight. The rugged line of his jaw held a hint of stubble, and she had the sudden urge to touch that roughness, to feel his skin beneath her fingers.

"Who is she?" he asked.

"Mrs. Lutton." Her heart beat faster than it normally would for a waltz. She'd never been so close to him for so long, not even when he'd carried her across the stream. She looked away from his face, trying to distract herself.

"And why does Mrs. Lutton dislike you?" he asked.

"It is unimportant." She stared at his shoulder, trying not to think about how delightful his hand felt against her waist and how gently his warm, strong fingers pressed against her own. His touch was so disconcerting that she nearly tripped as they made a turn on the dance floor. If he noticed her clumsiness, he gave no sign.

"The price of my rescue is that you tell me," he said, smiling down at her, "or else when the set is over I shall take you right back to her and insist on being introduced."

"She is the wife of Mrs. Hunter's former landlord," she said, unable to resist looking at his face again. Why was he being so pleasant and playful?

"Ah. She was less than pleased when you took in her tenant?" Again, he gave her a teasing smile.

She couldn't help but smile back. "Yes, especially when I rented her a much larger cottage for a quarter the price."

He laughed. He looked so happy and relaxed. She suspected even more that Lady Stratford was the cause of his good mood. He must still have feelings for her after all this time.

"You have kept very busy with charities and running the estate these past years," he said. "Is that why have you haven't married?" He shifted his hand slightly on her back. Despite the respectable distance between them, she felt exceedingly conscious of their bodies, as if they were dancing too close.

He wanted to marry her off and be rid of her. That was why he was suddenly being friendly again, and why this afternoon he'd been so interested in what had happened with Mr. Harley. The idea that briefly sprang to mind, that he might be simply be interested in her, she immediately dismissed as preposterous.

"I told you," she said, "I will not be pressured into a match. I prefer to wait for Madeline to marry."

"But you might have married and taken her with you to your new home," he said, looking doubtful, as if he didn't quite believe her reasons.

"Wareton is her home," she said, "and she belongs there. And I have always wished to see her happily settled first." The words came easily. She'd repeated them so many times to Madeline and to her friends and neighbors. She'd even convinced Madeline they were true.

But Lord Wareton was different. He watched her too closely, and he saw too much. He sensed she was hiding something.

And after years of having never spoken the truth to anyone, she suddenly wanted to tell him everything.

"So you have discouraged suitors these past six years?" He still looked skeptical. "And you have simply not allowed yourself to become attached to anyone?"

It was true, or it had been true. Until she'd met him again. But she said nothing. She would be a complete fool not to try to conceal her feelings for him. He was hopelessly far above her in rank and situation, making any honorable relationship impossible. He was her stepsister's guardian. He had a reckless, disreputable past. He currently had a mistress, perhaps two.

And yet, he'd answered Madeline's plea to rescue her. He was kind, so handsome, and tonight he was as warm and friendly as the day they walked together.

Slowly, his eyes moved over her hair and her face. Was she imagining it, or did his gaze linger on her lips? Surely after this afternoon he knew that he affected her, so what on earth was he doing?

He pulled her closer, until only a few inches separated them, a barely respectable distance. She dropped her gaze to his shoulder, too startled to look into his eyes any longer. His fingers moved on her back, brushing briefly above her waist, the touch feeling as decadent and warm through her silk gown as if he touched her bare skin. Was it merely an absent movement of his fingers, or was he deliberately caressing her?

The waltz was ending. As they slowed for the final notes, he drew her even closer.

"Six years, Miss Colbrook," he whispered, his breath warming her hair, "is a long time to hide from the world."

Hide from the world?

The music stopped. He released her and stepped back, his face once again a mask of polite indifference. She was suddenly aware of the dozens of people nearby, some glancing at them curiously.

She curtsied quickly, hoping the other guests were merely interested in the new earl and that she hadn't betrayed her feelings to the entire ballroom.

"Adrian!" Lady Carlton marched up to him and grabbed his arm. Cecelia and Madeline followed in her wake. Despite the cool breeze where they stood near the open windows, Lady Carlton flapped her black fan furiously.

"You must come with me and meet some very important people." Lady Carlton glanced disapprovingly at Anna. "You must not be wasting your dance sets, either."

Lord Wareton inclined his head at Anna, a flash of anger

in his eyes, but he allowed his aunt to lead him away. Lady Carlton commanded Cecelia to follow. Madeline took Anna's arm, and they strolled out of the ballroom into an antechamber where several small groups of people were escaping the crush.

"She is so ill-mannered," Madeline said. "I cannot believe how she speaks to you."

"She is ill-mannered to everyone," Anna said. They stopped in a quiet corner, watching guests pass by on their way to the refreshment table in the adjoining room.

"Yes," Madeline said, "but she is particularly rude to you." Madeline's face was unusually grave. "She is angry with me for asking Lord Wareton to save you from Mrs. Lutton. Why do you think that is?"

"You dared to interfere with her plans of whom he should dance with." Anna looked away. "Is that not reason enough?"

"It is not only that." Madeline stepped closer and lowered her voice. "When you were dancing together it rather looked like..." Madeline hesitated and glanced around before adding, "Are you growing fond of him, Anna?"

"Who?"

"You know perfectly well who," Madeline whispered. "Lord Ware—"

"Do not be ridiculous." Guilty as she felt for lying, she couldn't tell Madeline the truth. Admitting her foolish feelings would make it far too real, and she wasn't even sure how real it was. She was simply indulging in a pointless infatuation, while the strongest emotion he likely felt was amusement at discovering how much he could unnerve her.

"I thought not." Madeline sighed with relief. "I told Lady Carlton about Sir Neville but she hardly seemed reassured. She believes you are distracting Lord—"

"What did you tell her about Sir Neville?" Anna asked.

"Do not be angry. Anyway, she would see for herself

soon enough."

"You mustn't say things like that, especially to her. Sir Neville is my friend, nothing more."

Madeline shook her head, sighing. "If you hadn't told him that you refused to marry before I do, he probably would have declared himself already. I do not understand why you insist on denying the obvious."

"Madeline—"

"He was so despondent after his wife died, yet you were the one who drew him out from his grief. He has become devoted to you, it is evident to everyone. And I believe you like him as well. He is a wonderful gentleman, if you would only let him know you are agreeable to an offer—"

"I am not agreeable to an offer," Anna whispered. "I will not consider it until you are happily settled." The familiar answer came easily, but she felt a pang of uneasiness. Lately she'd wondered if it wasn't time that she told Madeline the truth about why she hadn't married. Madeline was old enough now that, as much as the terms of the settlement would upset her, Anna might be able to convince her that she wasn't to blame. But to reveal the secret after so many years made her exceedingly uncomfortable. Soon, she vowed, she would tell Madeline. Soon, but not yet.

"But I shall likely be married before long," Madeline said, "now that I am out. And until then, I have Miss Cecelia and Lady Carlton to keep me company." Madeline took Anna's hands in her own. "I will miss you terribly, but I will feel even worse if you continue to delay your happiness on my account."

"But if I choose to—"

"You would not be far away at all." Madeline stood taller. "And besides, I am not a child anymore." It was true. Madeline's head would never reach above Anna's chin, but there was no mistaking her for a girl any longer.

Lord Wareton's final words during their waltz repeated in her mind. He might not know anything about the terms of her inheritance, but she had a horrible feeling that he was right all the same. After so long without risking her emotions, was she hiding?

"Sir Neville should arrive soon," Madeline said as she squeezed Anna's hands. "Perhaps tonight you will let him know how you feel?"

"I do not know how I feel," Anna said. She hadn't been sure of her feelings for Sir Neville before Lord Wareton's arrival, and ever since, she'd given Sir Neville little thought. Shamefully little, considering how attentive he'd been to her over the past months.

"Remember, gentlemen as fine as Sir Neville are rare." Madeline sighed. "I might fancy him myself were he not so obviously devoted to you."

"Would you?" Anna said, surprised. Madeline had always admired Sir Neville and had seemed especially sad for him after his wife died. Yet he was more than a decade older than Madeline, and it had never occurred to Anna that her sister might have any romantic interest him. Surely, she was only saying that and meant little by it?

Madeline released her hands. "But I must go; I am promised for the next dance. It is only with Mr. Stanhope." Madeline rolled her eyes. "Still, a dance is a dance. Think on what I said," she added before hurrying away.

Anna watched Madeline return to the ballroom. She wasn't ready to face Sir Neville. She turned in the opposite direction and slipped out an open door that led outside.

The veranda was empty. Lanterns cast a soft glow along the balustrade and illuminated the central garden path, with everything beyond it falling into darkness.

She stood in the center of the terrace, staring out into the shadows, and considered what Madeline had said. Did Sir Neville truly wish to marry her?

She'd known Sir Neville for over fifteen years, ever since moving to Wareton, but it was only in the past year that they'd become close friends. She'd been the first to persuade him to socialize again after his wife died, and he'd sought out her company more and more.

Over the past few months, since he'd officially come out of mourning, his attentions had increased. Proper as he was, the signs of his interest were subtle, but they were becoming harder to deny.

What puzzled her was why she wished so strongly to deny that Sir Neville liked her.

To have captured the attention of a man of his rank and situation was unlikely enough, but at her age, it was practically a miracle. Sir Neville was a renowned hero, considerate, intelligent, and wealthy enough to marry a wife with no money if he wished. He was handsome too.

And if he did want to marry her, she should probably leap at the chance to secure such a match.

A man stepped through the doorway on the far side of the veranda. He strolled to the edge and leaned forward, his long arms resting on the railing. With the dim glow of a lantern directly behind him, he was little more than a silhouette, but she immediately recognized Lord Wareton's tall form.

Apparently, he hadn't seen her in the shadows. He leaned forward even more, resting his elbows on the railing, allowing his head to drop. He'd seemed so happy earlier, so excited about seeing his former love again, but now he looked weary, even troubled. What could be distressing him?

She felt guilty for watching him without his knowledge, and oddly uncomfortable to see him appearing so vulnerable.

She moved, intending to slip back inside unseen, but her shoes clicked against the stone floor. He straightened and turned towards her. All signs of weariness had disappeared.

"Hiding out here, Miss Colbrook?" he said quietly. It was the second time that evening he'd accused her of hiding. For some reason, it made her feel terribly out of sorts.

"I might say the same of you," she said.

"You would be correct." He walked towards her. As he passed through a circle of lantern light she could see that he was smiling. "But I fear I will not be safe from my aunt for long."

He was right, and should Lady Carlton hunt him down and find them together outside in the dark, it would be extremely unpleasant for everyone. Anna most of all.

"If you will excuse me, I've had enough fresh air." She turned toward the nearest doorway.

"Running away?" He sounded amused. "Do I frighten you?"

She stopped. Yes, she thought, even more than your aunt does. And that was saying quite a bit.

"No," she lied, turning to face him. He stood only a few paces from her. "Why should you frighten me?" He knew very well that he unnerved her. How could he not, after her ridiculous display that afternoon in the sitting room?

"A good question." He stepped closer. "Why should any gentleman frighten you?"

"They do not."

"I think they do." He stopped barely an arm's length away. She stood at the edge of a circle of lantern light. If she moved backwards one step, she would be in the shadows. "And I believe I know why."

What was he about? Was he trying to coerce more information out of her in his attempt to marry her off?

"I'm sure your theory is terribly fascinating," she said, "but I have no wish to hear it."

"The old earl refused Mr. Harley, and it broke your heart." He spoke casually, as if it were a game to him. Why had she ever told him the old earl had turned down Mr. Harley, not her? What had made her confide in him when she should have known he might use it to try to push her to marry?

"And now you use Madeline as an excuse," he added,

"and you hide yourself in plain gowns—"

"Plain?" She crossed her arms. "How charming you are—"

"All because you are afraid." He moved forward until she was forced to step back into the dark to maintain a respectable distance. He stood at the edge of circle of lantern light, his face now in shadow. "Do you fear some gentleman might desire a kiss?"

She inhaled sharply. "Why fear it, when my plain dresses will clearly prevent such attentions?"

"That sounds like a challenge," he said softly. He stepped even closer. He was almost as near to her now as when they were dancing. This time she didn't step away.

Was he only trying to frighten her, or did he truly want to kiss her? Would he dare?

They stared at each other in the low light, the music and sounds of conversation from inside seeming to fade. He stepped forward into the shadows, closing the slight space that remained between them, his legs brushing the skirt of her gown.

Only a complete fool wouldn't turn and run inside this moment. If anything should happen between them, he would only wish to find her a husband even sooner once he regretted his actions. And he would surely regret them. As would she.

Then he reached out and slowly, he cradled her face in his palms. The music from the ballroom seemed even quieter, softer than the calls of insects in the garden and the whisper of their mingled breathing. His breath smelled faintly of brandy, sweet and warm.

He bent his head towards her. She closed her eyes, trembling as she lifted her mouth to meet his.

CHAPTER SEVEN

FOR A MOMENT, THEIR MOUTHS remained separated by a whisper of air, the sweet promise of his kiss and the warmth of his body a breath away. Then he pressed his mouth softly against hers, at first merely brushing her lips with his, then drawing her closer for a deeper but still gentle kiss.

Anna couldn't move. She didn't breathe. She accepted the kiss, too shocked to kiss him back, amazed by the velvety warmth of his lips and the heat of his palms on her cheeks.

"Miss Colbrook?" A man called out from close by.

Lord Wareton abruptly ended the kiss and stepped back. She turned to see Sir Neville crossing the veranda towards them, his walking stick tapping against the stone floor.

"Miss Madeline said I might find you here, getting some air," Sir Neville said as he approached.

"She knows me too well," she said, vowing to admonish Madeline later for sending him to search for her.

Sir Neville caught sight of Lord Wareton and stopped short.

Lord Wareton inclined his head. "Sir Neville."

"Lord Wareton." Sir Neville didn't bow. His eyes narrowed as he glanced from Lord Wareton to Anna and back to Lord Wareton. "Rather a cool night to be out of doors long."

"A brief respite from the crush." Lord Wareton's tone was mild, but he stood stiffly, his hands clasped behind his back.

"Indeed." Sir Neville drummed his thumb against the gold handle of his walking stick.

Clearly Sir Neville knew of Lord Wareton's past reputation and was assuming the worst. Would he be so wrong? At least she knew Sir Neville would keep quiet about finding them alone. He would never do anything to harm her reputation.

Footsteps broke the awkward silence as a woman stepped out onto the terrace and looked in their direction. She was a petite blonde that Anna didn't recognize. The woman glided forward, her eyes on Lord Wareton.

For an instant the woman's face was expressionless, and Anna thought her almost plain. But then she smiled, and her long nose and deep-set eyes were suddenly beautiful.

"Lord Wareton," the woman said in a sugary voice, "how wonderful to see you again." Her honey blond hair was upswept and held in place with diamond pins that sparkled in the soft light.

Lord Wareton stepped forward and lifted the woman's hand to his lips.

"*Lady* Stratford." He smiled as he kissed her jeweled fingers, and Lady Stratford stepped closer to him. As she moved, her necklace glittered, a string of emeralds that drew attention to the low neckline of her green and silver crepe gown.

Lady Stratford glanced at Sir Neville and Anna. "You must introduce your companions."

Lord Wareton introduced Sir Neville first. As Lord Wareton presented Anna, he kept his gaze on Lady Stratford.

"Miss Colbrook," Lord Wareton said, "Lady Jane Stratford." Anna forced a polite smile. "Lady Stratford," Lord Wareton continued, "my cousin's stepsister, Miss Anna Colbrook." Anna curtsied, and Lady Stratford quickly assessed her from head to toe.

Lady Stratford smiled. "You never mentioned that you had any cousins." Her voice was warm, as intimate as if they hadn't been apart for the past several years. "I saw your sister just now, dancing with the Duke of Dulverton.

How lovely she looks. Has she caught his eye?"

"They have only just been introduced," Lord Wareton said.

"Sometimes it takes only a few moments to become completely enraptured," Lady Stratford said, her eyes locked with his. There was a brief silence while they continued to stare at each other. Lord Wareton smiled, but the happiness Anna expected he would show seemed to be missing. Or was she merely seeing what she wished to?

Barely realizing what she was doing, Anna drew her arms around herself.

"You are cold," Sir Neville said, offering her his arm. "Shall we step inside?"

Anna nodded.

"Will you join us?" Sir Neville asked, looking to Lord Wareton and Lady Stratford. Sir Neville's tone made it clear that he hoped they wouldn't.

"Thank you," Lady Stratford said, smiling at Lord Wareton, "but I wish to remain here a while longer. The night air is so refreshing."

"Excuse us, then," Sir Neville said.

Anna glanced back as Sir Neville led her towards the ballroom. Lady Stratford leaned scandalously close to Lord Wareton, murmuring something in his ear. As Anna stepped inside, blinking in the brightness, Lord Wareton's deep laugh echoed behind her.

Soon after Sir Neville escorted Miss Colbrook inside, Lady Stratford returned to the ballroom for a dance. Adrian remained on the terrace, looking out across the shadowy gardens but seeing nothing. His mind was filled with thoughts of Miss Colbrook and Sir Neville. He hadn't noticed any signs of it during his brief encounter with Sir Neville on his second day at Wareton, but tonight there was no doubt in his mind.

One look at Miss Colbrook and Sir Neville together, and Adrian knew the situation, already ridiculous, was truly impossible. A man recognized possessiveness in another man, and Sir Neville had made it clear that he believed Miss Colbrook was his to protect.

Of all the men who might be Miss Colbrook's suitor.

Were it any other man, Adrian might have reacted differently. He might not have stifled the surprising rush of competitiveness he felt over Miss Colbrook. He might not have backed away and forced himself to seem interested in Lady Stratford. But seeing Sir Neville's interest in Miss Colbrook had stopped him cold.

Now he understood why Sir Neville had kept secret what had happened between them. He'd told Adrian it was for the sake of the friendship between their families. Obviously, there was far more than friendship at stake for Sir Neville.

He must love Miss Colbrook deeply, to have gone to such lengths to protect her. And Sir Neville was far enough above Miss Colbrook in situation that only a great deal of passion could explain such a match.

Sir Neville's anger at finding them alone in the dark was completely justified. Being discovered in that situation with any man could compromise her reputation, and Sir Neville believed Adrian to be especially dangerous. Many men would have reacted violently to such a scene, but Sir Neville remained calm, saving Miss Colbrook from embarrassment. And shaming Adrian even more for his behavior.

Adrian strolled to the far end of the veranda, stopping before an open doorway that looked in on the ballroom. Sir Neville stood nearby, chatting with Madeline but keeping his eyes on Miss Colbrook. Adrian followed Sir Neville's gaze.

Miss Colbrook was dancing with a young, freckle-faced gentleman. Her hair shone like copper in the bright candlelight. Her gown rippled as she moved, the silk lifting just enough to reveal her slender ankles and the silver bows on her shoes.

She was captivating.

She wasn't the most stunning woman he'd ever seen, and she usually dressed so plainly that a man could almost miss her beauty at first glance. Yet that afternoon he'd wanted to kiss her with a single-mindedness that alarmed him. Soon after, he'd thought that he'd banished such foolish ideas from his brain.

Until he danced with her.

Holding her so close was distressingly arousing. He'd been acutely aware of every movement of her body, each intake of breath and shift of her gaze. Her back had felt molded to his hand, and her long fingers, warm within her soft gloves, fit within his own as if they belonged there. As he'd leaned close to whisper to her, the scent of her had drawn him even nearer, urging him to press his lips against her skin right there and then.

When the dance ended, he'd quickly regained his senses. But later, when he stepped outside to escape Lady Carlton, he'd still been thinking of the dance when Miss Colbrook suddenly appeared in the shadows.

As she stood before him in the dim light, annoyed with him for his personal remarks, nervous but stubbornly refusing to admit her fear, alarming ideas stirred in his brain, thoughts he hadn't allowed himself in a long time. For years, he'd been a man who thought little of consequences. Once, whether the impulse was an outlandish bet at cards, a reckless carriage race, or the seduction of an attractive woman, he'd acted on his desires almost immediately, with rarely a second thought, drinking away any troublesome pangs of conscience. Three years in the military had finally taught him discipline and restraint. He no longer acted impulsively—until today.

He'd half-believed that after wanting to kiss her so

desperately, the reality would be disappointing and would quickly bring him to his senses. Instead, his desire for her was now far stronger. Her skin was silken, even softer than he expected. And he'd had barely a taste of her soft, full lips before they were interrupted.

He was shocked that she'd even allowed him to kiss her, and that she hadn't run away long before he took her in his arms. She was clearly drawn to him, but she must know as well as he did how hopeless such an attraction was.

Yet it was a powerful temptation, catching him pathetically off guard. Touching her had been a grave mistake.

For a moment after he'd kissed her, he'd wondered— what if he seduced her? Why shouldn't he take his pleasure with her and then see her married off? He could add to her inheritance and make her an excellent match, find her a husband who would tolerate an indiscretion in his wife's past.

The thought of behaving so sordidly filled him with disgust.

Even just kissing her had been shameful. Of all the women with whom he could possibly dally, choosing her was the height of insanity. She was too beneath him in position for an honorable courtship, and she was too virtuous for anything else. Worst of all, even if he wasn't her guardian, she lived in his household under his protection. To compromise her was to dishonor his own family.

Even without the complication of Sir Neville wanting her, it was impossible, unthinkable, ridiculous. He must forget all about his attraction to her. By interrupting them, Sir Neville had saved him from possibly making a grave mistake. He would go inside and find Lady Stratford. His future might be with her; it certainly wasn't with Miss Colbrook. Pursuing her would only lead to scandal and pain that could extend far beyond the two of them.

As the set ended, he turned and walked toward the doorway that led to one of the ballroom's antechambers.

He stepped inside, turned a corner in the hallway, and nearly stumbled into Miss Colbrook.

"Lord Wareton," she stammered. He couldn't tell whether she'd been searching for him or not. If she was angry with him for having stolen a kiss, she gave no sign of it.

"How are you enjoying the party?" she asked. Her cheeks were attractively flushed from dancing.

"It is tolerable." He took a step back and brushed imaginary lint from his sleeve. He glanced at her only long enough to notice her face lose some of its color. Had she really expected him to react differently, and not immediately regret kissing her?

"Miss Colbrook," he said, "allow me to apologize for my behavior earlier. It was inexcusable." He adjusted his cuffs while he spoke. Coward that he was, he couldn't meet her gaze. "It was a foolish impulse."

Except he wanted to kiss her again. And do a great deal more. Which is why he must keep his distance from her, at least until his absurd infatuation passed.

"Even if it were more than a fleeting impulse," he continued, his voice a harsh whisper, "such a relationship is simply not possible." He met her gaze, and the pain in her eyes shamed him.

He had to get away from her. Now.

"Excuse me," he said. "I have promised the next set to Lady Stratford." He stepped around her and strode away.

Anna watched him disappear into the ballroom. She was a fool to be surprised. Of course, he was right. It was impossible. He was an earl, descended from noble bloodlines on both sides of his family, and she was a commoner. Nothing could erase the fact that her father had worked for a living and his father before him. But a foolish impulse? Those words stung far too much.

For a few absurd moments after he kissed her, she'd dared

to hope he was as attracted to her as she was to him. He must find her attractive or he wouldn't have tried to kiss her, but he obviously regretted his impulse as soon as he saw Lady Stratford. And why shouldn't he? Lady Stratford was beautiful, titled, rich, the daughter of a gentleman, and descended from nobility—his equal in every way.

But why had he toyed with her? His actions didn't match what she believed of him, or at least, what she wished to believe of him.

She must force herself to see him clearly and not be blinded by her attraction to him. He couldn't be trusted. She knew he'd behaved dishonorably, as he evidently kept mistresses, and still she'd allowed him to kiss her. What man, with a woman as moon-eyed over him as she was, wouldn't be tempted to steal a kiss? She had no one to blame but herself.

She stepped back out onto the veranda and wandered towards the spot where they'd kissed. A gentle breeze tickled the back of her arms and the nape of her neck as she stopped at a window that looked in on the crowded, noisy ballroom. Even outside, the sweet aroma of beeswax from the scores of melting candles permeated the air.

A new set had just begun, an allemande, and Lady Stratford and Lord Wareton were paired in the center of the ballroom. The contrast between them was striking. Lady Stratford's petite curves and sparkling jewels were all the more stunning against Lord Wareton's tall, muscular build and unadorned clothes. Both were handsome and elegant, and they moved together with breathtaking grace. They had obviously danced together many times.

After a moment, Anna forced herself to look away. There was a sinking feeling in her abdomen, similar to when she'd indulged in too many glasses of Madeira at a dinner a few months before, only this time the balcony didn't spin along with her stomach.

She wished she could return home, but she couldn't go

alone. Cecelia was having a grand time. Many gentlemen, including the duke, had taken an interest in meeting Cecelia, and she was never without a dance partner. She glowed under the attention, her eyes bright with happiness.

Madeline was enjoying herself as well, chatting with friends and dancing. This was one of the first balls she'd attended, and she looked so cheerful that Anna couldn't bear to ask her to leave. Lady Carlton would never abandon Cecelia and as for asking Lord Wareton to escort her home—Anna would sooner spend the evening with Mrs. Lutton.

But leaving early would only let Lord Wareton know how deeply he'd upset her. She drew herself taller. Let him believe her feelings were no more than a fleeting impulse as well. Indeed, perhaps they would turn out to be only that. They must be, for anything else was pointless.

The set ended and the musicians paused for a break. Soon people would wander onto the veranda, and she didn't wish to be seen out here, moping. She tucked her loose hair back into her chignon and stepped into the ballroom. She scanned the room for Sir Neville but instead caught Lady Stratford's eye. She was with Lady Carlton now, and Lord Wareton was nowhere to be seen.

Lady Stratford smiled at Anna, and she and Lady Carlton strolled in her direction. Lady Carlton looked smug, fanning herself slowly, the feathers on her headdress fluttering as she approached.

"There you are, Miss Colbrook," Lady Carlton said. "Have you met Lady Stratford?"

"I have already had the pleasure," Anna said.

"Then you know Miss Colbrook is Miss Madeline's stepsister?" Lady Carlton asked, turning to Lady Stratford. "Her mother was Lord Gerard's second wife. Her father was a shipping merchant." Lady Carlton smiled at Lady Stratford as if this were a private joke she would understand. To Anna's surprise, a slight wrinkle appeared in Lady Stratford's brow and she narrowed her eyes at Lady Carlton.

"Lady Carlton," Anna said, peering over the older woman's shoulder, "I do believe Cecelia's lace is slipping."

"Heavens!" Lady Carlton said, "And she is about to dance another set with the duke. I must go." Lady Stratford nodded graciously as Lady Carlton turned and pushed her way through the crowd toward Cecelia.

Lady Stratford smiled. "I am eternally in your debt, Miss Colbrook."

"I shall have to make it up to Cecelia somehow," Anna said.

Lady Stratford laughed. "If you will not think me too forward, I was hoping you would answer a question. Would you sit with me for a moment?"

"Of course." Lady Stratford took Anna's arm and led her to an unoccupied settee at the edge of the ballroom.

"I may have only just met you," Lady Stratford said as she settled herself beside Anna, "but I know an honest face when I see one. Will you forgive me asking a somewhat indelicate question?"

"You have my permission to ask whatever you wish," Anna said, curious. Close up, she was struck by the contrast between Lady Stratford's porcelain skin and golden hair, which made her seem almost angelic, and her cool eyes which, pretty as they were, seemed to belong to a much older woman.

"Thank you. It concerns Lord Wareton." Lady Stratford made certain no one else was within earshot and lowered her voice. "I am sure you have heard that he and I once formed an attachment." Anna nodded. "I hoped you could provide insight into his current situation."

"I am not sure what you mean."

"I ask if he is currently involved with anyone," Lady Stratford said, "if he has formed a new attachment." Not unless a fleeting impulse qualifies, Anna thought. Or a mistress or two.

"I fear you are asking the wrong person," Anna said.

"I know it is terribly inappropriate of me to ask," Lady Stratford said, "but where Lord Wareton is concerned, I often lose my reserve. We were quite fond of each other many years ago. I should not press this upon you, having just met you, but I must know before considering renewing our friendship that I shall not be interfering with any present happiness of his."

Beautiful, apparently not snobbish, and goodhearted as well. Anna's mood plummeted.

"If I have embarrassed you," Lady Stratford said, "I am sorry."

Anna shook her head.

"Tell me then, is anyone else in his heart?"

Anna had the awful impulse to say yes. But it would be a lie, and what right did she have to try to deny this woman or Lord Wareton happiness? On the surface at least, they seemed well suited to each other. Both were handsome, elegant people of high rank and aristocratic backgrounds. What right did she have to be jealous?

"He does not seem to be a man who would let his heart go easily," Anna said. If he even had one to give. His behavior this evening made her wonder.

Lady Stratford's smile widened. "Thank you, Miss Colbrook. You have helped me immensely. I must admit that when I first saw you and Lord Wareton dancing together, I thought..." She smiled. "Well, you have reassured me."

Next to Lady Stratford's radiant beauty and elegant clothing, Anna suddenly felt plain. Then just as quickly, she felt angry. Why did Lord Wareton affect her so? She was nothing to him, he had said as much.

"I look forward to us becoming better acquainted," Lady Stratford added, glancing across the room. "We may be in each other's company quite often in the future."

Anna followed Lady Stratford's gaze to where Lord Wareton had just stepped into the ballroom. He stood with his hands behind his back, his face somber as he spoke with the Duke of Dulverton. The duke was widely considered a handsome man, with his blond hair and slim build, but Anna thought he looked quite plain beside Lord Wareton.

"I look forward to it as well," Anna murmured, forcing her gaze away from Lord Wareton.

Lady Stratford glanced at Lord Wareton and back to Anna, then raised one elegant eyebrow, a slight frown on her face.

CHAPTER EIGHT

SIX DAYS LATER ANNA SAT on a hillside at Sir Neville's estate. She traced the patterns on the blanket beneath her with one finger, admiring the flawlessly stitched wreaths of wildflowers. The grass all around was thick with nearly identical blossoms of blue and yellow.

"No doubt Sir Neville ordered that made to match this particular hillside," Lady Stratford said, watching her. "After knowing him only a short time, I can see he spares no expense in anything he does."

Several large picnic baskets and rumpled, empty blankets surrounded the two women. Below, where the hill flattened into a broad field, a dozen people were scattered about, most moving toward the glittering river at the far side of the meadow.

Anna looked past the servants who stood chatting at the base of the hill, to the front of the party. Mrs. Shelby was half-hidden by her large parasol as she walked between Lady Carlton and Mrs. Dunbury. Ahead of them, Agnes and Angeline Dunbury strolled with Lord Wareton, one on each side. Both young women tripped increasingly often as they crossed the field, forcing him to catch them.

"The Dunbury sisters are quite shameless," Lady Stratford said. "Not that I blame them. He is likely the most interesting gentleman these parts have seen in a long time. Wouldn't you agree, Miss Colbrook?" She smiled at Anna, her expression casual, but after spending time with Lady Stratford over the past several days, Anna had concluded that she never asked a question without a definite purpose.

"Lord Wareton is quite a catch," Anna said evenly. She

leaned over a basket and drew out an apple. As she began to polish it against her white muslin skirt she looked back to the field, where at the back of the parade, Madeline and Cecelia walked slowly with Sir Neville between them.

"Of course, Sir Neville might be considered a great catch as well," Lady Stratford said. "What he lacks in noble background one might argue is made up for by his heroism. And he is obviously rich enough to marry as he pleases. Is it true he was granted this estate and fifty thousand pounds for rescuing those nobles from robbers?"

"I am not certain of the exact amount," Anna said, "but the prince himself declared it enough so Sir Neville need never worry about money again."

"The income from his estate must be quite large," Lady Stratford said. "Yet even though he is out of mourning, the young ladies seem to leave him alone. Why is that?"

"I could not say." Lady Stratford had almost certainly heard the speculation about her and Sir Neville, but Anna wasn't about to share such personal matters with her.

"I understand Sir Neville had a ward," Lady Stratford said, "a young lady who went to Scotland just before his wife died."

Anna paused, about to bite into the apple. "Yes, Miss Julia Howe. Sir Neville sent her away to save her the pain of his wife's final days."

"Indeed? Yet I hear she never returned to Somerset, not even for the funeral."

Anna frowned. "Sir Neville said Julia was too grief-stricken, that she wished to remain with family in Scotland." What was Lady Stratford up to? Anna bit into the apple, savoring its crispness.

"I heard something quite different during my time in Kent." Lady Stratford leaned closer to Anna and lowered her voice. "I heard a rumor that the young lady had been sent away to conceal her condition."

Anna choked on a bite of apple. She finally swallowed,

the fruit scratching her throat. She reached for her napkin.

"Of course, rumors are often incorrect." Lady Stratford smiled. "And I see from your reaction that you've not heard the same talk?"

"No." Anna dabbed at her chin, sticky with apple juice thanks to Lady Stratford's shocking revelation. "There has never been a hint of scandal associated with Sir Neville's family." Could there be any truth to what Lady Stratford said? Anna doubted it, but even if so, it was none of her affair. Yet how awful for Sir Neville, if it were true, to have two tragedies strike so close together.

"Well…" Lady Stratford leaned back. "Perhaps the young ladies ignore the heroic and handsome Sir Neville because they know his interest is already captured?" Lady Stratford twirled a gold and onyx locket between her fingers. The necklace complemented her black and white crepe gown, sensationally patterned in stripes that varied in size and direction to accentuate her figure.

Anna smiled. "Perhaps."

Down the hillside, Madeline and Miss Cecelia moved forward to speak with the Dunbury sisters, and Lord Wareton slowed, allowing Sir Neville to catch up with him. The two men began talking, but it was soon clear that the conversation was unpleasant. Lord Wareton crossed his arms as he walked and even from this distance, Anna could tell that he was angry. Sir Neville gestured with his free hand, speaking emphatically about something Lord Wareton obviously didn't enjoy hearing.

Could Sir Neville be warning Lord Wareton about taking advantage of her?

If Lord Wareton were seriously interested in pursuing her, Sir Neville would be wise to be concerned. She barely trusted herself were Lord Wareton to embrace her again as he had at the ball. Even now, she shivered at the thought of kissing him. She'd been unable to stop reliving the heady shock of their kiss and her disappointment when he quickly dismissed what happened.

But Sir Neville need not worry. She wasn't likely in any danger from Lord Wareton. Not only did he immediately regret kissing her, he'd barely glanced at her since the ball. He seemed to have quite forgotten all about his foolish impulse. She wished she could forget it so easily.

"Why do Lord Wareton and Sir Neville dislike each other?" Lady Stratford asked, startling Anna from her thoughts.

"I could not say. Perhaps you should ask Lord Wareton?"

Lady Stratford smiled. "I would never be so blunt."

Anna laughed. Lady Stratford was sly and often unnerving, but at the same time, it was difficult not to be affected by her charm. Anna understood why Lord Wareton liked her. Even so, Anna watched them together, and despite his clear admiration for Lady Stratford, he didn't seem captivated. He was charming and attentive, but he didn't stare into her eyes or touch her, despite the fact that she was constantly touching him.

"I hope you will forgive a personal question, Miss Colbrook." Lady Stratford dropped her locket and sat straighter. "You and Sir Neville appear to be good friends. Have you never considered him for yourself?"

"Surely Sir Neville's position makes any such hopes foolish," Anna said. "He can do far better than a wife whose father was in trade."

"Perhaps, but he can apparently also afford to marry as he pleases. And his birth is not so far above yours. He has relatives in trade on his mother's side, does he not?"

"Yes. But his achievements have elevated him far beyond his birth."

"I was not born to wealth," Lady Stratford said after a moment. "My family was so poor that I was told I should be fortunate to marry a rich farmer, told so even by ladies whose backgrounds were no better than mine except that chance had brought their fathers a few hundred more pounds a year." Lady Stratford looked toward the field. "People like Lady Carlton, to whom rank and wealth determine a person's value." She paused, her eyes glittering. "I have proven them wrong."

"You are a remarkable woman," Anna said. She meant it. She had little doubt if Lord Wareton didn't already view Lady Stratford as a potential wife, Lady Stratford would do her best to convince him of it. She had a hunger in her eyes that made it clear she wasn't content to remain a mere baroness.

"We have much in common," Lady Stratford said, turning back to Anna. "You know what it is to be treated as inferior to those around you, yet if you wished to, you could marry quite well."

"I do not have your noble bloodline. And my father was not a gentleman."

Lady Stratford flipped open the nearest picnic basket and reached into it, searching for something. "Tell me, Miss Colbrook," she said, keeping her gaze on Anna, "if you could have any man in the world, from king to fisherman, who would you have?"

Anna forced herself not to glance down the hill at Lord Wareton. For some reason it mattered intensely that Lady Stratford not know about her foolish attraction to him. Not that it would change anything if she did know. It was only senseless pride.

"No one I know now," Anna said. As she spoke, there was a shout from below which she immediately recognized as Lord Wareton's voice, followed by peals of feminine laughter. Anna fought to keep her gaze focused on Lady Stratford, realizing her mistake too late. Lady Stratford also resisted the natural impulse to look toward the noise, staring back at Anna, her arm suddenly still in the basket.

"Finally, I knew I should find it eventually." Lady Stratford drew out a smaller basket. She removed the woven lid and held it out to Anna.

"I am guessing you also like peppermint biscuits," Lady Stratford said softly, smiling. Anna nodded, reaching out to accept the biscuits. "Another thing we have in common."

A short time later Anna watched the rest of the party return from their walk. The Dunbury sisters plodded up the hill together, their shoulders slumped, glancing at each other with sour faces. The hems of their walking dresses were smudged with dirt from all their stumbling. Behind them, Lady Carlton jabbered at Mrs. Dunbury and Mrs. Shelby while Cecelia and Madeline strolled shoulder to shoulder, their bonnets touching as they whispered to each other. Lord Wareton and Sir Neville walked far behind the others, both looking displeased.

"It is your fault, for hanging on him so much he could not bear to walk back with us," Angeline whispered loudly as they neared Anna and Lady Stratford.

"It was not I who kept falling on him," Agnes said. "You have no doubt bruised him so badly he will never wish to see either of us again."

"Bruised him!" Angeline said. "I did not—"

"Hush!" Agnes grabbed her sister's arm and smiled at Anna and Lady Stratford.

"I trust your walk was a success, Miss Dunbury?" Lady Stratford asked as the sisters sat on a green blanket some distance from hers.

"A success?" Agnes smoothed the ribbons of her pink bonnet. "Whatever do you mean?"

"I meant you successfully found the river, of course." Lady Stratford smiled. "You seemed to have difficulty crossing the meadow. You and Miss Angeline both."

Anna stifled a laugh as Angeline and Agnes scowled, and Lady Stratford smiled sweetly.

Madeline stopped at the edge of Anna's blanket, twirling her lilac and ivory striped parasol. "Anna, will you come for a stroll? That walk was not nearly long enough to suit me." Madeline widened her eyes. She had some gossip to share, something about the Dunburys' behavior during the walk, no doubt. Madeline wasn't one to wait and tell her anything later if she didn't have to.

Anna nodded and stood. The sky was clouding up, but they should have enough time for a quick walk.

They strolled down the hillside in silence. They waved to a scowling Sir Neville and stone-faced Lord Wareton as the men passed some distance from them. Once they were far enough away to not be overheard, Madeline spoke in a rush.

"Can you believe how brazen Angeline and Agnes are?" Madeline said. "As if Lord Wareton could be in any doubt now of their desperation. You were wise to remain behind." Madeline lowered her voice. "Did you see Sir Neville and Lord Wareton glaring at each other? Why do you think they dislike each other? Do you think Lord Wareton disapproves of Sir Neville's regard for you?"

Anna laughed. "I have no doubt Lord Wareton would be ecstatic if I were to marry Sir Neville."

"Then why...?" Madeline frowned. "Why do you say it like that? Tell me what is going on."

They turned onto the path that followed the river, and strolled toward an enormous willow hanging partially over the flowing water.

"You have been behaving strangely ever since the ball." Madeline stopped suddenly. "Did Sir Neville propose?"

"No." Anna shook her head and began walking again, faster than before. Madeline hurried to keep up.

"I have no doubt that he will," Madeline said, apparently misreading the look of anxiety on Anna's face for disappointment. "If you would only give him a hint that his offer will be welcome."

The breeze grew stronger, and Anna tugged her shawl tighter around her shoulders.

Madeline pulled her parasol closer to block the wind. "I have half a mind to tell Sir Neville myself—"

"No, please. Do not say anything to him." Anna glanced at the clouds. They were thicker than before and deep gray. "Perhaps we should turn back. It looks about to..." A raindrop hit Anna's bonnet, followed quickly by two more. "Rain."

The drops, thick and slow at first, rapidly grew steadier. The only shelter nearby was the willow.

"Under the tree," Anna said, taking Madeline's arm. "Perhaps it will pass quickly."

As they hurried beneath the willow, the rain increased, beating on the branches around them until drops began to pelt them through the canopy of leaves.

"We shall be wet through if we return now," Madeline said above the rain. She crouched close to Anna, trying to share the parasol with her, but it was barely large enough to keep Madeline's head and shoulders dry. Madeline started to shiver.

"Let us run back to the carriages," Anna said. "You will catch cold."

Madeline shook her head. "You will get soaked." A moment later she sneezed.

"You go back alone then," Anna said. "You can stay somewhat dry with the parasol. I shall wait and see if it lets up."

Madeline sneezed again and nodded.

"Take my shawl." Anna wrapped the thin blue muslin around Madeline's shoulders and tied it in the front.

"I shall send someone back with a blanket for you," Madeline said as she ducked beneath the branches.

Anna peered through the boughs of the willow, watching Madeline hurry up the hillside, her parasol clamped to her shoulder to deflect the rain. Rain trickled through Anna's bonnet and plastered her sleeves to her arms.

Most of the party had taken refuge in the carriages. Only

Lord Wareton, Sir Neville, and the footmen remained outside. Lord Wareton spotted Madeline hurrying up the slope, and he gestured to one of the footmen. The servant disappeared around the coach and quickly returned with a blanket.

Lord Wareton snatched it up and hurried to meet Madeline. He draped the blanket around her and escorted her to the carriage. As he helped her into the coach, she hesitated and gestured toward the hillside. Another blanket was handed out to Lord Wareton, but when he turned to start down the hill, Sir Neville stopped him.

Even through the gray film of rain, Anna could tell that Sir Neville wanted to bring her the blanket. There was a brief argument before Sir Neville seemed to concede. Of course, it would take him far longer to reach her. He couldn't run like Lord Wareton.

Lord Wareton drew his coat tighter around himself, secured his hat, and hurried down the hill. Behind him, Sir Neville disappeared into his own carriage.

Anna moved back to stand by the trunk. She caught occasional glimpses of Lord Wareton through the drooping branches as he neared.

After a moment he ducked beneath the willow, his hat striking leaves and showering water on him. He straightened and stepped towards her, his gaze falling on her body. He stopped suddenly and nearly dropped the blanket, catching it just before it hit the damp ground.

As he straightened, his gaze faltered on her chest. She was suddenly aware of how drenched her clothes were and how tightly her bodice clung to her. He slowly held out the quilt and met her stare.

In the instant before he looked away, she saw it in his eyes.

He wanted her.

She took the blanket from his outstretched hands and drew it around her shoulders, shivering less from the cold than from pleasure at the fire in his eyes. He wasn't so indifferent to her after all.

As she adjusted the blanket he strolled behind her, his broad form blocking the worst of the wind. She snuggled into the covering and leaned against the trunk once again, turning to watch him.

"Delightful weather," he said. He took off his hat and shook it, spattering raindrops across the ground. His hair was disheveled, dry to his ears but dampened to a dark brown and curling up at the ends. His jacket, the front of his shirt, and nearly all of his trousers were soaked. He still looked entirely handsome.

She realized it was the second time he'd come to her rescue recently. First at the ball, saving her from Mrs. Lutton's company, and now this.

"Thank you for the blanket," she said.

He nodded, still not looking at her. "It looks as if the rain may let up shortly." The patter of raindrops immediately grew dramatically louder, and he frowned. "Shall we wait a few moments to see if it stops before I escort you back to the carriage?"

"Yes." She regretted her answer immediately. She didn't know how long she could remain with him in such stifling awkwardness. Perhaps he wasn't as uncomfortable as she was, and perhaps he wasn't thinking of their kiss at the ball. But then why was he trying so hard not to look at her?

"Not too long," he said, finally glancing at her, a hint of a smile softening his face, "or Sir Neville may come looking for us."

"He should not," she said, eager to fill the uneasy wait with conversation. "With his leg, he probably shouldn't have walked down the hill once today, never mind again and in the rain."

He jammed his hat back on his head. "Your concern for him is admirable." His voice was clipped.

"You and Sir Neville do not like each other," she said.

"Why?"

The blunt question clearly caught him off guard. "I ... do not know him well enough to dislike him," he said stiffly. She could see from the resolve in his eyes that he probably wouldn't answer her question, at least not directly.

"I saw you arguing with him earlier," she said. "What were you talking about?"

"You can guess well enough what we were discussing," he said. "You."

He leaned away, as if he were afraid of being too close to her. Yet the shelter of the tree was so small that he was still disturbingly near. Close enough that she could see the faint lines around his eyes as he frowned and smell the damp wool of his coat.

"Sir Neville is my friend and wishes to protect my reputation," she said. "No doubt because of what he saw at the ball, he fears that you might take advantage of me. Any gentleman would—"

"It is because he wants to marry you." The stiff, restrained expression he wore around her lately gave way to one of annoyance.

"He told you this?" she asked.

"It is obvious." He rested one arm against the tree trunk. "He pays no particular attention to any other woman, only you." He glanced away and idly traced a finger along a line in the bark. "Why do you seem reluctant to accept the idea?"

She could hardly keep her mind on Sir Neville. She stared at Lord Wareton's hand on the tree and recalled the pleasure of his touch the night of the ball. How would it feel to have his touch elsewhere on her body? She twisted the blanket around her fingers, trying to force away such wicked thoughts.

"Because it would be foolish for a man of Sir Neville's situation to marry me," she said.

"Indeed." He straightened and crossed his arms. "And

yet, in his position, he can afford to be imprudent."

Anger flared in her for a moment, then quickly faded. Why should she feel bitter towards him for speaking sensibly, for holding an opinion that merely reflected the truth of his upbringing and his position? Even she acknowledged it would be a poor match for Sir Neville, so why did it anger her that Lord Wareton agreed so heartily?

"I intended no offense," he added, glancing at her, his voice softer. "Only that the right woman can cause any man to act rashly, even when it comes to something as important as marriage."

"Not you, however," she said.

"No." He smiled grimly. "I am not free to behave with such recklessness." Of course, he intended to marry Lady Stratford or another lady of equally high birth. As he should. She glanced away, trying to hide her senseless disappointment.

As if the one kiss they shared meant anything, even if they suited each other—which they clearly didn't. And as if the fact that her father was in trade didn't make her utterly beneath a man of Lord Wareton's illustrious rank. He was an earl, for heaven's sake.

"At least," he added, shifting closer to her, "I cannot be reckless in whom I choose to *marry*."

The suggestion in his words sent her heart racing.

His gaze swept from her eyes to her lips and chest before returning to her mouth. He clearly wanted to kiss her again. And despite knowing nothing honorable could come of it, despite her awareness that to him it was probably only a game, she still wanted him to.

She looked at his handsome mouth, down across his firm jaw, to his broad chest. His wet shirt revealed a shadow of dark hair. How would it feel to run her fingers across his skin and against the soft hair beneath his shirt?

He stepped even closer. "Lately I, too, have been tempted to recklessness," he said softly. He lifted a hand to her cheek and caressed her face with his fingertips, tracing the curve of her chin, pausing as he brushed her lips. "Ever since the night of the ball, I have wanted to steal another kiss."

She stared at him, unmoving, unable to speak.

"Why do you not run away from me?" he asked softly. His collar and cravat were loose from the rain. The pulse in his neck seemed abnormally fast.

"I do not wish to," she whispered.

He smiled. The egotistical devil. He knew that he captivated her.

He continued to stare at her, caressing her cheek.

"You are beautiful, you know," he murmured. His breath warmed her face as he gazed down at her, his mouth inches from hers. The wind shifted and spattered rain onto her face and her lips. He slowly brushed the drops away, his thumb lingering on her mouth.

Then he tugged the blanket open and dragged her into his arms.

He kissed her.

The quilt slid from her shoulders and pooled at her hips, held there by the crush of their bodies. He slid one arm around her, pulling her tighter against him, while with his other hand he slipped his fingers beneath her bonnet.

She'd dreamed of kissing him again, but this was nothing like she imagined—it was both more wonderful and more frightening. Her body responded to him quickly, to the warm press of his broad chest, the clinging dampness of their mingling clothes, and the delicious warmth of his mouth.

This time she returned his kisses, slowly moving her hands up his arms and wrapping her fingers around his shoulders, grasping at his damp coat. She moved her hands higher, tentatively drawing her fingers over the smooth skin of his neck, across the roughness of his cheeks, until she brushed her fingertips against his soft hair. She parted her lips, allowing him to deepen the kiss, until she could taste the faint sweetness of apples and brandy from the picnic that clung to his mouth.

They kissed.

They kissed and the rain roared around them, so loudly that they didn't hear Sir Neville until he was nearly upon them. They separated just as Sir Neville stumbled underneath the tree, spraying them with water as the branches snapped back behind him.

They stood only a few paces apart, and if Lord Wareton's guilty expression was any indication, the kiss they'd just shared was likely evident in her face as well.

Sir Neville stared at them a moment, water dripping from his dark hat. "I have brought you a parasol, Miss Colbrook," he said slowly, frowning.

Lord Wareton stepped further away from her. He leaned against the broad trunk and crossed his arms, stone-faced, gazing at Sir Neville as if nothing unusual just occurred, and it was perfectly normal to find them standing so close. There was a challenge in Lord Wareton's eyes as he and Sir Neville stared at one another. Sir Neville's expression was one of blatant hostility and challenge met.

"Thank you, Sir Neville," she said, forcing a smile, "you are very thoughtful. But you should not have come so far with your leg—"

"You should not remain here in the cold in wet clothes," Sir Neville said. "You could fall ill." He glared at Lord Wareton. "Someone must be mindful of what is best for you."

"You are too kind," she said quickly. "Would you escort me back to the carriage now?"

Her mind was spinning.

Lord Wareton had kissed her again, despite apparently intending to wed Lady Stratford. What did it mean? Would he try to seduce her and then see her married to another, a gentleman more suitable for her position? He couldn't make her his mistress even if he wished to, even if she was mad enough to accept. Their family connection made it unthinkable. They should never have allowed anything to happen. They were behaving selfishly, dishonorably.

"You will be forced to walk slowly with me," Sir Neville said, tapping his walking stick, "and become more soaked. Perhaps Lord Wareton will help you back to the carriage since I am incapable of hurrying." He glared at Lord Wareton.

"I am already drenched," she said quietly. "I welcome your help."

"As you wish." Sir Neville snapped open the parasol and held it over her. "I can at least ensure you do not slip and come to harm." He scowled at Lord Wareton again.

Together she and Sir Neville stepped to the edge of the tree. Sir Neville pushed the branches out of her way with his walking stick. Lord Wareton followed behind them.

Sir Neville paused before they left the shelter of the willow. "Miss Colbrook, would you do me the honor of joining me for a carriage ride tomorrow morning? There is an important matter I wish to discuss with you."

"Of course," she said.

An important matter?

She felt a chill that had nothing to do with the rain. Was Sir Neville going to ask her to marry him? And if he did, should she accept, if only to escape Lord Wareton and save herself from ruin?

"We shall not have dinner at Highton Park tomorrow," Adrian said.

"You are being unreasonable," Lady Carlton said from beside him in the carriage. "We must go."

"We are attending the ball later this week," he said. "And we picnicked there today. That is enough time spent there for one week."

He was grateful for the rain that had finally put an

end to what—with one exceptional, far too delicious moment—was surely the most miserable picnic in history. Unfortunately, the rain also meant that he chose to return to Wareton in the carriage rather than ride. Now he regretted that decision. Being drenched through might be preferable to enduring the ladies' displeasure, not to mention having to look at Anna after what had happened. He was already nearly soaked anyway. His breeches stuck to his legs, and his coat sleeves and shirt were cold and damp.

The flooded roads forced them to drive slowly, drawing out what was normally a quick journey. Cecelia and Madeline both pouted, staring out the window nearest them despite the film of raindrops, looking as if he'd just announced they weren't going anywhere for a year, rather than missing one dinner.

Anna sat beside them wrapped in a blanket. She stared straight ahead, frowning. Her eyes matched the blue flowers on the fabric tucked beneath her chin. He recalled vividly how she looked under the willow, her white dress clinging to her chest and hips in a way that had made him forget everything else. It wasn't an image he would ever forget.

Fool that he was, he'd kissed her again. And it had been far more maddening than the first kiss because this time she'd responded. She'd kissed him with such longing, such sweet innocence, and such long-stifled passion that, had they carried on much longer, he would have been ready to take her right there against the tree or on the muddy ground.

His aunt's sharp voice interrupted his thoughts. "I already told Sir Neville that we would attend," Lady Carlton said. "We cannot refuse now without offending him. To do so would be foolish anyway." Lady Carlton leaned closer to him. She'd escaped the worst of the downpour, but the swansdown trim on her walking dress was damp enough that she smelled faintly like a duck pond. He shifted away. "He might not be the most appropriate match for anyone here," she added, "but he is a close friend to several eligible gentlemen, including the duke."

"Sir Neville is honorable, wealthy, and a hero," Madeline said. "He would be a fine husband for any woman of any rank."

"Let us be realistic, dear," Lady Carlton said. "No matter how many carriages full of people he saved from ruffians, nothing would make him suitable to marry into the upper ranks of the nobility. He would be aiming too high were he to court you or Cecelia." Lady Carlton glanced at Anna and added quietly, "Now I believe he may be aiming too low."

Anna ignored her, her gaze focused straight ahead. Madeline bit her lip, frowning. Adrian resisted the urge to unlatch the carriage door and give his aunt a hearty shove.

"At any rate," Lady Carlton continued, "we simply must have dinner there tomorrow."

They would likely be celebrating Miss Colbrook and Sir Neville's engagement by tomorrow. It was exactly what Adrian would have wished when he first arrived at Wareton. He should be relieved.

Instead, the idea twisted his stomach into knots.

"Very well," he said, his mood dropping even further. "You may attend without me." The carriage lurched and a spatter of raindrops pelted the window.

"Attend without you?" Lady Carlton's gaze darted from him to Miss Colbrook. Her lips thinned. "If your duty to your sister and cousins is not enough to sway you, Lady Stratford has also been invited. Perhaps that will change your mind?"

"No," he said, "and I shall not discuss it any further."

"But Adrian—"

"I said I shall not discuss it." His expression and tone must have been fierce because his aunt actually fell silent. She mumbled something under her breath and busied herself smoothing Cecelia's pelisse.

Adrian stared out the window.

Sir Neville would propose to Miss Colbrook tomorrow.

When Sir Neville had caught them under the tree, there was a near desperation, a struggle between anger and faltering hope in his manner. He obviously suspected what had happened, and if he wanted Miss Colbrook, he would try to convince her to marry him soon. If Sir Neville did ask for her hand, it would be an exceptional marriage offer, and if she had the least bit of sense, she would accept.

He had no right to be jealous. It wasn't as if he could offer her as much as Sir Neville. He could give her nothing— not the honor of marriage or even the protection afforded a mistress. His position came with great responsibilities, and one of his most important duties was to marry well. He must choose a wife of high status who would add to his family's wealth and influence. To wed a woman of limited means whose father wasn't even a gentleman would be scandalous and reprehensibly selfish.

In the past, he'd been scandalous and selfish, but now he was a changed man. He refused to fail in his duties again.

The best he could do for Miss Colbrook was to see her married to Sir Neville, and the best he could do for his family was to marry Lady Stratford. He could make her a countess, and she could make his family even more wealthy. Lady Stratford and he would suit each other far better than Miss Colbrook and he ever could.

Jane Stratford. Beautiful and amusing as she was, he found it increasingly difficult to keep his attention on her, especially when Miss Colbrook was present. Though he tried not to even look at Miss Colbrook, he still heard every word she said to others, was aware of her every move, and was constantly battling sinful thoughts about her.

He suspected Lady Stratford had noticed he was distracted. She'd questioned him about Miss Colbrook rather strangely earlier, during a moment of privacy. What were Miss Colbrook's marriage prospects? Why was she still unwed? Only minutes ago, when he leaned into Lady Stratford's carriage to say goodbye, she'd commented wryly on what a disappointment the rain was. The gleam in her eye told him that she hadn't missed him gaping at Miss Colbrook as they returned to the carriages. He was only human. A man would have to be dead not to notice her in a pale, wet dress.

The thought of kissing her again sent heat through his body and an immediately response in his loins.

His lack of control was pathetic. He'd been so long without a woman that he was being driven mad by kisses—very delicious kisses, true—but kisses from a woman who was unsuitable for him in nearly every way.

And he was behaving as recklessly as he had five years ago, kissing a woman without any thought to the consequences. Yet even back then, would he have been so foolish as to try to seduce his cousin's stepsister and a member of his own household?

If the woman were Miss Colbrook, he likely would have.

The irony of his situation didn't escape him. Now that he was reformed, now that he could no longer behave as he wished, he was suddenly infatuated with a woman forbidden to him.

He glanced at her again. The blanket concealed her well, all except for one calf, clearly outlined against her soaked skirt. How he would like to raise that wet skirt and bare her legs. And do a hundred other, far more wicked things to her.

He forced himself to look away.

He couldn't risk such a scene again. It would ruin everything. The honor and duty he'd built his existence around could be shattered by another indiscretion. The stakes were too high for such a gamble.

Adrian stole one last glance at her as the carriage slowed before the entrance of Wareton. She shifted in her seat, sinking deeper against the cushions, and pulling the blanket higher over her shoulders. Her bonnet cast her eyes in shadow. He could see only her smooth chin and full mouth above the crumpled and rain-spattered satin bow. Even cold, her lips looked soft and pink, more tempting to him at that moment than a warm fire and dry clothes.

She tilted her head slightly, revealing her entire face in the gray afternoon light, meeting his gaze in silence. He allowed himself to look into her blue eyes for one long moment, to savor the sweep of her dark lashes below her delicate brows. Even as his body responded to her beauty, he knew he must overcome this attraction. He had no choice.

As the carriage slowed again, he tore his gaze from her and stared out at the gray walls of Wareton Manor, darkened with rain. He had no choice because, without abandoning the very honor and duty that had saved his miserable soul, he could never have her.

CHAPTER NINE

ANNA TRIED TO CONCEAL HER anxiety as she climbed into Sir Neville's curricle.

"Shall we visit May Gardens?" he asked while he helped her to her seat.

She forced a smile. "That would be lovely."

They rode at a leisurely pace out to the main road and then to the west, towards Highton Park. As the carriage climbed a long hill, she turned back to take in the view of Wareton and watched as the manor vanished into the trees.

She couldn't help but wonder what Lord Wareton was doing. At dinner last night, he'd avoided her gaze, and soon after, he'd disappeared into the study for the rest of the evening. She also hadn't seen him at breakfast that morning, which suggested he was deliberately avoiding her. He obviously regretted what they'd done as keenly as she did.

Or did she?

She should feel relieved that he wasn't trying to seduce her. Instead, she quietly fumed. How could he kiss her so passionately one moment and then ignore her the next? Had he no concern for her feelings? For all she knew he might toy with her again, and who knew how far he might take it next time. Most frightening of all, she didn't completely trust herself to resist him if he did decide to seduce her.

There was one way to escape the problem. Should Sir Neville make an offer, she could accept and leave Wareton before the situation became any worse. Sir Neville had become a good friend. She didn't love him romantically, but so many marriages that weren't love matches were still quite content, oftentimes more successful than marriages where strong emotions were involved. After all, a husband who could never claim a woman's heart could never break it, either. Married to Sir Neville, she would never suffer as her mother had, even if he had half a dozen mistresses. Yet knowing Sir Neville, who was so proper and had always seemed so devoted to his wife, he likely had none.

She turned back around in the carriage and glanced at him. He smiled fleetingly, his dark eyes warming, but he said nothing. She studied his thick, chestnut hair streaked with gray that curled out from under his dark hat, his intelligent eyes, and his elegant clothes.

He was a good, honest man and a just landlord. He gave to charities regularly and attended church without fail. In everything he did, he was the model of an honorable gentleman. He would be a fine husband, she was almost certain, and he would treat her well.

By society's standards, such a marriage would be far beyond her reasonable hopes, and everyone would expect her to accept without hesitation. Marrying him would enable her to have what she'd always wanted: a home of her own, far grander than she ever imagined, and perhaps even a family.

So why did the idea leave her feeling so...empty?

Her strong desire to refuse Sir Neville had nothing to do with any foolish ideas about Lord Wareton, absolutely nothing.

She forced her thoughts back to the man beside her. Sir Neville drove with his head held high, practically looking down his nose at the road. He allowed the horses not the tiniest bit of freedom, but kept them carefully paced as they climbed a hill.

"You have a new pair of matched grays," she said.

"Yes." He appeared pleased that she noticed.

"They seem eager to go faster."

"Not to fear. Not in your presence, Miss Colbrook. They are powerful horses, and I wouldn't wish to frighten you." He lifted one hand from the reins and briefly patted her fingers.

She was about to reply that she would enjoy it if he gave them freer rein, but his caress startled her into silence. Sir Neville was always so restrained. He never touched her outside of offering his arm for a stroll or assisting her in and out of carriages. He'd patted her hand without lingering, but that he had touched her at all was unusual.

She swallowed hard on the knot forming in her throat.

They rode in silence until they reached the south end of Highton Park. Sir Neville's gardens were among the most impressive in Somerset, with plants imported from throughout the world. He had several hothouses and employed over a dozen gardeners. In that respect his estate was even more impressive than Wareton.

Sir Neville halted the carriage at the arched stone gate. As he helped her down, she couldn't help but compare him to Lord Wareton. Sir Neville's hands were strong but his touch felt ordinary, with nothing like the intensity she felt from Lord Wareton's touch. And Sir Neville released her the moment she had both feet on the ground, lingering not one second past what was proper.

He secured the carriage and turned to her.

"There is something particular I wish to talk to you about," he said. "I have wrestled with it for some time, but now I cannot keep it from you any longer." He didn't smile as he offered her his arm. "Perhaps we could walk to the vista and speak there?"

She nodded. As they strolled slowly through the garden, she held on to him lightly. They walked in silence, the only sounds the soft crunch of their boots and his walking stick scratching on the gravel path. She let her eyes wander over the lush vegetation, inhaled the perfume of greenery and blossoms, and all the while her heart ached.

Only some of the ache was from worrying about Sir Neville proposing to her. Much was from thinking of Lord Wareton and their embrace yesterday. She had lain awake most of the night, alternating between emotional extremes, thinking of the joy of kissing him and the pain of knowing that what they did was wrong and should never be repeated. Little could distract her from thinking of him for long, and after yesterday, it was even worse.

"You seem troubled," Sir Neville said softly. "I'm not surprised, given the situation you find yourself in."

She said nothing. What could she say? She could hardly discuss her feelings for Lord Wareton with Sir Neville.

The path widened into a circular clearing, bordered by blooming hedgerows and half a dozen curved stone benches. Highton Manor sat on a hill in the distance, as impressive as a castle, its square towers rising high above the main building. And Sir Neville had been given all this magnificence as a gift. She often forgot that he hadn't been born to such wealth. He behaved as if he'd been bred to the upper levels of society when in fact his father had been a gentleman of modest fortune, generations removed from any rank, and Sir Neville's maternal grandfather had been in trade.

"It is so beautiful here," she said, "and you have made it even more remarkable."

"I have tried to care for the estate as it deserves," he said, pride evident in his tone. "His Highness was most generous with me."

"No more than you deserved." They'd had a similar conversation several times before, but she knew it always pleased him to speak of it. "Few would have acted as bravely as you did. You risked your life against four armed men, even after you were wounded."

"I had the cover of the woods," he said, "while they were in the open road."

"Still, it could not have been an easy thing to shoot

them."

"It was not as difficult as you might imagine." His tone was casual. "They deserved it."

She nodded. "You probably saved the lives of everyone in the carriage."

"And I saved the constable the trouble of hanging them later," he added dryly, smiling.

"True," she said. But she couldn't think of it lightly, even though she knew what he did was right. She thought of Lord Wareton and how he refused to speak of the violence he'd endured. How different he and Sir Neville were. But so were the circumstances of their heroics, so it seemed unfair to compare them.

Sir Neville frowned. "You seem distressed. Forgive me for going on about such an indelicate subject. Let us speak of something else."

Her gaze returned to the garden. "This is my favorite place on your estate."

"My wife designed it," he said. "She had three different sets of benches made before settling on these." He stared at the benches.

"You miss her," she said gently. "I'm sorry."

"I do, but..." He looked at her again. "Perhaps lately not as much as I should." He stopped walking and turned to face her. She dropped her hand from his arm and took a step back.

"Miss...Anna," he said softly. He'd never called her by her given name before. "I hope it comes as no surprise that your happiness is of particular concern to me." He stared at her, carefully assessing her reaction.

She fought the sudden urge to move further away from him. To stop him before he could propose.

She was being utterly senseless. She should be afraid of staying at Wareton, not of leaving. She should let Sir Neville make an offer, accept immediately, and leave Wareton as soon as possible, before disaster struck. Disaster in the handsome, disturbing form of the Earl of Wareton.

He cleared his throat. "I believe it also comes as no surprise that I fear Lord Wareton may be a threat to your future happiness." A delicate way of phrasing the situation.

"I had thought to wait longer to make my intentions clear," he said. "I made a promise to my late wife that I would wait longer before I…" He hesitated and cleared his throat. "And, well, I also know it has long been your wish to see Miss Madeline settled before thinking of your own happiness. However, recent events—"

"Sir Neville, before you go any further, please understand that is still my wish."

He frowned. "But under the circumstances—"

"I am resolved not to consider my own future until Madeline is settled." She could hear the panic in her own voice. "I cannot be persuaded otherwise. Forgive me, but I shall hear nothing else on the subject."

He stared at her a moment, then nodded. "I expected as much." She was prepared to argue with him further, and she felt a wave of relief that he had given in so easily to her protests. And a touch of surprise.

"I have always respected your deep concern for your stepsister," he added. He almost seemed relieved that she'd rebuffed him.

But now she understood.

She never doubted that Sir Neville cared for her, and his protectiveness towards her seemed genuine, but sometimes she wondered at his reserve. She sensed his restraint wasn't only due to a strict sense of propriety. Despite his attentions to her, there were times, like now, when he seemed conflicted about his feelings. But she hadn't known until now that he'd promised Lady Mary to wait longer before remarrying.

Yet he had been ready to offer marriage to protect her from Lord Wareton, even if it meant breaking that vow, even when in his heart he clearly wasn't yet ready to marry again.

He stared at her, his expression growing increasingly grave. "There is something I should tell you," he finally said. "I have debated the wisdom of it for fear of distressing you, but now I believe, under the circumstances, it is the right thing to do."

He tapped the handle of his walking stick. "But it brings me no joy, you must believe me."

She frowned. "What is it?"

He stilled his hand and gripped his walking stick tightly.

"I made it known that Julia went to Scotland to be spared the pain of my wife's passing."

"Yes." Julia? What could he have to tell her about his ward?

"That is not the truth." He let out a long breath. "While we were all in London before Mary's death, Julia was in fact…compromised."

She stifled a gasp. Lady Stratford's rumor was true after all.

"I tell you this," he continued, "only to try and protect you from a similar fate." He clearly could see that Lord Wareton was toying with her, and he feared that she would be ruined like Julia.

"Sir Neville, I am grateful for your concern, but my situation is different—"

"Please, there is more." He held out a hand. "I have reasons beyond simply the shame of the scandal for concealing what happened."

"What do you mean?" she said.

"I learned who the villain was almost immediately. I longed to call him out for what he did." Anger flashed in his dark eyes. "Yet I couldn't bear the pain I knew it would bring to others close to me. I especially feared what it would do to our friendship. But now I find what I once did to protect you and your family, now puts you at great risk—"

"Protect *me*?" Her heart raced. Even as she spoke, she knew what he was about to say. Yet foolishly, she hoped that it was all a terrible mistake.

"Yes," he said, "the man who ruined Julia is Lord Wareton."

No.

She clutched the nearby bench and lowered herself onto it, her hands shaking. How could it be? It was almost too much to believe, and yet, everything made sense. Lord Wareton and Sir Neville's animosity went beyond anything to do with her. It explained the strain between the men, and the fact that they wouldn't speak of how they'd met.

Sir Neville gently touched her shoulder. "I had to let you know that he cannot be trusted. I am sorry."

She shook her head. "You have behaved with such admirable restraint. To have endured his company after what he has done, to extend your friendship to him, to all of us..." She couldn't continue. Her mouth felt dry, and her throat tight.

Sir Neville was an even better man than she'd believed, and Lord Wareton was far worse, a scoundrel who had toyed with her emotions and risked bringing scandal on their family. He'd claimed to be reformed, and she'd believed him. She'd opened her heart and extended her friendship to him, accepting that he'd become a new man. She thought of the day they'd walked together and how candidly they had spoken. He must have been amused at her naiveté. Likely just as he was for her allowing him to kiss her.

She glanced at Sir Neville. His eyes were narrowed, his face dark with concern.

"Forgive me for telling you," he said. "I have shocked you."

"You owe me no apology. I am grateful for what you have done to protect my family." She reached out and took his hand, squeezed it briefly, and let her hand fall back into her lap. Her fingers still trembled.

Sir Neville was a noble gentleman who was willing to marry her in order to protect her. Lord Wareton was a shameless villain who only wished to seduce her.

Yet her foolish heart ached for the villain.

After his second ride around the estate, Adrian stopped deceiving himself that he wasn't waiting for Miss Colbrook's return. He passed the main road to the manor half a dozen times before he finally spied Sir Neville's carriage. Adrian kept his horse still and watched from the trees as Sir Neville helped her down from the curricle. Adrian was too far away to see their faces clearly, and he couldn't ascertain anything from their body language. Sir Neville climbed back into the carriage and nodded farewell.

Adrian vowed he wouldn't ask what happened. Either Miss Colbrook would tell him soon enough or Sir Neville would call, requesting the formality of Adrian's blessing. And when he did, Adrian would give Sir Neville his approval, because that was what he should do. It was the best thing for everyone.

Sir Neville was a wealthy and respectable man. He would make her an excellent husband. And they were well suited to each other. Weren't they?

No. For no logical reason, Adrian was certain they weren't.

Sir Neville was honorable but he was too restrained, too proper, too much of a cold fish. Oddly, those were words that not long ago Adrian would have used to describe Miss Colbrook as well. Now he knew better.

He thought again of kissing her. Would she kiss Sir Neville as passionately? Why did the idea make his gut ache?

Foolish, unreasonable jealousy.

As much as he hated to admit it, there was nothing

lacking in Sir Neville as a potential husband, especially for a woman of Miss Colbrook's background. It would be a highly advantageous match for her. Adrian should be pleased for them both, and yet not only wasn't he happy that Sir Neville wanted Miss Colbrook, but irrationally, he couldn't bring himself to like Sir Neville. In fact, he liked him less and less every day. It was to the point where even the mention of Sir Neville's name was beginning to grate on his nerves.

Yet it wasn't just about Sir Neville. He admitted that he didn't want her to marry anyone—not right now, anyway. He wanted her badly, enough to feel a strong sense of possessiveness, stronger than he'd felt for any mistress or lover in the past. Perhaps his feelings were so intense because he'd been so long without a woman. No matter, it was pointless.

He turned his horse away from the manor and urged him to a gallop, heading north. One more long, exhausting ride was what he needed to clear his head and get over the absurd jealousy he was feeling. Anything was better than returning to the manor, for his aunt had invited Lady Stratford over for the afternoon, and he was in no mood to speak with either of them right now.

Two hours later he was back at the manor, sweaty and tired, striding to the house from the stables, when he caught sight of Miss Colbrook's bonnet above the hedgerows in the garden. Unable to help himself, he changed direction.

He found her by the rose arbors in the center of the garden. She was kneeling before a rose bush with her back towards him, a basket several paces behind her lying on its side with several red roses spilling out onto the gravel. Her sapphire blue shawl had fallen from her shoulders, and the edge touched the ground.

He bent down and picked up the roses, brushing the gravel from their petals.

"Did you accept his offer?" He blurted out the question

despite all the promises he'd made to himself not to ask. She hesitated at the sound of his voice, then continued cutting the stem.

"There was no offer to accept." She snapped the rose off sharply with her knife. Her voice was strangely flat.

"No offer?" He stood, leaving the basket on the ground. She almost seemed devastated that Sir Neville hadn't proposed. Did she secretly want an offer from him after all? His chest felt strangely tight at the possibility.

"I stopped him before he could propose." She laid the knife carefully on the ground, her hand trembling. She slowly rose and turned to face him. As he looked into her eyes, Adrian felt the breath leave his body.

She knew about Julia Howe.

Foolishly, this possibility had never occurred to him. He was so sure that Sir Neville would propose today, Adrian never considered that Sir Neville would tell her about his ward. After all, Sir Neville was the one to insist that she and her family never know what happened. Obviously, catching Adrian and her together had changed Sir Neville's opinion of what she needed to be protected from. There was nothing else short of Sir Neville eloping with her that could so guarantee that she'd never be in Adrian's arms again.

Even while he respected Sir Neville for fighting for the woman he wanted, Adrian felt another surge of dislike for the man. And yet Sir Neville had every right to tell her what he believed was the truth. Indeed, Sir Neville was acting honorably, trying to protect her from ruin. No, it wasn't Sir Neville who deserved his anger.

It was Edmund.

Adrian wanted to tell Miss Colbrook the truth. Badly. To erase the shock and disdain for him from her face.

But he couldn't. Not without putting his brother's life at risk all over again.

"Why Julia?" she asked softly, stepping closer to him. If

she'd yelled, the words couldn't have been more of a blow. "Why a respectable young lady with every chance of an honorable life?"

His throat tightened. "I will not speak of it." He turned and strode toward the manor.

"Was it because she was illegitimate?" She hurried to keep beside him. "Did you believe her birth put her beneath respectability?"

"It is not your concern." He felt a sharp pain in his right palm and realized he still clutched the roses. "Sir Neville should not have told you."

"You are criticizing him for trying to protect me?" she said. "You? You claimed you were a reformed man, and I was foolish enough to believe—"

He stopped and spun around so quickly she nearly crashed into him. Instinctively, he reached out to steady her, gently grasping her arm. Her delicious scent washed over him, and he had the sudden inappropriate desire to not let her go, but to drop the roses and take her in his arms.

"I am reformed," he said. She gazed at him for a moment, and then jerked away as if he were the worst sort of villain. Indeed, that's what he was to her.

"Do you deny you ruined Julia?" She stared at him, and the anger in her eyes made his heart sink. He wanted desperately to gain her understanding, to tell her everything. It was madness to even consider it. She would almost certainly feel obligated to tell Sir Neville if she learned the truth. Or she might let it slip to Madeline or someone else who would tell him, and then Sir Neville might very well be furious enough to challenge Edmund in vengeance. Adrian couldn't take such a chance with Edmund's life. As long as Miss Colbrook hated him and believed he was the villain, Edmund was likely safe.

And her believing him responsible would solve the problem of his increasing attraction for her. Already, her fury at him for what she believed he'd done was evident in her eyes, although it was tempered with a small flicker of hope. He must dash that hope. This was exactly what he needed to ensure that he didn't make a fatal mistake and carry their indiscretions too far. So why did he feel no relief, only a raw ache?

He gripped the roses tighter in his fist, feeling the thorns press against his skin. He forced the words from his mouth.

"I do not deny it," he said.

She stepped back, startled, as if she'd hoped he would refute it. "You ruined Julia's life," she said as if she didn't quite believe it. "Ruined and abandoned her."

"I have not abandoned her. She is being cared for."

Her eyes widened. Sir Neville apparently hadn't told her that detail. "You are taking care of her?" she asked.

"Yes."

Realization shone in her eyes. "She goes by the name Miss Carpenter?"

"Mrs. Jameson," he said, struggling to control his anger. He wasn't surprised that she remembered the names she read in the ledgers. No doubt she now believed Miss Carpenter to be another young woman he ruined. He felt fury churn inside him—at Edmund for forcing him into this position, at himself for allowing it to happen, at Sir Neville for telling Miss Colbrook, and even at her for the accusation and hurt that shone in her eyes.

"Where is she living?" she asked. "I wish to write to her."

"She resides not far from Eastgate. But it is better that she has no contact with anyone from her past—"

"I must know that she is well."

He stared at her for a moment. "You may give me a letter," he finally said, "and I shall see that she receives it." He lowered his voice. "I ask you not to tell Miss Madeline of this."

"Do you think I would bring her such pain?" She curled her hands into fists. "She adores you!" *As I once did*, her eyes said. "She would be heartbroken if she knew."

"Miss Howe chose to do what she did," he said quickly. "I shall not speak of it again."

He couldn't endure to look at her any longer. He turned and strode away. Halfway to the manor, he hurled the roses to the ground, cursing as one blossom stuck, its thorns deep in his palm. He plucked it free, tossing the flower onto the stone walkway with the others. He wiped the blood on his dark coat as he continued to the house. It was without a doubt far less painful than his conversation with Miss Colbrook.

An hour later Anna tossed the letter, two pages thick and sealed with a dark red stamp, onto the table before Lord Wareton. It landed atop his crisp, unwrinkled newspaper, slid off, and came to a stop when it met his teacup and saucer.

"When can I expect it to be delivered?" she asked.

His chair creaked as he leaned back, frowning at her. His eyes looked paler than usual in the brightness of the drawing room, a soft green, not, she thought bitterly, reflecting the truth of his soul. He was no gentleman, only a selfish rake.

If he were wholly without admirable qualities, she might despise him less, but she'd been deceived by his charm and the good she saw in him. Since the moment he'd admitted to ruining Julia, she'd felt a growing hatred for him. When her anger threatened to subside, the sorrow that was ready to take its place frightened her even more. So she nurtured her rage, reminding herself of what he'd done. But one question plagued her.

Did Julia love him?

She'd never known Julia well. Sir Neville's ward had spent most of each year away at school, and when she'd come home to visit, she generally didn't socialize but remained at his invalid wife's side. Sir Neville had said that Julia was a gifted pianist and that his wife had loved to hear her play and that Julia would perform for hours to comfort her. As far as Anna knew, Julia had been a devoted and obedient ward, and in spite of her illegitimate parentage, a respectable young woman.

To have been seduced by Lord Wareton and to have behaved so shockingly, Julia probably loved him desperately.

But did he love her in return? Julia was the daughter of a gentleman, a distant cousin of Sir Neville's, but because she was illegitimate, even if Lord Wareton wished to, he could never marry her without disgracing his family. Yet he didn't behave like a man in love, only as a man with a mistress whom he visited once a week while flirting with other women. Women such as Lady Stratford, and, if ever so briefly, Anna herself.

He was the worst sort of libertine.

She should be relieved she found out in time, before she'd allowed herself to become completely carried away by his charm. Her foolish heart should know better than to trust a man like him. Some men were surely capable of profound change, but in his case, he'd only changed in appearances. Even if he hadn't gone so far as to seduce her as he had Julia, he still risked a scandal that could devastate their family.

She'd been weak and imprudent. Sir Neville might have saved her from making a horrible mistake. She owed him a great deal.

"If there is a reply, you will receive it within a fortnight," Lord Wareton said quietly.

"If?"

"I can make no promises."

"I would not believe them if you did." She swore for an instant that he looked wounded or ashamed or both, but then it was gone, and his expression was impassive again.

"You are no fool, Miss Colbrook."

She glared at him. "Not anymore."

"There you are, Miss Colbrook!" Cecelia bounded into the drawing room, a large basket of flowers in her hands. Lady Stratford glided in a few steps behind her.

"Where did you disappear to?" Cecelia said in a rush as she hurried towards them. "We were waiting for you to bring more roses." She didn't wait for a response before turning to her brother. "Look, Adrian, the most beautiful flowers in the garden. They are for the arrangements for the dinner party tomorrow."

"Have we interrupted?" Lady Stratford asked as she swiftly scanned his face and Anna's.

"You have not," he said quickly. He snatched up the letter and slipped it into his coat.

"You are writing someone," Lady Stratford said, touching his arm. Her voice was soft, teasing. "Or is it a letter for you? Do share. You know how I love secrets."

"Is it from Edmund?" Cecelia asked, smiling. "Saying when he will arrive?"

Lord Wareton drummed his fingers against the table. "Since when is Edmund expected?"

"Lady Carlton said he would likely visit within the week," Cecelia said, her smile fading. "She wrote to him."

"Of course she did," he said.

"I am looking forward to making your brother's acquaintance," Lady Stratford said. "I have heard so much about him."

Lord Wareton glanced at Lady Stratford, and his face softened. "You may be one of the few people who won't regret those words," he said mildly. "I would not raise your hopes, however, as Edmund only appears about half the time he promises to."

"He is a rogue, then? Like his elder brother once was?" Lady Stratford's husky voice made the word "rogue" sound indecent. She caressed his arm through the sleeve of his coat.

"Indeed," he said. "Worse."

Anna felt a stab of anger, watching him smile at Lady Stratford. With everything he'd done, he still felt free to flirt and complain about a troublesome younger brother. She couldn't believe she'd thought him so reformed, and so noble, that she'd allowed him to kiss her. Twice!

Lady Stratford laughed. "He sounds fascinating. Wouldn't you agree, Miss Colbrook?"

"In comparison to his brother, I have no doubt he will be delightful." Anna barely realized what she'd said until she saw Cecelia and Lady Stratford's eyes widen. Cecelia giggled. Lord Wareton scowled.

"Come, Cecelia," Lady Stratford said, smiling. She released Lord Wareton's arm and took his sister's hand. "We shall join Miss Madeline and Lady Carlton in the sitting room. The duke is to call shortly." Lady Stratford led Cecelia away, her words lingering in the air after her. "We shall let your brother finish his conversation with Miss Colbrook."

Lord Wareton watched her leave, frowning. He looked to Anna and his frown grew. "I believe our conversation was concluded."

"Yes," she said. "It is quite over."

As were any foolish hopes she'd had. She would no longer have any difficulty fighting her attraction to him. No matter how reformed he was in appearances, what he'd done was too horrible to be forgiven. She only hoped that she could endure living with him.

CHAPTER TEN

ONE WEEK LATER ADRIAN LOUNGED in the library, reading. The ladies had gone calling, and he was hidden in the farthest corner of the room, slouched in an oversized armchair behind an enormous potted plant. He'd come to the library thinking he might reread *The Odyssey*, his favorite, or perhaps indulge in some Milton, when he'd spotted the red-bound book on the table. He'd picked it up, intending to return it to its proper spot, but had absently flipped it open and scanned the first page...

Many chapters later, a shadow abruptly fell across the pages. He looked up to see Miss Colbrook standing in front of him. He slammed the book shut and covered it with his arms.

"Good morning, Miss Colbrook."

"Good *afternoon*. What are you reading?" She was wearing the plain blue gown that she'd worn his first day at Wareton. She looked beautiful.

"Nothing interesting." He shrugged.

"It looked like..." She crossed her arms. "Let me see it."

"No."

Her lovely eyes narrowed. "Why not?"

"Because, quite frankly, it is none of your concern what I read."

"You were very enthralled. Perhaps I would like to read it when you are done."

"You would not."

She continued to frown at him. Despite the fact that she now clearly despised him, he still thought of her constantly. He must do a better job of fighting it. After all, was she really so ravishing? There were far more gorgeous women in the world. So why did he keep fixating on the fullness of her mouth and breasts? And why, even when she was scowling at him, did he have the strong desire to take her in his arms and kiss her again and—

He *must* stop thinking this way. Even if he weren't convinced she would slap him soundly if he should so much as take her hand now, it was an impossible situation and a pointless attraction. He tried to find something about her that wasn't appealing. Looking her over, his frustration and annoyance grew. Her feet, he thought, seeing the dark toe of one of her shoes poke out from beneath her dress as she tapped her foot impatiently at him. She had rather large feet for a woman. Unfortunately, thoughts of her feet—which were, in fact, perfectly suited to her height— led to memories of glimpses of her slender ankles and long legs. Like when her dress had slipped as he'd carried her across the brook. Or when he'd followed behind her as she climbed the hillside in the rain, her skirt hiked, her ankles and nearly everything else visible through her wet, tight clothing...

"Was there some reason you came in here," he said, too loudly, "other than to bother me?" He'd been extremely irritable the past week, ever since their confrontation in the garden. They both had.

Two days ago, she'd finally started to speak with him again, although her manner was still far from pleasant. They couldn't tell anyone else in the manor about what had happened, or talk to each other about it, and they were both so frustrated by each other's presence, he wondered how much longer they could possibly endure the situation.

Unlike him, she at least wasn't suffering from their mutual attraction any longer. She despised him so strongly, any affection she once had for him had clearly ended. He could see it in the way her eyes narrowed, her back stiffened, and the way she frequently clenched her hands in his presence. She loathed him. How else should she feel about the man she believed ruined her neighbor, and who'd made scandalous advances on her as well?

"I need a new book," she said. She wandered over to the bookshelves and ran her hand along a shelf. Her slender fingers stopped before an empty space.

"*The Guide to Game Keeping* is missing." She turned and glowered at him.

He sighed. "Very well. Here is the damned book." He held it out to her. "Go ahead, take it." He shook it at her.

"Oh no. I would not want to read that. It would mean admitting to ignorance."

Deserved or not, he didn't think he could suffer her temper much longer. But what could he do? Sir Neville hadn't offered for her. Adrian couldn't order her to leave Wareton, and he refused to leave himself. He would have to find a way through it.

"You have made your point," he said. "Why are you here? Weren't you and the others out calling on the Dunburys?"

"We went out hours ago. You must have been so lost in your reading that you were not aware of time passing."

The butler entered the room at that moment.

"Excuse me, Lord Wareton, Miss Colbrook," Smith said, "a message just arrived for your lordship." Smith handed him the note and left. One glance at the handwriting and Adrian knew his day was about to get much worse.

"Edmund," he muttered. He stood, dropped the book onto the chair, and strode towards the windows. Did Edmund need money? Or help getting out of some scrape, likely involving a female? Adrian unfolded the paper.

"Bad news from your brother?" Miss Colbrook followed him across the room.

"The worst," Adrian said, refolding the paper. "He's coming for a visit."

"When?"

"Today." Adrian sighed. "No time to escape."

She frowned. "Will his visit be so terrible?"

"You clearly don't remember him well."

"Well enough," she said. "Mr. Sinclair was always quite charming and well-mannered." She glared at him. "Much like his sister."

And there was the sharp wit he recalled so well from London. He'd been reintroduced to it at length the past two days. Not that he blamed her, given what she thought of him. If only he didn't wish to kiss her so badly, he might not care so much.

"Edmund has done little but cause trouble for some time," he said. "He is described as many things, but never well-mannered."

Miss Colbrook turned and walked to the chair where he'd been reading. Her hips swayed enticingly, and the curves of her backside were tantalizingly evident beneath her pale skirt. What would it be like to undress her, to free her voluptuous figure from the confines of corset and gown, to see and feel her naked beneath him—

"He could hardly be so terrible," she said as she snatched the book from the chair, "or Lady Camden never would have invited him to her estate last month."

Adrian frowned. "What?"

"I heard that he attended her recent house party." She turned and clutched the book against her delightfully full chest. He forced his gaze away.

Edmund, they were speaking of Edmund...

"Lady Camden," Adrian said, "the queen bluestocking herself?" He shook his head. "Clearly someone with a ghastly sense of humor started that rumor."

"I heard it from a very reliable source that your brother attended and spent a great deal of time shooting."

"If your friend lived to tell the tale, he didn't go shooting with Edmund. He can't shoot."

He wondered though. Several weeks had passed without any news of Edmund, when he was unaccounted for in either London or Easton. But Lady Camden's respectable gatherings were hardly Edmund's style. If it were true, some mischievous reason must have drawn him there.

Miss Colbrook craned her neck and stepped close to the window. "The duke is calling," she said.

Adrian moved to her side. And wished he hadn't. That damned, delicious perfume.

As she watched the duke's carriage stop out front, a wrinkle appeared in her brow and her lips thinned.

"You do not care for the duke?" Adrian asked.

She shook her head. "I do like him. He is a pleasant… honorable man."

"Such enthusiasm," Adrian said.

"I simply do not believe he suits Cecelia. He is so serious and quiet."

Adrian frowned. Startlingly blunt, even for Miss Colbrook. Who was she to decide what was best for his sister?

"He is the highest ranking noble around, a good man, and close to her in age." He took a few steps away, but still the scent of roses lingered. Miss Colbrook was likely being contrary just to bother him. What could be better than Cecelia becoming a duchess? Adrian would be more than a little proud if they wed, and securing her such a grand match would more than make up for his past neglect. "And Cecelia seems quite happy with his attentions," he added.

"Does she?" Miss Colbrook turned from the window to look at him. He met her gaze. And immediately wished he hadn't. After having known, however briefly, how it felt to have her look at him tenderly, he wondered if he would ever grow accustomed to the anger and disappointment in her eyes. "Perhaps you only see what you wish to see," she added.

What the devil was that supposed to mean?

She spun around and swept from the study, leaving the scent of roses in her wake.

A short time later in the drawing room, Anna leaned forward in her chair by the fire. "You play very well, Mr. Sinclair," she said.

Edmund Sinclair pounded the keys, sending the crystal vase and pink rose skipping across the top of the pianoforte. He grinned whenever he glanced up and saw she was watching him. He was so enthusiastic that Anna couldn't help but smile back. When she saw Lord Wareton step into the room, her smile faded.

Lord Wareton's gaze swept the room. "Where are the others?"

Mr. Sinclair stopped playing and waved his hand toward the window. "Outside. They wanted to stroll to the pond. We decided to stay behind." He broke into another grin. "Miss Colbrook has excellent taste in music."

"You flatter me too much," she said.

"It is not flattery when it is so deserved." Mr. Sinclair swung his legs over the stool and stood. His outfit would be the envy of any London dandy—pea-green and black, shockingly tight, and embroidered with gold on the coat cuffs and trouser seams. With the fancy clothes and the same sandy hair, Anna thought Mr. Sinclair looked a great deal like his brother had six years ago. Although even back then, Lord Wareton would never have worn such outlandish apparel. But it definitely suited Mr. Sinclair's flamboyant personality.

"Good God, Edmund," Lord Wareton said, "you look horrid."

Mr. Sinclair smiled. "A warm welcome to you, too, brother." Next to his younger brother's clothes, Lord Wareton's elegant tan coat and black trousers looked practically somber.

"It is the latest thing." Mr. Sinclair lifted his arms to reveal more of the embroidery. "I had it made while I was in London last month."

Lord Wareton scowled. "That is the most repulsive shade of green ever."

Anna frowned at Lord Wareton. Did he always speak so harshly to his brother?

"I suppose that explains the bill I just received," Lord Wareton said. "The second bill in as many weeks. For half a dozen new outfits you do not need."

"I do need them," Mr. Sinclair said. Almost in unison both brothers stood taller, crossed their arms, and glared at each other. The similarity in their mannerisms was remarkable.

"The bill included two hunting outfits," Lord Wareton said. "Is it true you've actually been hunting recently, at Lady Camden's?"

"I may have." Mr. Sinclair shrugged. "Or I may not have."

Lord Wareton shook his head. "Since when can you shoot anything? The last time I went hunting with you, you missed a pheasant that was running straight at you."

Mr. Sinclair sniffed. "The sun was in my eyes."

"It was cloudy," Lord Wareton said.

Mr. Sinclair frowned at him, his expression one of mild annoyance, but fiercer anger flashed in his eyes.

"And where else have you been for the past month?" Lord Wareton said. "Creditors have been to Eastgate three times in recent weeks searching for you. A Mr. Collins also paid a visit. Apparently, he wishes to call you out for some offense you caused his wife."

Anna had never heard Lord Wareton sound so angry, not even when he was vexed with his aunt.

"Indeed," Mr. Sinclair said, "I thought that might happen. None of it is true, mind you—well, almost none of it— but I still thought it best I spend some time elsewhere." Mr. Sinclair glanced at her and smiled apologetically. "But let us not discuss such unpleasantness now. I'm sure Miss Colbrook has no desire to hear you rant."

Mr. Sinclair was right, Lord Wareton was ranting.

Mr. Sinclair strolled over and sat on the small sofa beside Anna. "Brandy, Miss Colbrook?" he asked, smiling.

"Thank you, no."

Mr. Sinclair leaned forward and helped himself to some from the nearby table. He took a sip and made a sour face. "What is this, Adrian? Surely, you can afford something better? I can't drink this for a whole month." He quickly downed the entire glass.

"A month?" Lord Wareton stopped before him, glaring. "I do not recall saying you could stay one night."

"You wouldn't refuse your own brother?" Edmund smiled. "I've not seen Cecelia in ages. Is it fair to deny me a visit with her?"

They stared at each other for a moment. Lord Wareton's expression softened. Mr. Sinclair had apparently chosen the right leverage.

Lord Wareton sighed. "A week—at most." He looked as if he wanted to say more, but he kept silent. Silent and glaring. More so at his brother than at her.

"Well, pleasant as it is to see you, dear brother…" Mr. Sinclair rolled his eyes and turned towards her. "I wonder, Miss Colbrook," he said, smiling, "if you would do me the honor of showing me more of Wareton Manor? I saw only a glimpse of the gardens earlier today, and they looked enchanting."

"I would be delighted." She smiled and stood, smoothing her blue gown. "Would you care to join us, Lord Wareton?"

"No," Lord Wareton said quickly. He wore a strange, pained expression, as if he were suffering from a headache. He glanced at his brother again. "Actually, yes." He glanced back at her. "No."

She laughed. "Which is it?" It was quite unlike him to seem so flustered. His brother's presence definitely had a peculiar effect on him.

"It is no. Thank you." Lord Wareton turned and strode

from the drawing room.

"I see Adrian is as jovial as always." Mr. Sinclair sounded like Lord Wareton for an instant, with the same dry humor and deep timbre to his voice. Then his face brightened and the resemblance faded. "I cannot say that I am overly disappointed he won't be joining us." He smiled and offered her his arm.

"I don't blame you," she said, taking his arm, "if he usually treats you so unkindly,"

"Elder brother's prerogative, I'm afraid," he said as they stepped outside. He was slightly shorter and less muscular than Lord Wareton, with blue eyes instead of green, and there was a boyishness about him that made him seem at least ten years younger than Lord Wareton, rather than only five. But the biggest difference between them was how they treated her.

Unlike Lord Wareton lately, Mr. Sinclair was charming, considerate, and flattering. Even so, when he wasn't trying so hard to be dramatic, his gestures, phrases, and even his laugh echoed his elder brother. Anna had trouble forgetting about Lord Wareton while she showed Mr. Sinclair the gardens.

She'd done everything to try and push away her feelings for Lord Wareton, to constantly remind herself that she should hate him for what he'd done. Yet despite her anger, thoughts of kissing him came to mind whenever she was around him. She was so obsessed that even when she'd asked him if Julia had sent a reply to her letter, she'd been distracted by how handsome his mouth was and the intense green of his eyes.

Adrian claimed that he'd sent the letter, but so far there was no reply. Each passing day Anna grew increasingly worried Julia wouldn't answer. What would she do then? She couldn't simply give up. She wanted to know Julia was all right. Selfishly, she was also hoping to learn what had happened between Julia and Lord Wareton, and if it had been merely one reckless indiscretion or if their hearts were involved. She glanced at Mr. Sinclair, studying his face. What did he know, if anything, of Julia?

He abruptly stopped walking and glanced back towards the manor. Anger flashed across his face.

"What is wrong, Mr. Sinclair?"

"We are being followed," he said quietly. He began strolling again, leading her towards the center of the gardens.

She peered back. "By whom?" She caught a glimpse of red servant's livery through breaks in the shrubbery.

"A footman, likely sent by my brother to watch us."

She frowned. "Watch us?"

"Adrian is no doubt concerned with protecting your virtue," he said. Bushes rustled some distance behind them, sounding as if the footman had stumbled into a hedgerow.

Protecting her virtue? From Edmund Sinclair, who despite his flattering attentions to her, seemed about as dangerous as a kitten? If there was any man in the household who had proven a threat to female virtue, including hers, it was Lord Wareton.

She'd heard that Mr. Sinclair had been in London with him for the season last year. What did he know of his brother's troubles?

"Mr. Sinclair," she said, "are you acquainted with Sir Neville Kent?"

"Not really." He paused as they strolled beneath the rose arbor. "Tell me about these roses. I have never seen ones quite that shade." He pointed to the clusters of pink-orange flowers on the canopy above them.

"They are a French hybrid," she said, "I do not recall the name. Are you at all familiar with Sir Neville's family?"

"I'm afraid not."

"Perhaps you met his former ward, Miss Julia Howe, while in London?"

Anxiety flickered in his eyes. He definitely knew about

his brother and Julia.

"Why do you ask, Miss Colbrook?" He began walking again. She would probably have to tread carefully to have any chance of learning something from him.

"I thought that we might have a mutual acquaintance to speak of," she said.

He glanced at her, a brief smile lighting up his face. It seemed he knew exactly why she was asking.

"I am afraid my acquaintance with Miss Howe was far too brief to have anything of interest to say."

Of course. Unconventional as he was, she didn't really expect he would betray his own brother's confidence. It really was none of her concern anyway, and yet she was desperate to know what had happened. She wouldn't deceive herself as to why she cared so much.

Yet she suspected if she was patient, Mr. Sinclair might reveal far more about the situation than his elder brother ever would.

"You will be joining us for the concert tonight?" she asked. "I would be pleased to introduce you to our neighbors, although an introduction to Sir Neville will have to wait for another night. He is not expected to make it back from Taunton in time to attend."

Mr. Sinclair grinned. "I wouldn't dream of missing it."

Early that evening Anna sat in her dressing gown as Sophie brushed out her hair. Anna rolled a hairpin between her fingers, the metal cool against her skin, the small red stone at the end sparkling in the candlelight. A carved wooden box lay open on the dressing table before her with a dozen identical hairpins inside. They were from her mother. She'd worn them only on Christmas and a few other special occasions, but tonight she decided she would look her best. It had been too long since she had dressed to draw attention to herself.

Lord Wareton was right; she had been hiding. His kisses made her realize how much she was denying herself. Why shouldn't she allow herself some happiness now? After all, Madeline would likely wed within a few years, and then Anna would be free to marry. She might as well begin looking her best. It had nothing to do with wanting to gain Lord Wareton's attention, nothing at all.

"Where are you off to tonight?" Sophie asked.

"A musicale at Smithfield Park," Anna said. Sophie pulled Anna's auburn tresses straight and began to build the usual tight knot. "Something different, please," Anna said. "I would like it pinned up gently."

"Pinned up?" Sophie let the hair slip from her fingers and stared at Anna's reflection.

"Yes. And these instead of the plain ones." Anna handed Sophie a hairpin. "And perhaps you could leave a few curls down?"

Sophie grinned. "You've your eye on a gentleman. Finally! Who is it, miss?"

"I do not have my eye—"

"It's Mr. Sinclair, isn't it? You can tell me. He's a handsome one, and much more affable than his lordship, I might add. And far more dashing than Sir Neville. I am not surprised—"

"I do not have my eye on a gentleman."

"Whatever you say." Sophie shook her head, still smiling as she began to arrange Anna's hair.

Anna picked up a perfume bottle from the back of the dressing table and lifted the top to her nose. Jasmine. Too heavy. She chose a second, crinkling her nose at the too-sweet lilac fragrance. Usually, she used only rosewater, but tonight she wanted something different. She tried two others before settling on a light lavender scent. She dabbed it on her neck and wrists.

"That smells pretty," Sophie said. "I am sure the gentleman you *don't* have your eye on will like it." She finished tucking Anna's hair into a loose chignon, and began to curl the tendrils she'd left free.

"I'm out of practice, but I believe it looks quite lovely," Sophie said as she finished. Sophie helped Anna put on ear bobs that she seldom wore, which were also from her mother, small teardrop rubies that hung just below her ears on thin gold chains.

"Which gown would you like?" Sophie swung open the doors to Anna's wardrobe.

"One of the new ones." Anna rose and went over to examine the dresses hanging in the back, the ones that she'd never worn from the most recent shopping expedition. She pulled out the most beautiful one, a burgundy silk gown with short, puffy sleeves and a low, square neckline.

"I have so wanted to see you in this," Sophie said as she took Anna's dressing gown from her. Sophie helped Anna with her corset, and Anna slipped into the new gown. The dress fell in shimmering folds from the high waist straight to the tops of her feet. Anna pulled on long, matching gloves and matching shoes. Sophie draped a flowered shawl with burgundy satin trim around Anna's arms.

The maid drew her before the tall looking glass next to the dressing table. "You are a sight, miss."

Anna looked at her reflection. The dress was lovely, brightening her face, but the neckline was far more revealing than she was accustomed to. She almost told Sophie to help her out of the gown.

"You look even more beautiful than you did at twenty-one," Sophie said softly.

Twenty-one. The last time Anna had dressed so elegantly. She felt queasy. It was foolish to be so nervous. She wasn't even in London, but had to face only familiar people. At least one familiar person, however, made her more nervous than a ballroom full of London *ton*. Would Lord Wareton notice her new gown and hair style? But she shouldn't care what he noticed. He was a libertine, a deceitful rake.

Sophie smiled. "The gentlemen's eyes will pop out of their heads when they see you."

Anna slipped her reticule around her wrist and headed downstairs. As she entered the drawing room, Madeline abruptly stopped playing the pianoforte.

"Oh, Anna, you look lovely." Madeline said. "I adore that dress on you. And what have you done with your hair?" Smiling, Madeline glanced at Mr. Sinclair and then back at Anna.

Mr. Sinclair rose from the sofa and bowed. "You look breathtaking, Miss Colbrook." He wore a yellow coat and breeches with a heavily-starched red and yellow striped cravat.

"You finally took my advice." Lady Carlton strolled away from the pianoforte where she'd been watching Madeline play. She snapped open her fan, cooling herself as she circled Anna. "What a difference a quality gown makes." Lady Carlton seemed as if she couldn't decide if she was pleased at the transformation.

Footsteps echoed in the hallway between the drawing room and the gallery. A moment later Lord Wareton strode into the room. He stopped short and stared at Anna.

Her pulse quickened as he slowly looked her over from her hair to the satin tips of her shoes. For an instant she thought his eyes widened as they had when he'd first caught sight of her under the tree at the picnic. But perhaps she'd imagined it. Now, he only stared at her with a somber expression.

"How do you think Anna looks, Lord Wareton?" Madeline asked, breaking the silence.

"She looks...not unpleasant."

Mr. Sinclair laughed. "You are fortunate you are handsome, Adrian, for you will certainly never charm the ladies with your eloquence." He stepped closer to Anna and raised her hand to his lips. "You look enchanting, Miss Colbrook, as beautiful as a Roman goddess."

CHAPTER ELEVEN

A DRIAN HATED THE CONCERT. HE sat beside Lady Stratford in the music room at Smithfield Park, but he couldn't enjoy the music or Lady Stratford's company because he was so distracted by Miss Colbrook and his brother.

She and Edmund sat a few rows in front of him, behind Madeline, Cecelia, and the Duke of Dulverton. Edmund hadn't left Miss Colbrook's side except to bring her refreshments, and he was constantly leaning close and whispering to her. Worse, she didn't seem to mind Edmund's attention. She laughed frequently, as if she were enjoying herself. And the way she was dressed tonight...

When Adrian first saw her in the new gown, her beautiful curves draped in burgundy silk, her hair soft around her face, he was so stunned he'd made a fool of himself in front of his entire family. She'd transformed herself into a glamorous beauty.

All because of Edmund.

The set ended and the audience applauded. People shifted in their seats or stood to stretch their legs while they awaited the next performance. Edmund and Miss Colbrook rose and faced one another. She spoke and while Edmund listened, he glanced quickly at Adrian then gazed back at her, a sly grin on his face. Adrian recognized that smile. Edmund wore it whenever he met a woman he was interested in a dalliance with. Adrian curled his hands into fists.

Miss Colbrook finished speaking and sat, but Edmund remained standing. As she bent to retrieve her reticule from the floor, Edmund stole a glance down the bodice of her gown.

"Damn him," Adrian muttered. He would put a stop to this right—

"You seem quite distracted this evening, Lord Wareton," Lady Stratford said, pressing his arm gently.

"Not at all," Adrian lied. He watched Edmund sit again and lean close to Miss Colbrook. Too close.

Miss Colbrook smiled and nodded at some comment of Edmund's before turning back to watch the musicians resume playing. Her hair sparkled from the jeweled hairpins she wore tonight. She'd never worn jeweled hairpins before that Adrian could recall. She'd never worn a gown so fashionably low. Too low, in his opinion. Even from here, he could see almost half her breasts, her beautiful, shapely br—

"Your brother seems to have you quite distracted." Lady Stratford smiled coolly. "Or is it not really your brother that has you at sixes and sevens?"

Adrian tore his gaze from Miss Colbrook. Perhaps he was jealous, but it was more than that. He was concerned for Miss Colbrook's safety. Edmund couldn't be trusted. Adrian would be equally concerned if his cousin or sister were in danger from a rake like Edmund. Wouldn't he?

"It is just Edmund," Adrian said quickly. "He drives me mad when he acts like this."

"He has been behaving like a perfect gentleman since his arrival," Lady Stratford said.

Perfect gentlemen did not steal glances down ladies' bodices, Adrian thought. However, she had a point, Edmund had been less trouble than usual.

All the more reason why Adrian was suspicious. Edmund must be very interested in Miss Colbrook, to not be distracted by other ladies. More than a few pretty young ladies had cast admiring glances at Edmund since they'd arrived, but Edmund seemed strangely uninterested.

Generally, Edmund went for the more flamboyant women with questionable reputations, those more like himself, whose behavior would generate the most gossip. Miss Colbrook, even as glamorous as she looked tonight, was still an entirely respectable bluestocking. It was very odd.

"Is it possible that he is truly smitten with Miss Colbrook?" Lady Stratford asked. She traced one elegant finger in a small circle on his sleeve. Normally he would enjoy her flirtations, but tonight Edmund and Miss Colbrook were ruining everything.

"No," Adrian said. "Edmund never wants more than a dalliance. And if by some miracle he did, it would take someone more...striking than Miss Colbrook to snare him." Surely it wasn't possible Edmund truly was forming an attachment to her? That would be horrible. Horrible beyond words.

Lady Stratford stilled her finger on his arm. "Why? Do you not think she is beautiful?"

"Tolerable. When she is being pleasant." Miss Colbrook was beautiful. Seeing her in that dress made it indisputable.

"Tolerable?" Lady Stratford laughed and squeezed his arm. "Come, you can be honest with me. Next you will claim she has no wit."

He said nothing. Miss Colbrook did indeed have an excellent wit; he could hardly deny that. She'd skewered him enough with it of late.

She was clever, no denying it. But even the cleverest woman could lose her sense when it came to men, and Edmund had been a bad influence on dozens of women to varying degrees—and those were just the ones Adrian knew of.

The music ended and applause echoed throughout the room. People slowly rose from their chairs and began milling about.

"Lord Wareton," Lady Stratford murmured, gazing over Adrian's shoulder. "Look. Your favorite neighbor. And I thought he wasn't supposed to be here?"

Adrian turned. Sir Neville stood just past the doorway to the hall. Madeline stood beside him, chatting, but Sir Neville's stare kept returning to Edmund and Miss Colbrook.

Bloody hell. Sir Neville must have returned early from Taunton. Adrian looked to Edmund, who was just noting Sir Neville's presence. Edmund's flinch was visible from across the room.

Sir Neville scowled at Edmund. He then turned his gaze to Adrian and made his way towards him.

"Lord Wareton," Sir Neville said as he stopped before him. "Lady Stratford." He never even looked at her, but kept his gaze riveted on Adrian. "May I have a word with you, Wareton?"

Lady Stratford politely excused herself.

"How unexpected to see your brother here," Sir Neville said grimly.

"He surprised us all with his visit," Adrian said.

Sir Neville glanced across the room at Edmund and Miss Colbrook. "Seeing him brings back many memories." He shifted his glare to Adrian again, and his dark eyes narrowed. "But it is not always good to stir up the past, is it? I am a patient man, but even I have my limit. I might have to revisit matters that you'd prefer left alone if you—or your brother—push me too far." He paused and added more quietly, "I never could decide who was the worse libertine. Perhaps I will finally have to. Always tempting to choose the weaker target though, isn't it, Wareton?"

Adrian struggled to keep his face impassive. Sir Neville knew. The bastard knew he was protecting Edmund.

Sir Neville nodded curtly. "Lord Wareton." He gave Adrian one final scowl and spun away.

Adrian felt a knot forming in his gut. He should never have let Edmund attend. He had to get him out of here.

Anna smiled at Mr. Sinclair, well aware that Lord Wareton glared at them from across the music room. How arrogant of him to treat his brother so harshly after his own outrageous behavior. He was conceited and unkind and an utter scoundrel.

And she still cared about him far too much.

She'd even enjoyed the anger that flashed in his eyes as he watched her with his brother. Savored the fact that he was distracted from enjoying Lady Stratford's company. Until she realized that Lord Wareton likely wasn't so much jealous of her as he was angry with his brother. There was long-standing resentment between them, anger that she sensed was growing increasingly dangerous, and not just for them but for anyone unlucky enough to be caught too close. Like her.

She'd also begun to suspect that Mr. Sinclair flirted with her not because he was enamored of her, but simply because it upset Lord Wareton. Mr. Sinclair's own mood seemed to improve with each scowl and dark look from his brother.

But when Sir Neville stepped through the door, Mr. Sinclair abruptly stopped flirting and suddenly seemed eager to speak with the Dunbury sisters. She was dragged into conversation with them for several minutes, with no chance to ask Mr. Sinclair what was going on. As Agnes and Angeline finally left to get refreshments, Lord Wareton strode over and dragged Mr. Sinclair away.

When Mr. Sinclair returned a short time later, he looked uncharacteristically somber.

"What is wrong?" she asked.

"I have developed a fearsome headache," he said. "I believe I shall return to Wareton for the evening."

She frowned. "You were fine a few moments ago. Tell me what is wrong."

"Please, Miss Colbrook," he said, his expression grave, "do not press me on this. Now if you will excuse me—"

"I shall go with you. I have a headache as well." She could interrogate him in the carriage. There was definitely something between him and Lord Wareton beyond ordinary sibling rivalry, and she wanted to know what it was. In a way, they were dragging her into the situation by using her to fight over, so didn't she have the right to learn the truth?

"Adrian will be even more angry with me if you leave too." Mr. Sinclair's eyes narrowed as he glanced across the room at his brother. "He'll be furious," he muttered, mischief sparkling in his eyes.

"So? I am going with you."

He smiled. "Shall I meet you in the carriage?"

A few moments later, after making the appropriate apologies and informing Madeline that she was returning home, Anna hurried into the foyer. Two servants swung open the doors and she stepped out into the cool air. She descended the stairs and a footman helped her into the waiting carriage.

When Mr. Sinclair didn't follow right away, she peered out the window. He stood at the bottom of the steps, speaking with a servant from the house. The man seemed to be insisting that Mr. Sinclair return inside. Mr. Sinclair looked towards the carriage and held up one finger, then turned and bounded up the stairs. The servant followed quickly behind him. The doors shut and Anna waited, watching the footmen stand like statues beside the steps, the lanterns flickering on their gold and crimson livery.

After a moment she lay back against the seat and closed her eyes. All evening she had tried not to look at Lord Wareton, and now when she shut her eyes, his image filled her mind. He looked terribly handsome tonight, as usual. His dark coat and breeches flattered his muscular figure, and the candlelight brought out the golden highlights in his hair. Even while glaring at her and Mr. Sinclair all evening, Lord Wareton had looked so compelling, she'd had to force herself not to dwell on the memories of their kisses. For days now, she'd obsessed about the delicious heat of his mouth and gentleness of his touch.

She must stop thinking of him.

Immediately, his face formed again in her mind, his eyes glittering at her as they had just before they kissed under the tree, his lips curving into a seductive smile—

Footsteps sounded on the stairway, and she opened her eyes and sat up. The door opened and the devil himself stepped inside.

CHAPTER TWELVE

LORD WARETON REMOVED HIS HAT as he fell into the seat across from her. The coach suddenly seemed too small and close.

"Where is your brother?" she asked.

"He is staying." As the carriage jerked forward, he stretched one arm out across the seat.

"Why are you here and not him?" She already knew the answer, but she wanted him to admit it.

"Because you should not be alone with Edmund."

"Why not?"

"Because he is a rake." There was no shame in his voice, no acknowledgement of his own guilt.

"A rake?" she said. "He seems to be a perfectly charming and respectable gentleman."

"He cannot be trusted."

"You being an excellent judge of untrustworthy behavior."

"A family trait," he said dryly. He dropped his arm from the back of the seat and leaned towards her. "And you are encouraging him," he added, glaring at her, "dressing like that."

She pulled her shawl tighter around her shoulders, covering her low neckline. If she didn't know better, she would swear jealousy burned in his eyes. The triumph she'd felt when she first walked downstairs that evening and seemed to stun him with her appearance had been fleeting, but now... No, he was merely being protective, much as he would be with Cecelia or Madeline. He looked at her with anger, not desire. His fury was all about his brother, not her.

"I assume this sudden transformation means you are interested in suitors again?" He drummed his fingers on the seat beside him. "If so, you must realize that Edmund is the last man who can be brought up to scratch."

"You think simply because I am civil to him, because I do not scowl and yell at him as you do, that I wish to marry him?"

"I must warn you that it is highly unlikely he has honorable intentions."

"Your hypocrisy is astounding," she said. The motion of the carriage pushed her forward until her knees nearly brushed his. Her shawl fell open as she clutched the edge of the seat to keep herself from sliding further. "Whatever his faults," she added, "he can be no worse than you."

Lord Wareton leaned forward from the shadows, the moonlight through the window revealing his narrowed eyes, his sensual mouth. He stared at her, his anger transforming into something far more unsettling.

"Perhaps you are right." The sudden softness in his voice sent a shiver through her. "Perhaps I am no better than Edmund."

He reached out and gently uncurled her fingers from the edge of the seat. Her heart pounded.

"I wish you had dressed that way for me," he said, the arrogance and anger suddenly gone from his voice, "not for Edmund."

"I did," she whispered, too stunned to lie.

In one swift motion, he pulled her across the carriage. He wrapped one arm around her and cradled her face with the other. He kissed her so quickly that she couldn't have protested even if she wanted to. Which she didn't.

His lips were velvet warmth, instantly melting away her anger. She returned the kiss, sinking against the wall of his chest. He smelled of shaving soap, cheroots, and midnight air. The clop of the horses' hooves and rattling of the carriage seemed to fade. He stroked her hair as he held her mouth to his in a lingering, gentle kiss, a kiss that made her ache everywhere with a sweet, dull pain.

She wanted more. Needed more.

She shifted, turning until her breasts brushed against his chest. She heard his breath catch in his throat, and his arm tightened around her.

He deepened the kiss, gently parting her lips with his tongue, pressing into her mouth, warm and soft and delicious. He moved his hand from her head, and she heard him strip off his gloves. Seconds later she heard the gloves slap gently onto the carriage floor behind her.

He curled a hand around her half-bare shoulder as they continued to kiss. Soon he drew his fingers lower and caressed her skin above the low neckline of her gown, wickedly close to her breasts. Her corset suddenly felt too tight, her gown too confining.

His kisses grew more demanding.

As did hers.

She leaned back against his arm, allowing him more freedom to touch her. Gently, he cupped her right breast in one large hand, and she moaned softly against his mouth. Even through her gown and corset, his strong fingers enveloped her with a tantalizing heat. He slid his mouth away from hers, across her cheek, her neck, her collarbone, and down to the bodice of her gown, until he warmed the skin between the swell of her breasts with his lips.

He moved his mouth lower and she gasped. He kissed one breast through her corset and gown while he continued to caress the other with his hand. He circled her breasts with his mouth and fingers, warm and teasing, brushing tantalizingly close but never quite touching her nipples.

She never knew—she had no idea that she could feel such pleasure, and through her clothes no less. Willing him to touch and kiss the one part he ignored, she lifted her chest towards him.

At last, he pressed his lips against her left nipple where

it jutted out against her gown. She cried out softly as his tongue swirled against her, dampening the silk. He groaned and moved his hand to her back, searching for the drawstring to her gown. Finally grasping the thin ribbon, he tugged it gently, slowly loosening her dress.

Then, abruptly, he stopped. He muttered a curse and let the ribbon slide from his fingers. To her amazement, he guided her head to his broad chest and slid both arms around her. His heart thundered against her ear.

"I am...close to doing the very thing I meant to prevent," he whispered, his voice ragged. "When I am near you, I cannot seem to help myself."

Neither could she. She could barely believe the liberties she'd just allowed him. To her shame, she'd not only permitted him to touch her so scandalously, but she desperately wanted him to continue. To pull down the bodice of her gown. To free her breasts from her corset. To press his mouth upon her bare flesh. And she wanted whatever might follow, no matter how sinful.

She should have pushed him away as soon as he kissed her. She should push him away now. Instead she kept close against him, her heart pounding as she struggled to calm her breathing. A brass button on his coat pressed softly against her cheek, a spot of cold amid the heat that surrounded her.

Senselessly, she felt safe, the safest she'd ever felt. How could she, lying in the arms of such a rake? What was wrong with her?

And yet, she had no doubt now that he wanted her, so why had he stopped? Why didn't he try to take advantage of her further? If he did, she might be able to rekindle her anger towards him, but this restraint and unexpected tenderness as he held her was something she had no defense against.

"I cannot believe you still care for me despite what you think of me," he murmured as he brushed his mouth against her hair.

At those words, the heat he'd ignited in her body dissolved. He must think she was so without scruples and so desperate for his attentions that she wouldn't let anything keep her from him. And would he be wrong? Against all reason, a huge part of her desperately wanted to let him seduce her.

The horrible truth was that he was behaving sensibly while she wasn't.

Yet even if he restrained himself now, for whatever reason, she quickly reminded herself she couldn't trust him. Julia's ruin was proof enough. But no matter how hard she tried, she couldn't despise him. Not when she saw how he cared for Cecelia and Madeline, and for the estate and its people. Even the way he treated his brother, harsh as it was, was clearly motivated by love. She couldn't control her attraction to him, for willingly or not, she was drawn to him, and this latest embrace only made her more certain of the strength of her feelings.

She was doomed. She lay in the arms of the man who had ruined her neighbor, and pathetically, she wanted him to seduce her as well.

She suddenly lifted her head and struggled in his arms. Silently, he released her, and she flung herself to the opposite side of the coach. She plucked her shawl from the seat where it had fallen and drew it tightly around herself. As the carriage shifted, she let herself slide against the wall of the coach. She stared out the window as they made the turn onto the main road of the estate.

She heard the sounds of him retrieving his gloves, the faint creak of the leather seat as he leaned forward, and the scuff of his shoes against the coach floor.

He said softly, "Miss Colbr—"

"Please, do not speak." She shook her head, keeping her

gaze on the lanterns lining the driveway. She must retain what little dignity was left to her, and she couldn't trust herself to do so if she looked at his face.

CHAPTER THIRTEEN

THE NEXT DAY ANNA SPENT as much time away from the manor as she could. She wasn't ready to face Lord Wareton after what had happened in the carriage. In the morning she rode, during the early afternoon she went calling with the other ladies, and afterwards she walked alone to visit Mrs. Hunter.

She was so reluctant to return home that by the time she left Mrs. Hunter's cottage, the sun shone low through the woods and cast long shadows on the path. She started across the stream, now shallow enough to cross by jumping from stone to stone. She stopped on a large, flat boulder in the center and stared at the sparkling water. Lord Wareton had carried her across this spot only a few weeks before, yet it seemed like months ago.

That day had changed everything. She hadn't fully realized it at the time, but that was when she first recognized how strongly she was attracted to him. No matter what she told herself at the time, even then part of her knew that her fascination with him wouldn't easily fade.

She was ashamed of how her own body betrayed her, and how passionately she responded to his touch and kisses. He threatened what she'd long believed about herself: that she was a sensible person who would never behave recklessly, never do anything that would risk her reputation or her family's honor.

He proved how shaky her self-control really was. She'd been so close to allowing him unthinkable liberties in the carriage. Had he decided to seduce her, anything might have happened. Yet he was the one who had shown restraint and stopped them from recklessness. He wanted her, she was certain now, but he hadn't taken advantage of her. He'd shown honor and conscience, and once again, he'd turned everything that she believed about him upside down.

She stood at the edge of the stream, lost in thoughts of him, when a gunshot rang out. The sound was so close, she nearly lost her balance. Once she'd recovered, she hurried across the stones to the far bank and paused on the path to listen. The woods were silent now, the only sound the low gurgle of the water. Likely someone was hunting close by.

Was it Lord Wareton? Her pulse sped up, and she walked faster. She rounded a curve in the path, where the trees opened into a small field. A man stood in profile in the center of the clearing, holding a small pistol close to his chest, the barrel pointed skyward. The setting sun behind him made him little more than a silhouette, but he was too short and thin to be Lord Wareton.

The man took several quick steps and swiftly lowered the gun, appearing to aim at a tree stump several dozen paces away. He fired. The shot echoed through the woods, making her jump. A stone smaller than a summer apple flew off the stump and into the grass beyond.

Whoever he was, he was an exceptional shot. He wore no jacket or hat, and the afternoon sunlight blazed on his hair, making the edges appear blond. As if he sensed her approach, he turned, and for an instant the way he moved reminded her of Lord Wareton.

It was Mr. Sinclair.

In his right hand, he gripped the pistol and in the other, he clutched a battered flask, the top undone.

They stared at each other in silence.

"Mr. Sinclair," she finally said.

"Miss Colbrook." He lowered the weapon. It was a pocket pistol, and not one she recognized from Wareton.

"You are an excellent shot," she said. He wasn't supposed

to be. Hadn't Lord Wareton said repeatedly that his brother was a poor marksman, that he couldn't shoot a pheasant right in front of him?

And even though it wasn't a dueling pistol—he could hardly carry one around without being noticed—she had a sudden, terrible suspicion.

"You are practicing to challenge someone?" She kept her voice calm.

"Perhaps." He seemed annoyed that she'd caught him and yet relieved as well. He raised the flask and took a long drink. He couldn't have been drinking much beforehand, not and still be able to shoot so skillfully.

"Whom will you challenge?" she asked. As if it weren't obvious.

"I'd rather not say." He placed the pistol on the ground, stood, and took another quick drink.

"You can resolve your differences without this," she said. "I know he treats you harshly, but he is your brother."

He retrieved his coat from the ground and slid the flask inside, a smile flickering across his face. "Tempting as the idea may be at times, I do not plan on challenging Adrian." He sounded truthful enough, but he avoided her gaze. She wasn't sure she believed him. This had something to do with Lord Wareton, she was certain.

"Then who?" she said.

Silently, he drew on his coat and began fastening it, his fingers slipping on one button. Was he more foxed than he appeared?

"You will not tell me?" she said. "What is so important that you would risk your life?" She bit her lip to stop herself from adding, *so foolishly.*

"Would it upset you if I was injured?" He sounded as if he were teasing her. He snatched up the pistol and slipped it inside his coat.

"Naturally."

"But not half as much as if Adrian were wounded." He

smiled, not a jealous or sad smile, but teasing... He *did* flirt with her just to upset his brother, she was now positive.

"Come, Miss Colbrook, shall I escort you home? At this hour, people will soon start worrying about you." He meant Lord Wareton, of course. Lord Wareton might indeed worry about her, if he knew she was with his brother.

He offered her his arm. She held onto him lightly as they strolled out of the field, heading back toward Wareton.

"Why do you and your brother fight?" she asked.

Mr. Sinclair smiled. "You noticed?"

"You joke, but I can see it is quite serious, and the resentment between you runs deep."

His smile faded and he drew away from her, letting her arm fall. He walked faster. "He makes no secret of it, that is certain," he said. He bent and picked up a stone from the center of the path.

"Why doesn't he trust you?" she asked gently. Perhaps she could help resolve the problem. The anger between them pained her, and not only because she had feelings for Lord Wareton, she quickly told herself. She hated to see bad blood between brothers. They should be close friends, not adversaries.

"What else could make two men act so foolishly?" He laughed dryly, echoing his brother's tone. "A woman." He hurled the rock into the woods.

"You both loved the same woman?" she said.

"Adrian?" He glanced at her and shook his head. "Perhaps you are not as observant as I thought, or you might have realized by now that my brother is incapable of such soft emotions." He spoke faster. "He is too wrapped up in honor and duty and being perfect. He cannot even forgive—" He stopped abruptly, and then sighed. "No, we were never in love with the same woman."

"Lord Wareton has never been in love?" she asked. They left the woods and walked between open fields bordered by low hedgerows.

"Not that I've ever known," he said. "Before he went into the army he was too much of a libertine, and since he returned, he's too obsessed with his responsibilities to allow himself to form any attachments." He kicked another stone, sending it skidding into a hedgerow.

If they hadn't both loved the same woman, what could it be? Had Lord Wareton disapproved of a woman his brother cared for? Did it have anything to do with Julia? Had Mr. Sinclair cared for her before Lord Wareton had seduced her?

"However," he said, "I must say that you have driven him to distraction far more than any other woman I can recall. I can tell he cares for you, as much as he is capable of caring for a woman, anyway."

She tried to suppress the thrill she felt at his words.

"Why does he punish himself?" she said. "Because of his past?"

"Yes. And everyone else along with him."

What exactly did he mean by that?

They climbed towards the manor in silence and paused on the top of a hill to look west. The sunset was just beginning, turning the wispy white clouds on the horizon pink.

"How lovely," Mr. Sinclair said, sounding quite sad. It almost seemed as if he'd forgotten she was there and spoke to himself.

"Mr. Sinclair," she ventured, "does the animosity between you and your brother have anything to do with Miss Howe?"

He blinked and the truth flashed on his face before his usual carefree expression returned. He tapped the side of his coat where the flask was hidden, as if he were considering another drink.

"It does," she said, before he could deny it, "I know it. Please tell me. Perhaps I can help."

"I assure you," he said, "you cannot fix what is between

us. Only I can." Determination flickered in his eyes. Despite his denial, she feared more than ever that he was planning on challenging his brother. His anger was undeniable—in his tone, the set of his jaw, and the way he curled his fists when he spoke of his brother. "Although," he added, his voice softening as he glanced at her, "I do appreciate your offer to help."

They began strolling once again, following the path down the hill. The manor glowed pink in the distance, reflecting the setting sun. She was surprised a servant hadn't been sent out after her. Dinner was not far off.

Mr. Sinclair took another long swig from his flask and began to walk faster. She had to try again to prevent whatever he was planning.

"You say that you do not wish to challenge your brother," she said, "but you hide your shooting practice from him."

"That is my concern," he said. They climbed a gentle rise and continued along the hedge-lined path that led to the gardens. He pushed the wrought iron gate open and held it for her as she stepped through.

He followed her a few steps and stopped abruptly, staring at the lights of the manor. "I have no wish to go inside now and see Adrian." He glanced at her. "Sit with me a while."

After only a second of hesitation, she nodded. Whether he asked her more out of a desire to upset Lord Wareton or a true wish for companionship, she wasn't certain. But if she stayed, she might learn what was between them. She watched him take another drink. Feeling only slightly guilty, she noted if he kept drinking the way he was, he might soon tell her anything she wished.

They settled themselves on a low stone bench at the edge of a steep slope that faced north, away from the manor. He sat a respectable distance from her, and they watched the sun disappear into the trees. The garden darkened abruptly, even while the sky remained light. A nearly full moon was rising, already bright against the shadowy sky.

Mr. Sinclair drew the brandy from his coat, tugged out the stopper, and offered her the flask.

She stared at him a moment, then took it.

He smiled. "I am surprised you accepted my invitation." His voice was soft, and now slightly slurred. "To be alone with a gentleman of my reputation, drinking, as night falls. It is quite shocking."

She realized then that she could be alone with him in any situation and feel completely at ease, unlike Lord Wareton, who made her heart speed up when he so much as walked near her. The fact that Lord Wareton was convinced she was in danger from his brother was almost absurd when she considered how many times Lord Wareton had kissed her. Yet Mr. Sinclair must have done something to make Lord Wareton distrust him, but what?

She swallowed a mouthful of the brandy, enjoying the warmth spreading down her throat. As she returned the flask to him, she said, "Tell me more of the woman who came between you and your brother."

He took another long drink and sat in silence for a moment, the only sound the croaking of frogs in the nearby pond.

"Why ask me?" he finally said, suddenly sounding childish and whiny, as he often did when he spoke with Lord Wareton. "Adrian will tell you how it is," he added, his voice rising, "after all, he always learns the truth."

"What do you mean?"

"I have made mistakes," he continued. "I shall not deny it. And Miss Carp—one mistake was especially horrid, I see that now. I *can* admit to my errors."

Had he been about to say Miss Carpenter, the name of the other woman in the account books?

"And because I've made some mistakes, Adrian now assumes the worst. Always." He leapt to his feet and marched around the bench. "And he has gotten harsher." He paced back and forth, swinging the flask in one hand. "He makes my life miserable," he said, his voice even louder. "Ever since he left the army, he acts like some bloody paragon of virtue. Like he has any right to tell me how to behave." His voice was now loud enough that she feared it might carry all the way to the manor.

"Mr. Sinclair." She stood and faced him across the bench, speaking softly. "You are being rather loud—"

"Loud!" He half laughed, half snorted. "This is not loud at all." There was more than a slight slur in his voice now. He put one foot on the stone seat and leaned towards her. His breath reeked of brandy.

"Lord Wareton, ha!" He swung away from her to look towards the manor. "Once he was a scoundrel too." He spun back around and stepped up onto the bench. "But now he's a man of honor, not a wastrel like me." He slid down on one knee; even in the dim light, she could tell he was grinning foolishly.

"Yes, he's truly reformed." He leaned towards her and swept his arm out dramatically, nearly hitting her. "And not just reformed, but a bloody earl now as well! So bloody noble that he'll lie, even risk his own life, to protect his pitiful brother." He spat out the last few words, spraying her face. Instinctively, she stepped back again, wiping her cheek.

Lie and risk his own life to protect his brother?

She'd just comprehended his words when her feet began to slide. She'd forgotten how close she stood to the steep slope. She knew immediately that she wouldn't be able to regain her balance. Mr. Sinclair lunged forward, trying to grasp her hands. But before he could reach her, she was already falling.

Adrian paced the length of the study, pausing to stare out the open window yet again. Edmund had been gone all afternoon and Miss Colbrook for nearly as long. Where in the blazes were they?

He scanned the grounds as far as he could see, watching for any sign of her return. A breeze cooled his face and stirred the papers on the nearby desk.

Perhaps Lady Stratford was right and Edmund's flirting, outrageous as it seemed, was harmless. Then again, Miss Colbrook wouldn't be the first intelligent woman to be seduced by his brother.

And she was vulnerable at the moment, as her behavior last night demonstrated. Adrian now felt certain that she was attracted to him, not to Edmund. Yet if she was distraught enough over her feelings for him, who knew what might happen under Edmund's bad influence?

A guilty thought pricked at him. Was he much better than Edmund?

Watching her last night, looking so radiant in her new gown, and seeing how much she seemed to enjoy Edmund's company, had been almost more than he could bear. He'd wanted desperately to take her away from Edmund, and at the same time, he feared his own behavior once alone with her.

He was being abominably selfish to even entertain such thoughts about her. But in the carriage, when she'd confessed that she dressed so beautifully for him and not for Edmund, his remaining self-control had shattered.

Until then, he'd believed that she despised him. To discover she still wanted him was both wonderful and terrible. He wanted so desperately to tell her the truth, to let her know he was innocent, at least directly, in Miss Howe's ruin. He wanted to banish the turmoil and anger in her eyes when she looked at him now, wanted to replace it with the approval and affection he'd known before.

Yet wanting to confide in her was a reckless impulse that could well make an already untenable situation far worse. And even if she did know the truth, what then? With one less obstacle between them, temptation and ruin would be that much closer. Even with her believing him to be Julia's debaucher, he'd nearly ravished her right there in the coach. It had taken all of his remaining self-control to stop kissing her, and to crush her against his chest instead of making an even graver mistake than he already had.

Yet he couldn't forget the feel of her against him, warm and soft, the lavender scent of her skin, and the delicious contours of her breasts. Strangely, he wanted to hold her close and simply wrap her in his arms for hours almost as much as he wanted to ravish her. He had never felt so powerless to control his emotions over a woman—

Shouting erupted from the gardens.

It was Edmund. Ranting in that particular tone he had. That particularly annoying tone. What the devil was he about now? Adrian knew that howling all too well. Edmund was foxed.

Miss Colbrook could be out there being subjected to heavens knew what horrid behavior. Adrian turned and strode from the study. It was time he put a stop to it.

Anna tumbled onto the slope and skidded downward, clutching at the dirt and grass as she tried in vain to stop.

When she finally landed at the bottom of the hill, she twisted her left ankle. Stunned, she lay still for a moment, listening to Mr. Sinclair curse as he stumbled down the embankment after her.

She sat up and straightened her now dirty gown. Her bonnet was gone, and her hair was half-fallen from its chignon. Footsteps pounded on the slope above them as Mr. Sinclair staggered to her side.

"I am so sorry," he said. "I tried, but I could not keep you from falling." He leaned towards her, offering her a hand up. Then he suddenly jerked backward. A shadowy figure had shoved him away.

Lord Wareton knelt beside her. He cradled her shoulder

with one hand and gently held her head with the other.

"Are you hurt?" he asked softly.

"I do not think so." She wiggled her foot. "I twisted my ankle, but otherwise it seems fine."

"Good." He carefully released her, stood, and turned to his brother.

"Damn you, Edmund." Lord Wareton's voice was fearsome. "I should thrash you within an inch of your life."

Mr. Sinclair rubbed his arm where his brother had shoved him. "Adrian, let me explain—"

"Not another word," Lord Wareton growled. "We will discuss this tomorrow."

"Adrian—"

"Leave. Or I swear, I'll—"

"I am injured—"

"You are foxed. And you've let a lady come to harm. Leave. Now." Lord Wareton stepped closer to his brother and curled his hands into fists.

Muttering under his breath, Mr. Sinclair turned, paused to retrieve his flask from a nearby patch of grass, and limped away.

"What in blazes is this?" Lord Wareton leaned down and grabbed his brother's pistol. He stared at it a moment then shoved the gun into his own coat, cursing the entire time. "Bloody, bloody imbecile." He turned back to Anna. "Idiotic bastard."

She stared up at him like a fool, her mouth open.

Lie, even risk his own life, to protect his brother…

"My apologies," he grumbled as he knelt beside her again. He thought she was shocked at his language. He slid one arm around her back and another beneath her knees.

"I can walk," she whispered, finding her voice again. He ignored her, lifted her up, and carried her toward the house.

"Do not blame your brother for my fall," she said. "It was my fault. I stepped back without looking, and I slipped. He tried to catch me."

He stopped walking. "Why were you stepping backwards without looking?"

"He startled me, and I stepped back and lost my footing."

"How did he startle you?" His breath was warm on her cheek.

"He was standing on the bench. He was foxed..." And insulting you at the top of his lungs, she added silently. "Did you not hear his shouting?"

"Yes, I heard it, and likely half of Somerset heard it. Unintelligible nonsense, like most of what he utters." He held her tighter. "I'd sooner believe that you fell trying to escape his advances—"

"No, he made no advances."

"Why should I believe you? You wouldn't be the first foolish woman to defend him, and he's been fawning over you since his arrival." He leaned closer as he held her, until his face was only inches from hers. "You even smell like his horrid cologne."

"He made no advances because you were not here."

"What?" He peered down at her. "Are you foxed as well?"

"He flirts with me only to annoy you."

"You are foxed."

"He wants your attention. Likely why he acts as he does about many things. Do you not see that?"

He said nothing, only frowned at her for a moment, then he began to stride towards the house again. He followed the long, gradual slope that led to the bench where she and Mr. Sinclair had been moments before.

"I understand your brother much better now," she said. "And you."

"God help us," he muttered.

Even carrying her this distance, he seemed to barely exert himself. Likely, he would carry her all the way to the house if she permitted him. Yet once inside, she might have little chance to speak with him alone.

"You cannot carry me inside like this," she said quickly. "The servants might talk."

He paused. "As you wish." He brought her to the bench. His hand brushed the back of her legs as he set her down.

He held her gently by the shoulders as he steadied her. "How do you feel?" he asked.

How did she feel? Her hands stung, her neck ached, her ankle burned, and in the morning she would likely be covered in bruises.

She'd never felt so wonderful in her whole life.

She reached out, grasped the sides of his face, and kissed him.

CHAPTER FOURTEEN

"WHAT THE DEVIL ARE YOU doing?" Lord Wareton said hoarsely, stepping away from her.

She rose and moved closer to him, ignoring the pain in her ankle. She wanted to kiss him again. To apologize for all the harsh words she'd said. To have him hold her again.

"I know it was your brother who ruined Julia," she said, "not you."

He stared at her, his silence confirming her words. Not that she had any doubt at this point. It all made perfect sense. It wasn't just that she wished him to be innocent. He was. He was as he'd said, truly reformed. He was everything she'd hoped.

"He told me you took the blame for him," she said. "You no longer need to lie."

He crossed his arms, but his shoulders relaxed and much of the tension seemed to leave his body. He appeared worried but at the same time relieved.

"Tell me what really happened," she said.

He began to pace back and forth before the bench, his boots whispering against the grass. After a moment, he stopped before her. "You cannot tell anyone," he said quietly.

"I won't," she said.

He let out a long sigh. "Julia Howe came to my townhouse one afternoon in London. She told me she was increasing and that Edmund was responsible. She said that she had told Sir Neville and now he would be forced to challenge Edmund." He raked a hand through his hair. "Apparently, Sir Neville was about to send her away that day, but she'd run off to my townhouse instead."

"Your brother was there?" she asked.

"Yes."

"And he refused to marry her?"

He nodded. "I tried to persuade him to do the honorable thing, but he refused. After denying that he'd touched her, he stormed off, but I knew he was lying." He lowered himself onto the bench and rested his arms on his knees. "This was only weeks after I learned that he'd seduced another woman while I was in the army. He'd denied ruining her at first as well. He only admitted his guilt when several people confirmed seeing them…in a compromising situation."

She sat beside him. "Miss Carpenter?" The other mysterious account entry.

"Yes." He straightened. "So I offered to support Miss Howe, to arrange for her to live comfortably somewhere no one would know her."

"And she agreed?"

"Not at first," he said, shaking his head. "She was near hysterical, and so angry and distraught that she seemed to *want* Sir Neville to shoot Edmund. Not that I blamed her," he added dryly. "But I finally convinced her that my offer was her best option. Sir Neville was furious with her and planned to send her away to a situation far less comfortable that what I offered. So we reached an understanding, and I immediately made arrangements to have her taken away and cared for."

"And Sir Neville?"

"I went to see him that evening. To let him know the arrangements I had made for Miss Howe, and, I hoped, to prevent him from challenging Edmund. He was clearly shocked to see me. And confused. Even more so when I told him that I had ruined Miss Howe, and not Edmund."

"But he believed you?" she asked.

He sighed. "I thought he did. I claimed that Julia told

him it was Edmund because she wanted to punish me, but she couldn't bear the thought of me being killed. He seemed to accept that." He paused and said more quietly, "Much as Edmund might have deserved it, he never would have stood a chance against a marksman like Sir Neville. I couldn't let him die."

"You were willing to risk your life for your brother," she said, "even after what he'd done?" She reached out to grasp his hands, but he shifted away.

He stood, clasped his hands behind his back, and gazed into the shadows. "I wasn't eager to die for Edmund's stupidity, but I'd just spent three years in the army. I knew Sir Neville was an excellent shot, but I hoped that I could still shoot first without wounding him too severely before he could kill me."

Anna stood. "What happened?"

He turned to face her. "Nothing. Sir Neville didn't call me out. Upset as he was, I don't think he ever intended to challenge Edmund—or me."

"And he didn't ask you to marry Julia?"

Adrian shook his head.

Of course, Sir Neville wouldn't. An earl marrying an illegitimate woman was unthinkable.

"And he didn't want her back?" she asked.

"No. He seemed more furious with her than with anyone. I think knowing she would disappear and the scandal would be hidden, he was content to have her become my responsibility."

Harsh as it seemed, Anna was not surprised. For a man like Sir Neville, who took such pride in his heroic and honorable reputation, Julia's ruin must have been especially difficult to accept.

"So I set her up in a house not too far from Eastgate," he continued, "under a new name, as a widow, to protect her and her child from scandal."

"And she and the child are well?" she asked.

"Yes." He stared at her in silence for a moment. "You do know the real reason why Sir Neville never challenged me?" he finally said.

"To avoid scandal."

He shook his head. "He told me he wouldn't because of the connection between us, the fact that you and Madeline were his neighbors. At the time I was stunned by the lengths he was willing to go to protect the friendship between our families. To be honest, I even questioned his bravery and wondered if it was an excuse and he really had doubts about defeating me in a duel." He shook his head. "Now I know it was all to protect you."

All to protect her. And all this before they'd even become close friends?

Guilt nagged at her, guilt at how much Sir Neville had done for her and her family. But her mind kept returning to the fact that Lord Wareton was innocent.

"But it now seems Sir Neville knows that I lied to protect Edmund. And with everything that has gone on with you..." His voice softened and he shifted towards her. "He has implied that he will challenge Edmund if he is pushed too far. Much as Edmund might deserve it, I cannot let that happen."

She listened to every word he said, but her mind kept returning to his innocence. The realization that he hadn't ruined Julia sent a wave of happiness through her. She pushed aside all the other reasons she should not do what she was about to do, and she stepped closer to him.

"So many things make sense now," she said. He moved backward, retreating towards the garden wall. She followed him until he was forced to stop, his back practically touching the ivy-covered stone. "These past days I've believed that you were the worst sort of man. I am so sorry for how I have treated you." She raised a hand to his face. As her fingertips brushed his rough cheek, he closed his eyes.

"You are playing a dangerous game," he whispered. He

opened his eyes and stared down at her. "Innocent as you are, you know that."

She did. But at that moment she didn't care. Rather than fear, desire and fascination led her. In that instant she realized that he was deeply affected by her, and the knowledge thrilled her. Amazed at her own daring, she raised herself onto her toes and pressed her mouth firmly against his.

He lifted his hands to her shoulders, and for a moment she thought he might push her away. He muttered something against her lips and then kissed her back.

He clamped one arm around her, nearly lifting her off her feet, and with his other hand he slid his fingers around her cheek. This kiss was far different from the gentle start of their other kisses. It was not a gentle suitor's kiss, but a lover's—unrestrained and demanding.

She responded instantly, wrapping her arms around him, and tangling her fingers in his soft hair.

He kissed her lips, her cheeks, her jaw, and the curve of her neck. He slid his fingers through her hair, loosening her already mussed chignon, and he pressed his lips against her over and over. She inhaled the delicious scent of him— soap, cheroots, and brandy—as she struggled to breathe amid the torrent of caresses.

He slowly turned her around and leaned her against the wall, pressing her back against the cool stone. He slid his fingers down her arms and took her hands, lifting them up, pressing them beside her shoulders, gently pinning her against the wall. He tore his mouth from hers only to rake her neck and throat with more kisses. Then he drew his mouth lower, down to the bodice of her gown. He slid his hands along her arms, letting them fall to her sides as he caressed her shoulders and the swell of her breasts.

His knee pushed against her skirt, parting her legs through the muslin. His thigh pressed against hers as he loosened her gown and drew it down, trapping her arms at her sides. With one strong finger, he traced the edge of her corset, then gently tugged downward.

He bared her breasts to the cool night air.

And to the hot, maddening caresses of his mouth and hands.

Without the wall holding her up, she felt like she might collapse. She began shifting beneath him, pressing her hips towards him.

As he continued to kiss and suckle her breasts, he moved one hand lower, finding the curve of her waist, and then her hip, and finally tracing his fingers down her thigh. The warmth of his touch left her for a moment and then returned to her calf as he trailed his fingers up over her stockings and slowly raised her gown.

He straightened, abandoning her breasts to kiss her mouth again. She returned his kisses and drew even tighter against him, her bare breasts against his soft coat, her hip pressing against his thigh.

He kissed her face, neck, and lips. He slipped one hand behind her, lifted her away from the wall, and held her by the hip. With his other hand, he pushed her skirt higher, baring one leg all the way to her garter.

She wanted to touch him as he touched her, but her arms were trapped in the sleeves of her gown. She could reach out just far enough to pull him even closer, until she felt his erection press against her. And heavens, he was well endowed, feeling as solid and unyielding as the wall behind her.

He was more than ready to fully compromise her.

Through the haze of passion, a stab of apprehension shot through her. She quickly pushed the fear away.

She would not think. Only feel.

He kissed her neck and caressed her thigh above her garter, edging closer, until his fingers played at the opening of her drawers. She wanted desperately for him to move his fingers even closer, to do whatever it took to end the delicious agony they'd started. She shifted closer to his touch, willing him to continue.

"Please," she whispered, uncertain of how to ask for what she wanted.

Her voice seemed to startle him. He cursed under his breath, withdrew his hand, and let her gown fall.

"God forgive me," he said in a rush of breath. He released her and stepped away. The only sounds were their labored breathing, gradually slowing.

She pulled her gown up to her shoulders, leaned back against the wall, and stared up at him. Even in the dim moonlight, desire and anger was evident in his narrowed eyes and the rigid set of his jaw.

"I will not do this," he said, his voice hoarse. His gaze drifted across her face and down her body. "I have never wanted a woman as I want you. Never." His words sent a thrill through her. "Probably because I cannot have you. Not without..." He looked into her eyes again. "I shall not dishonor you. I shall not bring any more shame to my family. Forgive me."

He spun away and strode toward the manor.

Anna listened to the sound of his fading steps. She slid back against the wall, her hands clutching at the ivy. Tilting her head back, she stared up at the dark sky with its dusty smattering of stars.

Desire for him still filled her body. Beneath her newly awakened passion, she felt something else come alive, an unfamiliar emotion...

Joy. So intense that it was almost painful. Her throat tightened and her chest ached. Tears filled her eyes, blurring the stars above to white globes.

She loved him.

She now realized that she'd loved him for some time, but what she learned tonight made her love for him irrevocable.

He was the finest man she'd ever known, quite likely that she ever would know. And the heart of what made him so noble—the love and honor and intense sense of duty that he felt towards his family—those were the same things that meant, even if he should wish it, they would never be together.

Suddenly, all the energy drained from her body. She lowered herself to the ground until she knelt on the grass. The happiness she'd felt was gone. Anguish filled her instead.

She curled up against the stone wall and wept.

CHAPTER FIFTEEN

EDMUND WAS BEHAVING STRANGELY.

Adrian watched his brother pace the study, his eyes darting everywhere and settling nowhere. Edmund had actually risen in time for breakfast but then eaten almost nothing, only fidgeted at the table, tapping his teacup and unfolding and refolding his napkin over and over. He'd also not said more than two words to anyone the whole morning, which Adrian couldn't recall ever happening before.

Adrian leaned his elbows against the desk and rubbed his temples. He had a headache, likely from lack of rest. Not surprisingly, he'd been unable to sleep after what happened in the garden. After about an hour of pacing the hallways, he'd come very close to slipping into Miss Colbrook's room in the middle of the night and finishing what they'd started. He'd been so near to losing all control that he only saved himself with a late-night swim in a frigid duck pond, followed by a vigorous early morning ride around the manor. Unfortunately, by breakfast, despite feeling utterly exhausted, he merely glanced at Miss Colbrook and his desire instantly returned. He did his best not to look at her again, but just knowing she was nearby was enough to torment him.

Her delicious mouth and soft skin and full breasts, her silken, supple legs that had parted so eagerly at his touch, the way she'd responded to him so passionately and willingly, all had haunted him through the night and morning. He wasn't sure how he'd found the will to stop when he had. He strongly suspected that she would have allowed him to take her right there in the garden, an idea that made him half mad.

He began to comb his fingers through his hair. He recalled the feel of Miss Colbrook's hands on his head and stopped, letting his hands fall onto the desk.

He truly was pathetic. And soon he would probably be mad as well, either from weariness or frustration. Even Edmund's odd behavior wasn't enough of a distraction.

"What in blazes were you doing last night," Adrian asked, "wandering around the estate with a pistol, foxed? You could have hurt Miss Colbrook. Or yourself. What the devil has gotten into you?"

"What's gotten into *me*?" Edmund stopped pacing and leaned against the mantel. "You're the one who looks two steps from death. What could have kept you from sleep?" Edmund smirked and began tapping his foot against the hearth.

Adrian sat up straighter. "Stop leering, it doesn't suit you."

"I've been told it does," Edmund said. There was no hint of jealousy in his teasing. Adrian couldn't dispel the idea Miss Colbrook might be correct about Edmund flirting with her merely to upset him. There was one way to find out for certain.

"What are your intentions towards Miss Colbrook?" Adrian said.

"Strange you should ask, as you always say my intentions can only be bad."

"I am serious, Edmund."

Edmund paused in his tapping and gazed at Adrian for a moment. He looked oddly solemn.

"You are indeed," Edmund said. "Even more than usual. How interesting."

"Answer the question."

"Well, I was rather taken with her at first, I must admit. She has a certain unconventional charm. And she is quite

attractive." Adrian curled his hands into fists. "However..."
Edmund reached up to the mantel and began fiddling with
a small wooden globe. "I decided last night that she is too
mentally unbalanced for me."

"Mentally unbalanced? Miss Colbrook?" What on earth
was he babbling about?

"Quite." Edmund gave the globe one final spin and set
it down again.

"How so?" Adrian leaned back in his chair and crossed
his arms.

"Well, she likes you. What more proof does one need?"

Adrian shook his head. "You really are an ass."

"Am I?" Edmund began pacing before the fireplace. "I
am not the one who has a beautiful woman pining after
me and behaves as if he's being tortured when instead he
should realize he's a bloody lucky bastard."

"I'm an earl, Edmund, not some gentleman who can
choose any woman he desires—"

"An earl, indeed, and you won't let anyone forget it for
a moment. You're puffed up like a peacock."

"You are accusing *me* of being a peacock?" Adrian said.
"*You?*"

"Yes." Edmund began carefully smoothing his hair. Just
to be more of an ass, Adrian thought, just to bother him.
Just as he flirted with Miss Colbrook. Damn it, she was
right. Why hadn't he seen it before?

Adrian frowned. Strange that Edmund should admit
he'd given up on her though. He'd expect Edmund would
use her to bother him even more, especially if Edmund
realized how desperately he wanted her.

Edmund finished with his hair and began fluffing his
ridiculous cuffs.

Edmund couldn't possibly know how strong his desire
for her was. He hadn't even known himself until he began
to think the unthinkable, late last night, lying on the grass
after his swim in the chilly pond.

What if he were to marry Miss Colbrook?

He could send Edmund away to protect him from any possibility of a challenge from Sir Neville. And it was possible that Sir Neville, even if he lost Miss Colbrook, might not carry through on his threats.

But how badly would such a match affect his family, and his sister's chances for a grand marriage? Would he be able to forgive himself for marrying for lust, rather than connections and prosperity and everything an earl should marry for?

He'd spent most of his adult life behaving selfishly. Now he owed it to everyone close to him to choose a wife based on what would be best for the family, not on his own base impulses. To marry her would be yet another selfish indulgence, worse perhaps than anything he'd done before, because it would affect so many people.

Yet he'd come so close last night to having to marry her, so dangerously close. Guilt had stopped him at the last moment; guilt over what he was doing to her and to his family had saved him from a fatal mistake. So why did he feel no sense of relief whatsoever?

Adrian rubbed his eyes.

"You really do look awful," Edmund said. "What are you thinking about to make you so miserable?" Edmund leaned beside the fireplace again and began gently kicking the stand that held the poker. It was like a tiny hammer magnifying Adrian's headache.

"Why are you here?" Adrian said, scowling. "Why aren't you out pestering women or wasting money or being a nuisance somewhere else?"

Edmund smiled. "I am awaiting the outing to Highton Park this afternoon. I am looking forward to seeing the grounds, I hear they are quite beautiful."

"You cannot be serious."

"Quite." Edmund stopped his fidgeting and straightened.

Adrian rose. "You will not go."

"I was included in the invitation."

"You cannot be in Sir Neville's company."

"Why? Do I not look guiltier if I avoid him?"

"He knows you are guilty," Adrian said.

Edmund's eyes widened.

"You were so nervous at the concert," Adrian continued, "that if he had any doubt, I'm sure that put an end to it. You should be hiding from him, not attending outings on his estate."

Edmund crossed his arms and jutted out his chin. "Perhaps I do not wish to hide."

Adrian suddenly recalled Edmund looking much the same when he was nine and had demanded to accompany his older brother to Eton. The battle had lasted days, and Edmund had backed down only after Adrian threatened to stay away longer if Edmund followed him. It was the most determined Adrian had ever seen his younger brother. The fact he remembered it at this moment made him strangely uncomfortable.

"Are you foxed?" Adrian said. "I lied to save your life, and I'll not let you risk throwing it away. I should never have allowed you to stay here—"

"Ah yes, you did indeed lie to save my life." Edmund marched to the brandy bottle on the corner table. "A fact you never allow me to forget." He poured himself a generous amount of brandy, so much that when he lifted it, some sloshed over the side of the snifter and spattered the sleeve of his fawn-colored coat. Adrian was astounded to see Edmund's hands were shaking. Edmund ignored the stain and gulped down half the brandy without his mouth leaving the glass.

"What in blazes is wrong?" Adrian strode around the desk. "You are behaving oddly, even for you."

"Am I?" Edmund grinned unpleasantly. "I'm only behaving as you always say I do. Recklessly, stupidly."

Adrian felt a burst of shame wash over him, and his

temper flared even higher. Edmund *was* reckless. In fact, he reveled in it, and made no attempt to reform himself. Adrian only treated him as he deserved. To try and turn the tables on him and imply that he was the victim in all this only proved even more how incorrigible Edmund was, how hopeless.

How strangely he was behaving, though...

"You let Miss Colbrook know about Miss Howe deliberately," Adrian said.

"I was foxed." Edmund shrugged. "I barely remember what I said."

Adrian scowled.

"Besides," Edmund added, "you should be grateful. You wanted her to know, don't deny it. You wanted her to know that once again, you are the reformed noble one, and I'm the good for nothing wastrel." Edmund tossed back the rest of the brandy.

"Stop the self-pity, Edmund, it grew tiresome months ago."

Edmund froze. He glared at Adrian and clutched the snifter as if he might crush it. "I've grown tiresome?" He slammed the snifter down on the table. "Maybe I am a wastrel, maybe I've made mistakes worse than anything you ever did, maybe I deserve to have you constantly remind me of the terrible things I've done, but at least I have the decency to treat Miss Colbrook with respect." He jabbed a finger at Adrian. "That's right. For once I'm behaving better than you. You always claim you've never ruined an innocent, and that makes you so much better than me, but how close have you come with her? Damn close, I'll wager. And that's what's killing you."

Adrian felt as if he'd been punched in the stomach. For a moment, he couldn't breathe.

"If you're so bloody honorable now," Edmund added, stepping closer to him, "you should marry her off to Sir Neville before it's too late. Lord knows he will treat her properly." Edmund's hands were shaking at his sides. "She certainly deserves better than this."

They stared at each other for a moment, the only sound the chiming of a clock in the hall.

"Leave, Edmund," Adrian finally said. "I expect you to be gone before we all depart for Highton Park. Go into town or do whatever, I do not care, but leave."

Something shifted in Edmund's expression. His anger drained away as he dropped his gaze to floor. He spun around and marched from the room.

Adrian turned and fell into his chair. He leaned forward and rested his arms on the desk, his body feeling strangely numb.

Damn it to hell, Edmund was right.

He'd merely said what Adrian already knew, that his behavior with Miss Colbrook was dishonorable. But to hear it spoken made the full horror of what he was doing sink in.

And Edmund was right about Sir Neville as well.

She deserved a man like Sir Neville. He obviously cared for her deeply, after all the pains he'd taken to protect her family from scandal. And even though she was far beneath his status, he was willing to wait patiently for her even if it meant several more years. To Adrian, such forbearance was unfathomable. How could the man endure it?

Furthermore, how could Adrian endure it? He would be forced to be in her presence for the devil knew how long, until Madeline married and Sir Neville finally offered for Miss Colbrook. Months, perhaps years, of seeing her nearly every day, at breakfast, dinner, parties, walking about the estate, sitting in the window seat...

It would be pure hell.

He couldn't bear having her in his home until Madeline married. Miss Colbrook had to wed Sir Neville as soon as possible. Why the blazes did she insist on delaying until after Madeline found a husband? Fear was a part of it, surely, but he was becoming increasingly convinced there was something more to it, some secret she kept from him. Whatever it was, he needed to find out, so he could convince her to marry Sir Neville as soon as possible and have the whole horrible mess settled once and for all.

Once she was Sir Neville's wife, Edmund would be safe from his challenge permanently. And Adrian would be forever safe from temptation.

CHAPTER SIXTEEN

THAT AFTERNOON ANNA SAT ON the terrace behind the manor at Highton Park. A large party had assembled at Sir Neville's home to enjoy the fine weather: the Dunburys, the Duke of Dulverton, Lady Stratford, Mrs. Shelby, Lady Carlton, Cecelia, Madeline and of course, Lord Wareton. Mr. Sinclair had left early that morning, supposedly to go into Somerton, although Anna wondered if Lord Wareton had asked him to disappear to avoid Sir Neville. Anna had seen Mr. Sinclair mount a horse and pat his coat pockets before he rode off. She strongly suspected he was taking a flask and pistol for another shooting session in the woods.

In all the madness of last evening, she'd had no chance to tell Lord Wareton about what she'd seen Mr. Sinclair doing, but today her head was clearer, and she knew she must speak with him about it. If only she could summon the courage to look him in the eye after what had happened.

He was definitely keeping his distance. She hadn't caught him looking her way once since breakfast. Now he kept close to Lady Stratford, his arm brushing hers as they stood at the edge of the veranda and looked out at the gardens.

The rest of the party sat around a large canopied table, sipping lemonade. At one end, the Dunbury sisters and Cecelia fought for the duke's attention. The duke seemed oblivious, sitting straight and somber as always, nibbling on an orange tart. Lady Carlton and Mrs. Dunbury watched him intently.

Madeline and Mrs. Shelby sat on each side of Anna, complementing Sir Neville on the beauty of his gardens.

Anna heard only half of what they were saying, as her gaze kept drifting to Lord Wareton. Lady Stratford was laughing and touching his arm as they spoke. She looked back toward the table and caught Anna staring at her. Anna quickly glanced away, but she felt Lady Stratford's stare follow her. Anna gazed where nearly everyone else did—at the duke, who was carefully chewing the final bite of his tart.

"I should very much like to walk to the lake," Cecelia announced, smiling and leaning close to him as he dabbed at his mouth with a handkerchief. "It is so fine out."

"Yes, of course." The duke nodded, frowning as if Cecelia had just asked him to answer a difficult mathematical problem. "A wonderful idea, Miss Sinclair."

There was a chorus of agreement from the Dunburys and Lady Carlton.

Madeline frowned. "But Sir Neville—"

"I shall be glad to wait here," Sir Neville said. "I would not ruin your fun. Though you are kind to think of me, Miss Madeline." He smiled at her and Madeline smiled back, her face suddenly bright.

"Then I shall wait with you," Madeline said happily. "And Anna," she added, "will you not rest with us? No doubt you are still weary from your long walk yesterday?"

Anna hid a smile. "I shall stay with you."

"Why do we not ride," Sir Neville suggested, "and meet the others at the lake?"

"A wonderful idea," Madeline said.

Sir Neville ordered a carriage brought around. While the rest of the party set out across the gardens, Anna, Madeline, and Sir Neville made their way to the front of the manor.

Sir Neville helped Madeline into the waiting curricle first. As she stepped up, the heel of her half-boot caught on the edge of the step, and she began to slip. Sir Neville caught her by the arm and steadied her. When Anna dropped into the seat beside Madeline, she was surprised to see her stepsister smooth her gown carefully where he had held her, a small smile on her face.

Suddenly, all the praise Madeline always heaped on Sir Neville, all the encouragement she gave Anna to marry him, looked very different. Did Madeline think so highly of him because she had romantic feelings for him?

No, Anna assured herself, Madeline was simply fond of him as a friend. She was making something out of nothing. She glanced at Madeline, who was still smiling at Sir Neville. Well, almost nothing...

Sir Neville took the reins and they set out, riding leisurely down the main carriage road to the lake. Soon they could see the rest of the party off to the east, following a footpath that crossed a field before rejoining the carriage road. After a few moments, the others passed out of view, and the trees that edged the lake came into sight in the distance.

Anna glanced at Sir Neville. Would he truly challenge Mr. Sinclair after all this time? Lord Wareton seemed convinced of the threat, but she had doubts that Sir Neville would do such a thing, no matter what happened.

"Much as I love the countryside," Madeline said, "I cannot wait for the season to begin. Will you be traveling to London this year, Sir Neville?"

"My plans are uncertain at present," he said. "But I have no doubt you will have a marvelous time and find many admirers in town, Miss Madeline." He added gently, "And I am certain it will not be long before you are no longer a 'miss'."

Madeline smiled. "And then Anna also, might not be a 'miss' much longer?"

Sir Neville smiled. "Perhaps not."

When Sir Neville had expressed his intentions towards her before, Anna had said little. She'd been too eager to stop him from making a formal proposal and then too shocked by his revelation about Lord Wareton. It was time she let Sir Neville know what her answer would be. It was the fair thing to do.

"I fear I may disappoint you both," Anna said quietly.

Madeline spun to look at her, frowning. Sir Neville's eyes narrowed, but he stared straight ahead at the road.

"What do you mean?" Madeline asked.

"I have been quite contented these past years," Anna said. "I have been thinking recently that I should like to remain just as I am, a spinster." She lifted Madeline's hand and held it gently. "I shall be content to help care for your children someday."

Madeline grasped her hand tightly. "Anna—"

Anna leaned forward to gaze past Madeline. "Sir Neville, would you be so kind as to stop the carriage? I believe I shall walk after all." He nodded without looking at her and drew the horses to a stop. "I shall let the others catch up to me," Anna added. "You and Madeline continue."

Sir Neville inclined his head and flicked the reins. As the curricle moved forward, Madeline turned and gazed back at Anna. The sadness on Madeline's face pained her, but she had to say what she did. It was well past the time that she dashed Sir Neville's hopes—and Madeline's as well—that she would ever marry him. If she'd ever seriously considered it, Lord Wareton had changed all that irrevocably.

Lady Stratford grasped Adrian's arm as they strolled toward the lake, trailing some distance behind the others. Her perfume seemed heavier and sweeter than usual this afternoon. Too sweet. Adrian looked towards the east, where Sir Neville's carriage moved slowly along the road to the lake. He could make out Miss Colbrook's pale bonnet above Madeline's darker one.

All afternoon he'd tried his best not to look in Miss Colbrook's direction. He'd attempted to focus on Lady Stratford and to not think about what he must say to Miss Colbrook. But he kept reminding himself that telling her to marry Sir Neville was for the best. It was sensible, the only practical things for everyone—

"I have been patient, Lord Wareton," Lady Stratford's voice broke through his thoughts, "but even I cannot wait for an answer forever." She tapped her fingers lightly on his forearm.

He snapped his gaze back to her. How long had he been staring after the carriage? And what the devil had been the question?

Lady Stratford sighed. "I asked about your plans for going into town next month."

"I have not decided yet," he said.

"Obviously." She was smiling, but her blue eyes remained cool. "You have been quite distracted of late."

"Forgive me."

"You know," she said, glancing towards the carriage, "he clearly has a great deal of affection for her. And she seems like a woman who would be far happier with a husband who can put his heart above other considerations." Lady Stratford sounded as if she almost admired Miss Colbrook for her romantic tendencies. Almost.

"Indeed," Adrian said, keeping his voice neutral.

"How wonderful that Sir Neville is also wealthy. And their backgrounds make them eminently suited for each other." There was an undeniable question in her tone. He glanced at her; she watched him with hard eyes, smiling faintly. "Anything else might only bring her heartache. And I can see how fond of her you are," she added, gently squeezing his arm. "I know you only want her happiness."

Adrian's throat tightened. As if he needed one more person to tell him how Sir Neville cared deeply for Miss Colbrook and how she would be better off with him.

"Yes, it is a fitting match," she continued. "He has no close family to be damaged by his choice of wife, no sisters or cousins. Rank, building connections—these things apparently matter little to him and even less to her." Lady

Stratford smiled up at him and lifted one hand to grasp the locket at her neck, a gold oval engraved with the crest of the Barony of Stratford. She tapped her finger gently against the metal. "She belongs in a different world from people like us, does she not?"

Adrian found himself unwilling to answer. He forced a smile.

"Here comes Mrs. Shelby to join us," Lady Stratford said, glancing ahead. Before Mrs. Shelby was within earshot she added, "You will have to let me know soon, Lord Wareton, whether I can depend on you in London next month. Or whether I should look for other company. I cannot wait forever."

CHAPTER SEVENTEEN

ANNA LEANED AGAINST THE STONE wall that lined the road and watched the rest of the party draw near.

At the front of the group, the duke and Cecelia walked side by side. As usual, he moved stiffly, his head held high, his arm rigid as he escorted Cecelia. In contrast, Cecelia leaned into his arm and spoke animatedly, seemingly unfazed by his stern demeanor. But sometimes, just for an instant, Anna thought Cecelia's eyes betrayed the truth: she didn't give a fig for the duke. She was merely doing what Lady Carlton and many others had told her time and again was expected of her. But above all, Anna suspected that Cecelia was trying to please Lord Wareton.

Anna frowned. Why on earth did he want his sister to wed such a dull man?

Because he was a duke of course, and because rank and money were everything, unquestionably far more important than compatibility or personal attraction. Lord Wareton had said as much last night in the garden. It was simply how it was done, but the idea of Cecelia trapped with the duke for a lifetime made Anna's heart sink.

Walking behind the duke and Cecelia, Lady Carlton looked smug but watchful, a displeased-looking Mrs. Dunbury at her side. Lady Carlton kept her gait purposefully slow, forcing the others to hang back, allowing a large space to open behind the couple. Whenever Mrs. Dunbury or her daughters, who walked behind their mother, tried to increase their pace, Lady Carlton slowed even more, using her broad figure to block them from moving forward.

At the end of the procession, Lord Wareton strolled with Lady Stratford and Mrs. Shelby. The two ladies were talking, but Lord Wareton seemed distracted, falling a few steps behind them. He looked up and caught sight of Anna; even a glance from such a distance made her heart speed up.

He was the handsomest and most intriguing man she'd ever met. For one instant she wished desperately that he wasn't an earl, that he was only a gentleman of modest means and background. Or not even a gentleman, but a tradesman or farmer or soldier—anything that could make their positions equal enough to allow her absurd dreams to come true.

Lady Carlton saw that the duke and Cecelia were just about to reach Anna.

"Miss Colbrook," Lady Carlton called out, "I wonder if I might have a word with you." Anna let the duke and Cecelia pass and waited for Lady Carlton.

"Yes, Lady Carlton?" Anna said.

"I, ah…" Lady Carlton apparently struggled to find a reason for having summoned her back. "Why did you not ride all the way with Sir Neville?" she finally asked, frowning.

"I decided I needed a walk after all."

"You should have at least brought a parasol. This is why you look positively brown. And that dress, the color is all wrong for you…" Anna half-listened as she droned on, wishing she could turn and see what Lord Wareton was up to. She could only occasionally hear him over his aunt's prattle.

Thankfully, after only a few minutes of being lectured, Mrs. Shelby rescued Anna from Lady Carlton's company. After joining them and chatting for a brief time, Mrs. Shelby took Anna's arm and drew her aside to examine some wildflowers. She only allowed Anna to begin walking again when Lady Stratford and Lord Wareton reached them.

For a few moments, Mrs. Shelby chatted about the scenery, but there was a sparkle in her eye and a slight smile on her face as she glanced around.

"Lady Stratford," Mrs. Shelby said, "would you care to walk ahead and speak with Cecelia? She mentioned earlier that she wanted our advice on preparing for the season." Mrs. Shelby smiled at Anna and raised one thin red brow, glancing at Lord Wareton.

Mrs. Shelby knew as well then. Was there anyone who didn't yet realize she had feelings for him? And good friend that Mrs. Shelby was, she was trying to be helpful. As if there were any real hope.

To Anna's surprise, Lady Stratford agreed to move ahead, leaving Anna with Lord Wareton. Lady Carlton glanced back, scowling, but she apparently feared leaving Cecelia too much to stop Anna and Lord Wareton from walking together. As Lady Stratford and Mrs. Shelby approached, making their way towards Cecelia and the duke, Lady Carlton seemed to forget about Anna entirely.

As she and Lord Wareton strolled silently, Anna forced herself not to look at him, but it wasn't easy. Just a glance at the sleeve of his coat, his strong legs flexing beneath his dark breeches, or his hand swinging gently as he walked was enough to re-ignite memories of the previous evening. She flushed to recall what he'd done to her, how he'd touched her and made her feel... And when he'd left rather than choose dishonor, his strength and integrity had made her realize how deeply she loved him.

Last night had changed everything.

And at the same time nothing had changed. They still strolled as if the day were an ordinary one, as if they'd never shared such intimacy, as if they meant little to each other. As if nothing had ever happened between them and nothing ever would in the future.

And likely it wouldn't.

His boots were dusty from the road and beneath the film of dirt, the leather didn't shine as it normally did. He was usually so meticulous with his appearance, but today in addition to his boots, the hair curling out beneath his hat was rumpled, his cravat was wrinkled, and a hint of stubble darkened his chin. He looked as if he'd shaved hastily or his valet hadn't seen to his duties as usual. Could it be because he hadn't slept at all? The shadows under his eyes also suggested as much.

Surprisingly, she had slept last night, exhausted from sobbing after he left her in the garden, but her dreams were troubled. She awoke twice, her bedclothes twisted around her, her skin as hot and tingling as if he were touching her. And in the morning she'd been restless, still aching from the memory of his caresses.

Could he be filled with as much longing for her? He'd said that he never wanted a woman as he wanted her. The memory of those words made her feel warm and a bit breathless. She tried to distract herself by focusing on the lake ahead.

The distance between them and the rest of the party had grown quite wide, far enough that no one could overhear them.

"Lord Wareton," she said.

"Yes?" His voice was tense, sharp. Did he fear she would mention what happened last night? What was there to say that would not cause them both more pain?

Mr. Sinclair, she reminded herself. She must speak to Lord Wareton about his brother and try to prevent a duel. Now was the best opportunity she might have for some time, for she doubted she would allow herself to be alone with Lord Wareton anymore.

"Did you ask your brother not to join us?" she said.

He frowned but nodded. "I sent him to town."

"Why?"

"To keep him away from Sir Neville." He kept his gaze

straight ahead.

Did Lord Wareton only fear Sir Neville would challenge his brother, or did he also suspect his brother wished to confront Sir Neville? She doubted Mr. Sinclair could be persuaded to stay away from Sir Neville for much longer, not if the amount of despair he'd displayed the other evening was any indication.

"There is something I never had a chance to tell you last night," she said. "I believe your brother may wish to fight Sir Neville."

"Nonsense." He scowled but his gaze shifted nervously, a hint of doubt in his eyes.

"The gun you found, I caught him practicing with it. I am afraid of what might happen—"

"Practicing? Why should he wish to admit his guilt to Sir Neville now, after all this time?" He shook his head. "I do not believe it." His tone made it clear he didn't wish to discuss it.

Could he really not see the truth, or did he simply not wish to? She sensed he might react badly if she pressed the issue, but she had no choice. He was the only one who had a chance of persuading his brother to stop.

She took a deep breath. "Perhaps he's tired of having you hold his mistakes over his head."

He stopped walking and glared at her. "What?"

She halted beside him and kept her head high, looking him directly in the eyes. "You are terribly harsh with him."

"Am I?" He crossed his arms. "Well, why shouldn't I be, after what he's done? Would you defend him, particularly after you were so unforgiving when you believed I was guilty?" He looked down at her with such anger, it pained her to meet his gaze. But she did.

"I do not defend what he did, but perhaps he's ready to finally take responsibility for it."

"Ready to commit suicide you mean?" Lord Wareton spoke a bit too loudly. Ahead, Anna noticed the others were glancing back at them curiously. "He would never," he added, his voice softer. "God forgive me, but even if Edmund were suddenly possessed with a fit of bravery, he would be slaughtered by Sir Neville. Sir Neville is renowned for his marksmanship. Edmund cannot shoot."

Stubborn man, he wouldn't admit what was right before his eyes.

"At least he would be doing what is right," she said, "even if he should be shot—"

"I'll not let him be killed." He began walking again. She hurried to stay by his side.

"You will not let him take responsibility for his own mistakes, the very things you criticize him for?"

"He became what he is following my example. They are my mistakes as well."

"Is that why you took the blame for him?"

He glanced at her sharply. "Should I have allowed him to be killed? And likely disgrace our family from the scandal? And yes, it was also my duty, for I was also to blame for what happened to Miss Howe."

"How?" She thought for a moment that he wouldn't answer her.

"Edmund copied me growing up," he finally said, some of the anger gone from his voice. "He saw how wild I was and behaved as I did. Only he carried it farther than I ever did. Too far."

"With Miss Carpenter?"

"Before then. Long before."

"What happened?" she asked.

He looked at her, considering, then sighed. "He was just out of school. I found him with a servant girl in our father's bed. I shall never forget how he looked lying there, drunk, foolish... He thought I would be proud of him. Proud." He shook his head. "I stopped my wild behavior. I went into the army a month later."

So that was what he'd held back from her before, the real

reason he enlisted in the military so abruptly. The shock of finding his younger brother in such a situation had apparently stunned him into finally recognizing his own failures and caused him to change. But did he still carry the burden of guilt after all these years? Was that why he seemed unable to forgive himself for his past or to forgive his brother?

"When I returned home," he continued, "and learned about Miss Carpenter, I should have watched him better, kept him from being alone with Miss Howe."

"You are not responsible for your brother's actions." She reached out to him, stopping herself an instant before she would have grasped his arm. She shouldn't touch him, not after last evening. Perhaps never again. The thought made her heart ache. She let her hand fall to her side.

"I was responsible," he said, still gazing down, apparently oblivious to her having reached out to him. "Our parents were dead. He looked up to me for guidance, and I failed him. Miserably. Cecelia too. I left her to live with..." He glanced ahead to where Lady Carlton marched angrily behind Cecelia, the duke, Mrs. Shelby, and Lady Stratford. "A less than ideal caretaker."

"What could you have done instead? You were but a child yourself much of that time."

He shook his head. "I was unforgivably selfish, wasting years when I should have been caring for them."

One word he'd said in particular echoed in her mind. *Unforgivably.*

That was what tormented him. Much as he insisted that others no longer judge him by his past, he refused to do the same. He was constantly measuring his behavior against a debt he believed he owed. The guilt was behind his every decision—whom to marry his sister to and whom to marry himself and how to treat his brother.

"Even the old earl despised my behavior," he said. "He told me once that the earldom would survive even a wastrel like me. I laughed at the time. It took me years to see the miserable old monster was right." He walked in silence for a moment, staring into the air.

"I have worked hard to become worthy of my inheritance," he continued, "to try and make up for years of mistakes. That is why now I must do the best to atone for my errors and protect Edmund from his folly. And see Cecelia settled well."

Cecelia. Another burden of guilt he carried. And one he was also trying to solve in completely the wrong fashion.

"You believe the duke is the best match for her?" she asked.

"Of course." His face darkened. "He is one of the highest-ranking bachelors in England. And the closest in age to her."

"But do you believe she will be happy?"

"It is what she wishes as well." His clipped tone made it clear he didn't want to discuss it. "And her future is also affected by the choices I make for myself. I do not deserve to make selfish decisions, choices that will not help my family."

He believed that if he married poorly, the duke might cry off Cecelia, and the status of the whole family would suffer. He was telling her again why, despite the attraction between them, they could never marry. As if she'd ever had any real hope. And yet, that he even defended his reasoning surprised her. Was the pain in his eyes simply from guilt over his dishonorable behavior, or was some of his anguish because he truly cared for her? At least he trusted her enough to confide in her. He must have some feelings for her besides lust, however they might pale compared to her own affection for him. It was the most she could ever expect.

Mr. Sinclair had said that his brother would never allow himself to fall in love, and now she saw that he was right. Lord Wareton was punishing himself so brutally for his past that even if he could love a woman, and even if she was his equal in birth, Anna doubted he would ever allow himself such happiness.

Adrian hated to look at her, yet he couldn't stop.

His gaze wandered to her constantly, devouring the sight of her. Every aspect of her tormented him. Her shapely ankles flashing beneath the flounced hem of her walking dress, the outline of her legs, her full hips, the luscious indent of her waist that seemed so slender beneath the swell of her breasts, breasts that he ached to caress again. Her beautiful face. Her striking blue eyes that saw far too much for his comfort. She was troublesome and infuriating, and even when he was angry with her, he wanted her with an intensity that terrified him.

And he was angry with her for implying Cecelia might not be happy with the duke, and even more upset at her for suggesting Edmund wished to fight Sir Neville. Yet as his temper cooled, he became increasingly worried that she might be right about Edmund. His brother was behaving strangely, and too many details didn't add up any other way. Miss Colbrook had said she heard Edmund went shooting while at Lady Camden's recently, something Adrian had dismissed as a false rumor. But what if it were true? And now he'd apparently been practicing with the pistol. And just this morning he said that he no longer wished to hide from Sir Neville. Adrian had tried to convince himself that his brother was merely trying to irritate him, but whenever he recalled the determined light in Edmund's eyes, his gut tightened.

He glanced at Miss Colbrook again. Damn it, she was probably right. Again.

He looked ahead at Jane Stratford, strolling beside the duke, her hips swaying gracefully, every movement alluring, every stitch of fabric and lock of hair perfectly arranged. She was the essence of wealth and aristocracy from her feathered hat to the tips of her kidskin boots. She was the picture of what a countess should be—elegant, sophisticated, regal.

He imagined her as his countess, as mistress of Wareton, and the manor filled with her tastes, her friends. There would be constant parties and fetes and breakfasts for the cream of the ton, and eventually, knowing her, the Prince Regent himself could very well dine at Wareton. A marriage to her would mean building even more powerful connections and undoubtedly grand marriages for his sister, cousin, and eventually their own children, should they have any. She would likely permit him two, he suspected, although he wondered if she would want many more. Yet any children she had likely would be doted on and would no doubt marry well, as nothing short of a match with nobility would likely satisfy her.

Undoubtedly, she would also expect him to have affairs, and wouldn't care so long as he was discreet and made the required appearances with her. He suspected she would wish to have her own indulgences as well. It would be a proper English noble marriage, effective at building connections and wealth and, therefore, by most estimations highly successful.

And marrying Miss Colbrook? A far different scenario leapt to mind. She would be a countess who could run the estate down to every detail and who would care for the tenants like an extended family. She would probably spend as much, if not more, of her time with her commoner neighbors as she did with members of the ton. A marriage to her could mean far more modest matches for his sister and cousin, and less prosperity for all of them.

Miss Colbrook wouldn't likely allow him to keep his distance, either. She would pry into nearly everything, not only matters of the estate, but his personal matters as well. She wouldn't likely tolerate a mistress, and she would spend a great deal of her time and his money helping those less fortunate. And as for children—the idea of having children with her made his chest tight—he suspected she'd be quite happy to have more than two.

Unquestionably, she would be a wonderful wife. But Lady Stratford was correct in her observation—not for him.

His family would gain even more status if he chose a wife like Lady Stratford. He must fulfill his obligations and act in his family's best interests.

And despite his rank, in some ways he thought Miss Colbrook deserved better. She deserved a gentleman who could put his affection for her above all other considerations. Lady Stratford had merely confirmed what his conscience already told him—that for her own happiness, she deserved Sir Neville. So Adrian must encourage the match, no matter how much jealousy he felt, and no matter how much he hated to do it. It was best for everyone involved that she marry Sir Neville.

Sir Neville waited for her even now. He and Madeline had descended from the carriage, not far from where the others strolled by. Sir Neville looked towards Adrian and Miss Colbrook, tapping his walking stick, waiting.

Adrian couldn't delay any longer. This might be the last time he would speak with her privately for some time.

He stopped walking. "There is something I must tell you."

She paused and turned to face him. Her eyes narrowed beneath the wide brim of her bonnet.

"Should Sir Neville make you an offer in the future, I would encourage you to accept it."

"Would you?" she said. "I suppose it would be the sensible thing to do." There was no accusation in her eyes. Only a horrible disappointment.

"He cares for you a great deal. Consider all he has done for you."

She stared at him, resignation seeming to settle on her face. That was how it should be. She must understand how impossible it was for anything to happen between them again. It would take very little encouragement on her part for him to give in to his desire. Even now, his mind drifted between anguish at what he must say to her, and the desperate desire to kiss her again, to caress her as he had the night before—

No. He forced himself to look away from her beautiful eyes, her full lips. He stared at the bow in her bonnet ribbon, just below her chin.

"Perhaps now you will change your mind about insisting Madeline marry first."

Miss Colbrook had to leave Wareton before it was too late, before she caused him to lose everything he'd worked for, and all he'd vowed to do.

"You truly wish me to marry Sir Neville?" she asked quietly.

He forced himself to meet her gaze. She stared at him, her face full of conflict. He gazed into her blue eyes, his stomach in knots, his fingers digging into his palms. He saw the weight of everything balanced in her eyes—everything he shouldn't want, all he couldn't have.

Behind her, Sir Neville waited not far away, standing at the end of the path, leaning on his walking stick, his eyes hidden by the shadow of his hat. Madeline stood beside him, fidgeting with the loose ties on her pale green bonnet, her face anxious.

"Yes," Adrian said. "As soon as possible."

CHAPTER EIGHTEEN

THREE DAYS PASSED. THREE DAYS in which Anna tried desperately to decide what she should do with her conflicting emotions. Three days and mostly sleepless nights of considering the impossibility of her situation.

She loved a man whom she could never marry, even if he were foolhardy enough to agree to it. If they did marry, he would almost certainly grow to resent her, and they would end up in a miserable marriage. Like her mother, she would be bound to a man who didn't love her in return. Even worse, a man who could very well grow to hate her for what he'd given up for her.

No. He would marry another woman. And she must marry someone else as well, or not wed at all. She would likely spend the rest of her life pining for him in silence, forced to see him and his wife socially. She would be left with memories of a few wonderful kisses and caresses and the rest only fantasy and unfulfilled dreams. It was still a better alternative than earning his lifelong hatred.

But there was a third option. It was shocking, but it would give her something, some small bit of joy, and it was all she could ever risk without bringing ruin to the family. A few weeks ago it would have been unthinkable, but now everything had changed; ideas that once seemed impossibly reckless looked more and more like reasonable choices.

She forced herself to interact with him as normally as possible. They both tried to behave as if nothing had happened, but they usually avoided each other's gaze and spoke with everyone else in the room but each other.

Once, when she ran into him unexpectedly as she strolled through the garden, he turned and quickly walked the other way.

By the third day she was desperate to escape the manor and spend some time away from the other ladies, so she declined to go calling with them. Instead, she went alone to visit some neighbors, saving Mrs. Hunter's cottage for last so she might stay there the longest.

It was a warm, fine day, and Mrs. Hunter's children played outside, running and laughing on the hillside behind the cottage. Mrs. Hunter and Anna sat on a wooden bench at the rear of the house, watching them frolic. A steady breeze carried the scent of freshly-turned earth in the nearby garden to Anna and cooled her half-bare arms.

Emma started to cry and Mrs. Hunter rocked her, humming softly until she settled.

"May I hold her?" Anna asked. "If you think she'll allow me?"

"By all means." Mrs. Hunter smiled and handed her the baby.

"Mrs. Hunter," Anna said, "there is something..." As Anna settled Emma in her lap, the baby looked as if she might fuss for a moment, but she stilled at the sound of her voice. "May I ask a very personal question?"

"It is about Emma, isn't it?"

"Yes."

"You have never asked, all this time. I wondered if you ever would."

"Do you have any regrets?"

"I should, shouldn't I?" Mrs. Hunter said. "Perhaps that's why some ladies—like Mrs. Lutton—are right about me being a bad egg." She smiled. "But I regret nothing. I wouldn't trade Emma, or that week, for anything in the world."

"Week?" Anna let the baby grab her finger and looked at Mrs. Hunter.

"He was a surveyor from Oxford, staying not far from my old house. I was missing my husband terribly when I met him. He had shoulders like this..." She swung her arms wide, grinning. "And the handsomest, most devilish eyes." She sighed and glanced at Emma. "He doesn't even know about her."

"You didn't try and tell him?"

Mrs. Hunter shook her head. "I didn't want him to stay for that reason. I wouldn't use a babe to try and force a man into something. I knew what I was doing, at my age, with the brood I already have.

"I won't lie and say we were madly in love, either," she continued. "We might have been, given more time. There was something so...well, I wondered if I might see him again."

"Then he might return?"

"I am not holding my breath." Mrs. Hunter laughed. Then her face grew more somber. "I suppose my only regret is that the babe may pay some price for my selfishness. And yet, here she is treated as all the others. Thanks to your kindness." Mrs. Hunter frowned. "But why do you ask?"

"I was just curious." Anna glanced down and adjusted the buttons on her gloves.

"Indeed? And you waited until now to ask, for no particular reason?" Mrs. Hunter's face changed to an expression she often wore just before she reprimanded one of her children. "Whatever you are thinking," she said, "remember, you and I are very different, in situation, in experience—"

"I know." Anna nodded. Kind and completely trustworthy as Mrs. Hunter was, Anna couldn't bring herself to admit what she was considering.

"A woman in your position has much more to lose...I would not wish to see you hurt."

"Of course not. Yet I cannot help but wonder which would hurt more?"

"What do you mean?" Mrs. Hunter asked.

"What if you hadn't had that week but wished you had?"

"That would be far worse than—" Mrs. Hunter stopped abruptly and cleared her throat. "I mean, I think it would depend on—"

"Thank you." Anna smiled, looked down, and stroked a lock of Emma's dark hair. It didn't really matter what Mrs. Hunter said. She merely confirmed what Anna had already decided.

Lord Wareton wished her to marry Sir Neville. Yet she would never marry him. Perhaps she wouldn't marry at all. But she wouldn't grow old without knowing what it was like to be with Lord Wareton, the man she loved with all her soul.

She would offer herself to him. This afternoon.

Not long after she returned home, Anna learned from Smith that Lord Wareton had gone for a swim, a new habit of his as far as she knew. She walked to the lake near the northern edge of the estate and soon found him, swimming in a cove sheltered by towering oaks. His coat, shirt, boots, and stockings lay heaped on a rock close to the water.

He was not far off, his strokes strong and smooth as he headed toward land. She stood in the shadow of the oaks and watched him glide closer. A few yards from shore, he stopped swimming and rose from the water. She stepped back, startled by the sight of him without coat or shirt. She stared as he wiped his eyes and combed back his hair with his fingers.

His hands, face, and neck were tan from all the time he spent outside. But the rest of him—muscular arms, shoulders, broad chest and back—was paler, normally hidden beneath clothes. Only a swath of hair shadowed his chest, a darker brown than the sandy brown of his head.

He turned and stood motionless for a moment, still

unaware of her presence, staring out across the lake. His face was somber.

She stepped out of the shadows. "You have learned how deep the water is."

He spun around, his eyes wide. "How long have you been here?"

"Not long."

He waded out of the lake. His breeches, the only thing he wore, stuck to his body like a second skin. His feet were bare.

He was the most handsome creature she'd ever seen. Yet he seemed self-conscious. Frowning, he quickly grabbed his shirt from the pile of clothing on the grassy bank.

"Please," she said softly, stepping towards him, "Do not put it on."

He stared at her in disbelief. After a moment he dropped his gaze and pulled the shirt over his head. He began to button the front.

She willed the fluttering in her stomach to stop. She forced herself to breathe slowly and speak calmly.

"Lord—" She paused. No. "Adrian." He froze. It was the first time she'd ever called him by his given name. "I want you to make love to me."

CHAPTER NINETEEN

ADRIAN THOUGHT HE'D LOST HIS mind. Surely, he was hallucinating. Sleep deprivation and sexual frustration had finally taken their toll.

"You want what?" he whispered. All the cool relief he'd felt from his swim vanished as he stared at Miss Colbrook, looking so beautiful in her simple white gown and blue bonnet, saying the unthinkable.

"I do not expect anything, I do not want anything else." Her voice was steady. "But I cannot bear the thought of never being with you."

"You know what you are asking?" he said hoarsely.

Of course she knew. She might be innocent but she wasn't ignorant. Barely a moment had passed over the past few days without him thinking about how she'd responded to him, how despite her inexperience, she was so unexpectedly passionate, so intoxicating she nearly overwhelmed his self-control.

"Please, Adrian," she said, a delicious huskiness to her voice. The sound of his name on her lips was as great an arousal as touching her soft skin or breathing in the delicious scent of her hair. In an instant he was fully erect, his heart racing.

He strode to her and pulled her against him. Raising one hand to her cheek, he tilted her face up towards his. He drank in the beauty of her blue eyes, dark lashes, and straight nose. Her cheeks were flushed and her lips parted, waiting for his kiss. He reveled in the heat of her body against his, the feel of her luscious curves that he ached to touch. And now she was asking him to make love to her, to explore with abandon what he'd merely tasted before, what he'd dreamed of for weeks.

Miss Colbrook. Anna. He returned his gaze to her eyes, the most beguiling eyes he'd ever seen, eyes that looked into his with not only naked desire but, at last, complete trust. He bent his head to claim the first kiss, no longer thinking of what it was to be an earl. Only a man faced with a breathtaking woman who wanted him as intensely as he wanted her.

Anna watched Adrian wade into the field. The grass was up to his knees, a lake of slender greens and browns. He knelt and used his body to bend the blades and carve a small clearing. He offered a hand to her and she took it, their fingers entwining as he pulled her down beside him. They knelt facing each other, their legs nearly touching.

She would know, if only this once, what it was to spend a few hours in the arms of the man she loved. To not do so, she knew, she would ache with regret the rest of her life.

Slowly, he drew her against him. When their lips met, she forgot her doubts and worries. She gave herself over to desire.

The gentle, smoldering kisses they'd shared before were gone. Instead he battered her mouth, cheeks, and neck with his lips. She responded to his delicious assault with equal passion, tasting the wholeness of his mouth, kissing the roughness of his face and the corded muscles of his neck. When she pressed her lips against the hollow of his throat, pausing to feel the hammering of his pulse beneath her mouth, he groaned.

He drew back and turned her around, her legs stretching out against the soft grass as he lowered her onto the ground. She let her head fall back as he again kissed her neck, moving closer to the bodice of her gown. He began to caress her through her gown, touching her only a finger's breadth away from her breasts.

"We should not do this," he whispered against her skin. "Tell me to stop, Anna. Tell me." He was giving her one more chance to be prudent, to keep them from taking a step that would change them both forever.

"No." She took his hand and drew it upward. She gasped as his fingers curved around her breast, and his thumb brushed her nipple. With his other hand he reached behind her and loosened the drawstrings of her gown. A moment later he lifted the white muslin skirt to her hips. She raised herself and arched her back, freeing the gown so he could pull it over her head.

Locks of hair slipped from her chignon as he tugged the gown off and tossed it onto the grass. He knelt over her, pulled all the pins from her hair, and dropped them to the ground. Then he lifted her hair and slid his fingers through her tresses, slowly letting the shining locks cascade around her.

"So beautiful," he murmured. He began kissing her again and rolled her onto her side, their mouths still joined as he reached behind her. The laces of her corset whispered softly as he pulled them free. A few seconds later the corset landed with a rustle in the nearby grass. Her chemise, trapped just above her hips, tore as she tried to wriggle free of it. Grasping it together, they finally cast it aside. Her stockings and garters followed.

Anna lay completely naked, the outdoor air cool and strange on her skin where it had never been before. And a man's gaze—*his* gaze—was on parts of her no male had seen before. She supposed she should feel shy or ashamed, but instead she stretched out fully, feeling a rush of joy.

He stared down at her, his eyes narrowed with desire.

She smiled. "You are wearing far too many clothes."

He grinned.

A moment later his boots, stockings, coat, and shirt vanished into the tall grass. As he began to unbutton his trousers, she grasped his hands.

"I want to," she said.

He lay back and she bent over him. She freed the buttons, and then tugged the damp trousers down his strong legs. Finally, he was as naked as she was.

For a moment she simply stared. He was so handsome, with rumpled sandy hair and a wide smile and a muscular body that she longed to touch more, and to see if he felt as good everywhere as she'd long imagined.

He did.

"It's like soft wool." Smiling, she gently pressed her hands against his chest, caressing the dark hair. She drew her fingertips along his tight muscles, across his wide shoulders, following the taut curves of his arm, the slight roughness of his elbow, to his broad, strong hand. She caressed his fingers, which seemed to make him breathe especially fast.

She followed the same path back, stroking up his arm and returning to his chest. Her nails brushed the smooth skin of his nipple and his abdomen tightened, drawing her gaze to the thin trail of hair that led down to where his erection jutted up against him.

She had felt that part of him before, straining against his breeches, pressing into her, but she'd never set eyes on his or any other man's until now. Did they all grow so huge when men were aroused?

He raised himself onto his elbows and watched her study him. She traced gentle circles on his stomach, her hands not quite touching that fascinating, most mysterious part of him.

How would he react were she to merely brush against it...

He breathed in sharply, his stomach tightening beneath her fingers.

Or touch lightly along its length...

He groaned.

Or slide her fingers around its width and grasp it, gently,

in her hand...

He growled and drew her hand away.

"Not yet," he said. "Or it will all be over too soon." He dragged her into his arms and rolled her onto her back.

He lowered himself over her, cupped a breast in one hand, and drew her nipple into his mouth. She gasped as warmth flooded her body, building to an agonizing pressure as he suckled and caressed her. Just when she was certain she couldn't bear any more, his hand left her breast and glided across her stomach, moving lower. She reached out, staying his hand. His whole body tensed, as if he feared she'd changed her mind.

Quickly she reassured him that wasn't the case, as her hands explored every part of him once more. She said with her fingers and mouth and body what she was afraid to speak—that she adored him, that she thought him the most wonderful man in the world, that she felt more passion for him than she'd ever thought possible.

That she loved him.

She knew, although he didn't love her, that he felt a passion for her more powerful than any ordinary lust. Skilled as he was at lovemaking, he still trembled and gasped from her inexperienced caresses, his response making it clear he was close to losing what little control he had left.

Finally, she allowed him to touch her again, to slide his hand across her stomach and between her thighs. His strong fingers brushed against her most sensitive flesh, caressing her with his fingertips, building the sweet pressure even higher.

She arched against him and he groaned.

"Adrian," she gasped. "Please."

His hands left her and he shifted until his erection pressed against her instead. She understood that he was only inches from taking her, from changing everything. But all she wanted was to feel him inside her.

"Anna," he whispered, "tell me now if you wish me to

stop. I can still—"

"No." She spread her legs wider and raised her hips, offering him all of her. He answered by pushing inside her. She gasped from the strangeness of it, and the wonder that he could fit.

For a moment he didn't move. His breath was ragged as he held himself over her.

"Am I hurting you?" he whispered.

"No. Please, do not stop." She reached up, pulled his head towards her, and kissed him.

He slowly began to move, lifting one hand to her hip and guiding her to his rhythm. Soon she matched his movements, her heart racing madly again, her breath shallow and fast.

The ecstasy he'd created with the gentleness of his fingers he now made her feel with each thrust of his body. She clutched him tighter, pressing her fingertips into the muscles of his back, savoring the delicious weight of him against her, and the fullness of him as he moved within her.

She breathed in the sweetness of the grass and flowers around them and the musk scent of him as their rhythm quickened and her heart raced ever faster. Each time they drove against each other, even more pleasure wracked her body, bringing her closer and closer to release.

He whispered her name and thrust hard, this time not retreating but holding her tightly against him. As she heard him moan and felt him shudder, the sound and feel of his pleasure and the wonderful pressure of him against her sent waves of ecstasy through her.

Soon after, as their breathing began to slow, she fell back against the earth and let her hands drop from him. After a moment she opened her eyes to see him still leaning above her. Sweat glistened on his brow and neck. His lips were parted as he caught his breath, his handsome mouth curled into a smile.

He kissed her tenderly, lingeringly. Then very gently, he

pulled out of her and lay beside her. He slipped his arm around her and cradled her against his chest. With the other hand, he stroked her hair.

"We shall marry as soon as I can arrange a license," he said. He pressed his mouth against the top of her head. "We shall tell no one beforehand, so no one can dispute it." He meant his aunt, of course. And there would almost certainly be others who would try and dissuade him from a match to a woman so beneath him in birth, circumstance, and connections. No matter what, the world would never judge her good enough for him.

But she refused to think about that now. She closed her eyes and savored the warmth of him, the softness of his chest hair beneath her cheek, and the gradually slowing rhythm of his heart that echoed her own.

He likely took her silence as assent, never considering that she would refuse him. To him there was no alternative. He was now bound by honor to marry her. She felt a twinge of guilt at deceiving him. By refusing him, she would be denying him the only noble course of action. Yet she tried to tell herself that if no one knew what had happened, it wasn't wrong.

Doubt gnawed at her, but she pushed it away. She couldn't marry him, not for duty or honor or even for such intense passion as they'd just shared. None of those were enough to claim his fidelity. Her unsuitability as a wife would likely hasten his resentment, but even if he didn't completely regret the match, he would probably give his heart to another woman someday and when he did, she knew she wouldn't be able to bear the pain.

She wouldn't end up as her mother had, wedded to a man she loved hopelessly, unrequited, while he shared his soul with a beloved mistress. She wouldn't make herself or her children so miserable.

Children.

It was unlikely she would conceive this once, but if she

did... If she did she could live like Julia, supported and protected, hidden from respectable society. She wouldn't be able to see her friends freely. She might not even be able to see Madeline as she pleased. But she knew the risks when she gave into her passion, and hopefully, it wouldn't come to such dire straits. Yet if it did, she was prepared to endure the consequences. But was it fair to allow a child to bear the shame for her selfishness? She had been selfish, yet she couldn't summon any real remorse for what she'd done.

"What are you thinking?" His soft voice startled her. "You look so serious. Do you regret what we have done?" He cupped her cheek with one hand and turned her head gently to look in his eyes. How she loved his eyes, the always-changing green color, the gold speckles in the irises, the thick, dark lashes. What would it be like to have those eyes look at her with love?

"No." She covered his hand with her own, feeling the roughness and strength of his fingers and wishing she could know their touch for years to come, until they were both white-haired and stooped. Until they were too old for a tumble in a field but would look back upon their lives with contentment, their hearts still full of love for one another.

A lovely, foolish dream.

She closed her eyes and snuggled closer against him. His pulse had returned to a steady, slow beat beneath her ear. His skin was cool against hers.

She wouldn't think of the future but only of this afternoon, until the shadows grew long across the lake and the darkness forced them back to the manor and back to reality.

Adrian held her. She smelled of lovemaking and grass and earth and the ever-present scent of roses that was uniquely her. He couldn't stop gazing at her. Her face was so beautiful, every part of it. Her dark lashes resting against her cheeks and now hiding her marvelous sea-blue eyes. Her soft, sweet mouth. The delicate skin of her cheeks, which had grown delightfully flushed with pleasure from his touch but now retained only a pale pink tinge in the afterglow of passion. Her body was equally beautiful, supple and curvy and velvety soft in all the right places.

He'd been with enough women—not half so many as the past rumors about him suggested—but still, he was experienced enough to know what just happened was extraordinary, and had little to do with the fact he'd been abstinent for so long.

He traced a finger down the valley of her spine and up again, his other hand still caressing her hair. The prim, frowning Miss Colbrook was banished forever from his mind. Never again would he see her as anything but what she truly was—a woman who awed him with her passion, her resilience, and her intelligence, a woman who made him feel joy he'd never thought possible.

For years to come, he wanted to find her reading in the window seat, hear the whisper of her shoes across the plush carpets, see her gaze at him challengingly across the broad dining room table, her eyes sparkling. He wanted her in his bed every night, as warm and sweet and eager as she'd been this afternoon.

How amazing she'd looked when she'd first reclined across the ground, naked and stretching out her long, ivory limbs, smiling up at him—a scene more breathtaking than any he'd imagined. Heat rushed through him at the memory.

Already he wanted her again.

And why not, since she would soon be his wife? What was a second dishonor when the first was so irrevocable? Yet as fevered with passion as she'd been only moments before, she now seemed almost sad. Despite her saying she had no regrets, he feared the shock of what they'd done was affecting her. Now wasn't the time to take her again. Instead, he held her, touching her hair with an almost reverent lightness.

He did not deserve her. He wasn't entitled to such happiness, not after the life he'd led, not after all the time he wasted in selfish pursuits, the mistakes he'd made, the pain he'd brought to his family.

He did not deserve her, but he wouldn't let her go. He'd decided as much when he took her innocence. He must marry her now, for no argument of birth or fortune could supersede a matter of honor. It was doubly so, for she was a member of his household, living under his protection, and he'd committed the most grievous trespass against her. The only answer was to give her the honor of his name.

Gently, he smoothed an auburn lock between his fingers. Her eyes remained closed, but she smiled, looking at peace for the moment.

He imagined holding her like this in the future, her beautiful body grown even more curvaceous, her belly hot beneath his hand, round with his child. His heir.

His throat and chest tightened as the realization hit him.

For the first time in his life, after over thirty miserable, selfish years, he was finally in love.

CHAPTER TWENTY

M R. SINCLAIR RETURNED TO WARETON that evening. Anna found him in the garden after dinner, sprawled on a bench not far from the manor, a drink in one hand. When he caught sight of her, he staggered to his feet, clutching a nearby tree for support.

"Miss Colbrook," he said, "you are one of the few people here I am actually glad to see."

She sighed. "Mr. Sinclair."

"Have a drink with me." He swung his cup towards her. It was polished silver, the initials AWS carved elaborately into the side.

Adrian's baby cup.

She took it and promptly tipped it over, watching the amber liquid splatter onto the ground.

"Ah, now why'd you do that?" he slurred, frowning. Then he shrugged. "Adrian's worse than you, anyway. He's ordered Smith to keep the best stuff away from me." He lowered his voice to a whisper. "I took some anyway."

"I wish you were not so foxed." She handed the cup back to him. "I need to speak with you about something very important."

He grinned. "Best that I am foxed, then." He spun around and flung the cup into the hedgerow behind him. Waving his arm toward the bench, he turned back to face her. "Will you sit?"

"No. Thank you."

"Well, I shall." He fell onto the bench and leaned his elbows on his knees, swaying slightly. He grinned foolishly as he looked up at her. "You really are quite lovely. Not my sort, mind you, but I can see why Adrian is so besotted. He could barely keep his eyes off you to cut his steak at dinner. Thought he might accidentally stab himself."

Adrian besotted? Over her? She wished it were true.

"And you have a glow about you this evening, I cannot say I've ever seen you look quite so radiant."

Dear heavens, did it show on her face, what they'd done?

"Mr. Sinclair," she said quickly, "do you ever remember conversations later when you are drunk?"

He sighed. "Unfortunately, yes."

"Good, then please listen to me." She moved closer, until she stood almost over him. "You must promise me that you will not confront Sir Neville."

He stared up at her, smiled sadly, and shook his head. "I'm sorry, truly, but I cannot. One of these days I shall summon the courage and do what I should have long ago."

"Please, I understand that you wish to do the honorable thing, to take responsibility for your mistake, but there must be another way for you to make amends without risking your life."

"Ah, Miss Colbrook," he said, "you make me sound so... noble, so heroic, wishing to finally make amends for my wrongdoing. Hearing you speak with such earnestness, I wish I were the man you describe, I truly do."

"But you are."

"No, I am not. I am spiteful and malicious and want vengeance on Adrian for the way he's treated me. If I have to die to punish him, then so be it."

"I do not believe you. If you truly wanted to die, you would not practice shooting."

"Only to prove Adrian mistaken on that count as well," he said.

"What do you mean?" She remembered something that had pricked subtly at the back of her mind for the past few days. The night when Mr. Sinclair had confessed Adrian wasn't the man responsible for Julia's ruin, he had admitted doing wrong in the past. But he'd also said something she'd wondered about, that Adrian now assumed the worst, no matter what the truth of the matter might be...

Good heavens, could it be?

"Mr. Sinclair, did you compromise Miss Howe?"

He looked startled, almost sober for a moment.

"Why, Miss Colbrook," he said, "you shock me."

"Answer me, please."

"Why should you doubt it?" His eyes narrowed. "A rakehell like myself? It must be true."

His expression was little proof of anything, as his face was so tight with anger and resentment towards his brother. But what if he wasn't guilty, after all? That would make the situation... More frightening than ever.

From what she'd observed, he and Adrian could both likely kill each other—if Sir Neville didn't kill one of them first—before the truth would come out. Mr. Sinclair would apparently rather die than try to convince Adrian of his innocence. Months of growing resentment had turned Mr. Sinclair's fury into something exceedingly dangerous. And Adrian's stubbornness and anger at his brother were hardly less of a peril to them both.

But if Mr. Sinclair wasn't to blame, why would Julia accuse him? Unless the villain had refused to care for her? Or perhaps the man had been poor, and Julia believed she'd be better off under the protection of a wealthier gentleman?

Anna imagined what Adrian's reaction would be to the idea. She shouldn't make such an accusation based only on a suspicion. But someone had to do something before disaster struck.

"I shall help you both," she muttered, looking down at Mr. Sinclair, "whether you wish it or not."

"Help us? Whether we wish it or not?" He belched softly. "Sounds like a very bad idea."

Anna had lain awake half the night, dreading what she must do.

She had to tell Adrian that she wouldn't marry him.

His sense of honor would likely make him argue, but in the end, she believed he would be relieved. After a night to consider what had happened, his passion cooled, he'd likely realized what a mistake it would be to marry her. Her reason told her that it would be for the best and that he would agree. At the same time, she hoped desperately that she was wrong.

The foolish part of her imagined that when he first caught sight of her today, he would smile, draw her into his arms, and act like a man very much in love. She fantasized that having been intimate would cause him to fall madly in love with her, change the rules of society, and bring instant peace to his troubled heart.

Not surprisingly, in the morning reality was quite different.

As she stepped into the study, he didn't even smile, only glanced at her and continued pacing the length of the room, from fireplace to window and back again.

"Adrian," she said as she shut the door, "I must speak with you."

"I am arranging for a special license." He stared at the floor as he paced. He sounded as excited about getting married as facing a firing squad. Her heart sank even further. At least it would make what she was about to do easier.

"We can be married as soon as Tuesday," he continued. "I realize you may wish to bring Madeline, but it would be better to tell no one ahead of time." No one meaning Lady Carlton, and anyone else who would try and dissuade him. He knew marrying her would have many serious and unpleasant consequences. Yet he would go through with it if she allowed him. Out of duty and honor, not out of love.

"No," she said.

He stopped pacing. "Not Tuesday? Then what day would suit you?"

Surely she was mad. Here was this wonderful man who, for all his troubles, was heroic, caring, titled, and wealthy, offering her far beyond what anyone could expect, and she was about to refuse it. Then she thought again of her mother and of the resentment Adrian would no doubt feel for her eventually and the misery their marriage would almost certainly become because he didn't love her.

"I will not marry you," she said.

"What?" The expression on his face made it clear he thought her mad as well.

"I am sorry," she said. "I am aware of the great honor of your proposal, but I must decline."

"You...must...*decline*?" He shook his head, obviously flabbergasted. "You cannot decline. There is no other honorable course after what has happened."

She shook her head. "I shall not marry you."

His eyes narrowed. "Why the hell not?"

She couldn't tell him the truth. If he knew why she refused, he would surely deny he would ever resent her, and he might even lie and say he loved her—whatever it took to do what he believed was right. So she must lie. A small wrong, but it would prevent a far larger mistake.

"I shall not forfeit my inheritance," she said.

"Your inheritance?" He looked thoroughly confused. "I do not understand."

"My inheritance has been settled that if I marry before Madeline I lose everything." A piece of the truth he'd long suspected. She hoped by giving it to him now, it would distract him from digging deeper.

"What?" His eyes widened, then narrowed again. "Let me guess who designed those terms."

"Yes. The old earl."

"Then I can change it."

"No, he made certain no one could. I have already considered every legal alternative."

"It was never your wish to stay with Madeline?" he said. She nodded.

"And you have never told her the truth?"

"Why would I?" she said. "Why burden her with such a thing? He was cruel to do what he did, and Madeline—you know her—she would almost certainly blame herself. Eventually I will tell her, but not yet. I have told no one until now."

"Why did you not tell me before? Surely you know I wouldn't tell Madeline?" He shook his head. "And I still do not understand why it is so important. You would live in continued dishonor for such a modest inheritance?"

"I have waited years for it," she said, praying she was convincing. "I shall not give it up now."

He curled his hands into fists. "Yesterday," he said, his voice cracking, "you agreed we should marry—"

"I never agreed. I said nothing, and you assumed I would marry you."

"Bloody right I did!" He strode closer and stopped before her. "How can you refuse? You are compromised. You cannot marry another. You could be..." He glanced at her stomach.

"That is unlikely," she said hastily.

"You would dishonor your family?" His voice rose. "Even Madeline?"

"There is no dishonor for others if no one knows what happened."

"We know," he growled. He grasped her shoulders, and his touch immediately brought intimate memories rushing back. She longed to fling her arms around him and have him hold her, not argue, not refuse him.

"No." She stepped back, letting his hands fall from her. She forced her gaze to the desk behind him.

"I offer you everything," he said, "rank, wealth, the home you have loved for years, and a marriage far beyond what you could have ever reasonably expected. I offer to elevate you at the expense of gaining far better connections for me and my family, and you *refuse*?"

"Yes." True as his words were, hearing him say how beneath him in position she was made her answer easier. He was obviously filled with anxiety over the idea of marrying her, and his words proved that eventually he would almost certainly resent her. She was doing the right thing by refusing him.

"I do not believe you," he said. "There is some other reason, something you will not tell me."

"I have told you why. My inheritance. And, as you said yourself, such a marriage would also cost you the chance to gain far better connections. It might even harm Madeline's and Cecelia's chances for excellent matches."

"That does not matter now." He frowned. "Honor forces us—"

"I simply cannot accept."

He glared at her in silence for a moment. "This is your final word?" His voice was ragged.

"Yes."

He turned and strode to the fireplace. He leaned one arm above the mantel, gazing down at the coals. She took a few steps towards him.

"Adrian." He flinched at her saying his name. "There is something else I must speak to you about."

"What?" He didn't turn around.

"It's about your brother."

His shoulders tensed. "What has he done now?"

"It's about him and Julia Howe."

He spun around, his eyes wide. "Has he said he will confront Sir Neville?"

"No, it is not that. Although I fear he will summon the courage to do so soon. It is something else..."

"What do you mean?"

"I think it's possible that he didn't ruin her."

He stared at her blankly for a moment, then scowled.

"What nonsense is this?" he said, rubbing his head. "Of course, it was him. You said yourself that he wanted to confront Sir Neville. If he was innocent, why on earth would he do such a thing?"

"I am not certain... To prove to you that he's a man? To prove it to everyone? Perhaps also to get back at you for not believing him?"

"He has acknowledged his guilt for months now!"

"Has he?" She tried to keep her voice soft. "Or has he simply given up arguing with you?"

"This is ridiculous," he said, his eyes narrowing. She could see the fury building in him. "Miss Howe said it was him. Why would she lie?"

"I am not sure. Perhaps the man who ruined her had already rejected her, and she was desperate and knew with your brother's reputation that she would be believed and cared for?"

"Absurd. Edmund is toying with you."

"He is not. He still claims he is guilty—"

He flung up his arms. "There. Even he admits it!"

"But I find him less and less convincing. Please, just consider that he might not have done it, that you might be wrong."

"You are telling me that Edmund's been innocent all this time? That I have—" He stopped abruptly.

She knew what he'd been about to say; the anguish of it was written in his face, in the thin line of his mouth and his clenched jaw. The possibility that he'd been punishing his brother for a crime he didn't commit was too much for him to accept. Knowing the level of rage the brothers felt towards each other and the history between them, she'd feared as much.

"Enough," he said. "This is ridiculous. I am sending

Edmund away as soon as he returns from wherever he's disappeared to. And you will stay out of it."

Mr. Sinclair was likely off practicing again, preparing for his duel.

"No," she said, "if you try and send him away, you will likely only force the issue. He will confront Sir Neville for certain, and Sir Neville might well be furious enough to—"

"If I send him away, he'll be safe." He resumed pacing.

"No, you mustn't do that." Suddenly, she grew more angry than fearful. Adrian's stubbornness might very well cost his brother his life. But she knew from the way Adrian's eyes flashed that he wouldn't listen to her right now.

"I am trying to save his life," she said. "If you do not listen to me, if you do not do something, he will become violent, I am certain."

"No." He took a step towards her. "You will stop defending Edmund with these wild ideas. And if you will not be my wife, you will stay the hell out of it."

He spun away, marched to the window and looked out at the gardens, his back to her.

In the silence, she thought she glimpsed movement in the garden, a flash of pale green through a gap in the hedges, but it was gone before she could be certain.

She noticed only now a window was ajar. She hoped to heavens that no one had overheard them arguing. Should the servants gossip about any of this, it could only make everything worse. She must act quickly.

Adrian turned until he stood in profile, but he still wouldn't look at her.

"Get out," he said.

"Please," she said, her voice cracking, "I only wish to help."

"Get the hell out of my house."

She paused, nodded, and turned away.

She knew what she had to do, and since she had no

choice, she would do it without his assistance. Besides, there was someone else who could help her.

CHAPTER TWENTY-ONE

A DRIAN STARED AT THE STUDY door, listening to Anna's fading footsteps.

She'd refused him. Refused him.

It was beyond comprehension.

He thought the same thing all day as he rode about the estate. He thought about it as he swam half a dozen times across the lake and then spent over two hours shooting into the air without hitting one bird. He was thinking of her rejection when, returning from shooting, he marched over a hill and the field they'd made love in came into view. Even at this distance he could see the hollow they'd carved out with their bodies, a tiny clearing in the tall grass.

He changed direction to avoid the field and took a longer way back to the manor.

Once inside, he kept to the study, thankful the ladies were busy with some outing. Edmund was still missing as well, which was just fine with Adrian. He wanted to be alone. Even the servants kept away from him, only Smith having the courage to occasionally venture near.

Adrian searched for the documents regarding Anna's inheritance, digging through every drawer and shelf in the study and library, but in vain. Finally, he sent a message to the old earl's solicitor, Mr. Roland, asking for both Anna's and Madeline's documents. At first Mr. Roland was apparently reluctant to divulge Anna's personal papers since Adrian wasn't her guardian. But in the end, he was more frightened of displeasing the Earl of Wareton and had sent a reply that he would deliver the documents as soon as possible.

Adrian kept to his room that evening and managed to avoid everyone, even his aunt, all night and the next morning as well. He skipped breakfast and called for archery equipment to be brought to a small clearing north of the gardens.

He glanced back toward the manor between shots, wondering if Anna would appear. Now that his anger had cooled somewhat, he wanted to talk to her again. But at the same time, he was still angry with himself for wanting to speak with her at all. The devilish woman had wrapped him around her finger, seduced him, and then unaccountably rejected him.

Given their different positions, it was unfathomable that she should refuse him under nearly any circumstances, but especially after having been so completely compromised. She'd said that she expected nothing of him when she'd seduced him, but was it possible she simply didn't want anything else from him? Had she merely used him for her own gratification?

He drew back on the bow and released it violently, watching the arrow sail wide of the target, just as most of his shots had all morning.

She claimed she didn't wish to give up her inheritance. When had a mere four thousand pounds ever been so valuable to someone? There was something she wasn't telling him. He'd seen it in her eyes when she rejected him.

It wasn't the money alone, certainly. Not merely wishing to wait for Madeline, either; that was too unreasonable, especially since Anna could marry him and remain in the same home as her stepsister. Could it be simply that her feelings forbade it? That she found him too disagreeable to marry?

He scowled. Impossible.

Obviously, she was insane. Or perhaps she merely took perverse pleasure in tormenting him. Was it all some game to her, to refuse his hand and then confound him further by suggesting he'd been wrong to blame Edmund all these months?

He released another shot that also missed. And another. His mind spun. She couldn't possibly be right, could she? Edmund had denied ruining Miss Howe in the beginning, of course, just as he'd denied compromising Miss Carpenter. Yet Edmund had admitted his guilt with Miss Carpenter eventually, while with Miss Howe he'd been stubbornly unrepentant, more angry than sorry.

Adrian heard someone approaching along the garden path, likely a woman from the light sound of the footfalls. Maybe Anna was coming to apologize at last, to admit she'd been foolish to reject him.

But it was only Anna's maid, Sophie.

Sophie bobbed a curtsy. "Lord Wareton." Perhaps the maid was there with a message from Anna, a test to see if he was still furious with her.

"Has my brother returned yet, Sophie?"

"No, my lord. I wished to speak with you about Miss Colbrook."

"What is it?" He let lose another arrow. It glanced off the edge of the target and fell into the grass.

"She wasn't in her room this morning before breakfast," Sophie said. "At first, I thought perhaps she went out riding early, so I didn't think much of it. But then the grooms said she didn't visit the stables this morning. The other ladies are all gone now, so I can't ask them if they know where she went."

"Miss Colbrook is likely just avoiding me. I shouldn't worry. She'll appear eventually."

"Pardon me, my lord, but I'm not so sure."

He lowered the bow and turned to look at the maid.

"I asked just now if any servants saw her leave," she continued, fidgeting with her apron. "One footman said he saw a carriage pull up before dawn and stay only a moment before driving away. He thinks Miss Colbrook left in it." Adrian's stomach tightened. The arrow fell from his hands. "My lord, I think she might have eloped with Sir Neville."

Adrian marched into the study to find a thick folder on the center of his desk. He realized only then that he still carried the bow. He tossed it onto a chair.

Smith peered into the room. "The papers you requested from the solicitor just arrived, my lord." After confirming that Adrian needed nothing else, the butler retrieved the bow and hurried away, shutting the door behind him.

Adrian tore open the folder and slid the documents onto the desk. He fell into his chair. Finally, he would read the details of Anna's inheritance. Perhaps he would find some clue to her odd behavior. He pushed aside his guilt for prying into her personal affairs. He wasn't her guardian or executor of her inheritance and had no real right to read the documents. The man who did would be Sir Neville, assuming she returned a married woman.

Anna. Married to someone else.

His hands curled into fists over the papers. Sir Neville might still marry her, even dishonored. Adrian didn't doubt she would tell Sir Neville first. She was too honest to deceive him that way.

But her excuse about the money must be a lie, because if she'd run off with Sir Neville, she would forfeit it now anyway. Unless her reason had been true until Adrian had ordered her away.

He'd treated her badly. He'd lost his temper when, misguided or not, all she'd probably wanted was to help Edmund. He'd likely pushed her right into Sir Neville's arms.

He put aside the set of documents that concerned Madeline's inheritance. He frowned. Many papers remained, far more than he expected for merely outlining

Anna's inheritance terms. He scanned the first page, his eyes stopping on the figure of four thousand pounds, listed as the money left to her by her mother, and given to Alfred Sinclair to pass on to Anna. He skimmed the details of how the terms of the inheritance couldn't be altered.

The second page was a surprise. The old earl had added to Anna's inheritance. He'd set aside an additional ten thousand pounds in an account for her, should she fulfill the terms of the contract and wait for Madeline to marry first. A generous sum, especially from a man as stingy with his money as Alfred had been.

Taken together, fourteen thousand pounds was a respectable dowry, enough to give her a good chance of marrying at any age. It was the least the old earl could do after refusing her fiancé and trapping her at Wareton.

But there were several dozen more pages. The solicitor was a meticulous note-taker, having listed every single time Anna visited him concerning the inheritance.

August 12, 1811, looked for ways to alter the terms without success. Informed Miss Colbrook it was watertight. September 29, went over possible ways out of agreement again, found nothing…

There were a few similar entries over the next few months, then something different. *February 11, 1812, Miss Colbrook inquired about investing the sum of £10,000. Found no legal barrier to such an endeavor, made arrangements to proceed with investments…*

He read on. Dozens of pages of notes followed, each transaction carefully recorded, every change in investment explained in detail. He scanned the pages. Anna had set aside the original four thousand pounds, but she'd not only invested the remainder of her pending inheritance, she'd reinvested it again and again. She must have achieved more than modest returns from the look of things. It also seemed she'd selected risky investments. He frowned. It seemed unlike her to be so reckless.

He flipped through the remaining pages, searching for

the most recent balance sheet. What kind of return had she managed on ten thousand pounds in five years? She must have at least doubled her funds from what he could see. He finally found the page. When he saw the sum, neatly recorded in the solicitor's angular hand, he nearly fell out of his chair.

It was six figures long.

CHAPTER TWENTY-TWO

A DRIAN STARED AT THE PAPER like a fool.
Anna wasn't merely rich, she was quite likely the wealthiest unmarried woman in Somerset. In her desire to protect Madeline from learning the details of her settlement, Anna had apparently kept her amazing fortune a secret as well.

No wonder she wished to wait for her stepsister to marry. Who in their right mind would give up such a fortune, especially one so cleverly earned?

Adrian frowned. Leaning over the desk, he flipped through the documents again, looking for one crucial bit of missing information. What happened to the money if Anna forfeited?

He dug through the papers again, finding the pages of the original settlement, until he located the clause:

Should Miss Anna Colbrook enter into matrimony before her stepsister, Madeline Sinclair, Miss Colbrook will forfeit, without any recourse, all funds in her account, including interest, and the sum will become sole possession of Madeline Sinclair, held in trust until the time she marries...

Madeline would get the money once wed, so essentially it would belong to her husband. A fortune Madeline hardly needed to bring to a marriage as she already had over fifty thousand pounds.

He could certainly understand now why Anna wished to wait to marry. But why hadn't she told him everything? Why hadn't she raised the possibility of them marrying later, but instead refused him outright?

He slammed the paper onto the desk. She must not wish

to marry him and for some reason had given that excuse, but why?

He tossed the paper aside, rose, and began pacing.

Did it matter? Whatever her reasons, she didn't wish to be his wife. Yet she loved him, he was almost certain.

So why had she refused him?

She'd said herself such a marriage would hurt the family, possibly damage Madeline's and Cecelia's own hopes for affluent matches. That had been true and might still be true to some degree, but her fortune would go a long way towards erasing the stigma of having a father in trade. She knew that, so that couldn't be the only reason she refused him.

He paused near the fireplace, his gaze resting on the portrait above the mantel, the one he'd once wanted removed but never did, the seascape with two smiling women strolling arm in arm on a beach. He always thought they looked like mother and daughter...

He recalled his second day at Wareton, when he'd asked Anna about her mother, and the ache in her voice when she told him her mother was miserable because she was married for her money.

Of course. It was so ridiculously simple. The same reason why she kept her fortune secret was also why she'd refused him.

She wanted to marry for love.

Yesterday he'd been too worried about what the consequences of marrying her might be to give her any sign of his affection. To let her know that despite his fears, he truly wanted her for his wife. Instead of letting her know he loved her, he'd even agreed that her birth put her beneath him and declared he was marrying her out of duty.

He was a bloody idiot.

After his behavior, he didn't blame her for apparently deciding to run off with Sir Neville, the one man she believed loved her.

And if she married Sir Neville, many problems would be avoided. He could fulfill his duty of making a prestigious match without fear of repercussions for his family. And if Sir Neville married her, their family connection meant Edmund would undoubtedly be safe from his challenge forever.

He should let her go.

And not long ago he would have. But now everything was different. He was different.

He only hoped he wasn't too late.

Adrian swung open the door and told a startled Smith to have his horse readied immediately.

"Adrian, where are you going?" Lady Carlton planted herself in the study doorway, her hands on her hips.

"All the way to Gretna Greene if I must." He grabbed his money purse from the top desk drawer and shoved it into his coat.

"Why?"

"You know why." He marched to the door. "Do not pretend you don't. Now excuse me."

She clasped her hands together and stood tall. Her broad figure blocked the entire doorway.

"I beg of you to think on what you are doing," she said. "It is an excellent match for her. If you disrupt it, Sir Neville may change his mind. Consider what is best for the family—"

"I've no time for this." He grabbed his aunt by her arms and lifted her off the floor. He carried her through the doorway and set her back onto her feet in the hallway.

"Adrian!" she sputtered, rubbing her arms. "You are quite out of your senses—"

"I said I have no time for this." He strode toward the foyer.

"Adrian." He could hear her heels clicking rapidly on the floor as she ran after him. "Adrian, stop."

He spun around. Panting, she grasped his arms.

"The irony is," he said before she could catch her breath, "that if I did not go after her now, later you would be furious with me."

"What nonsense. I won't allow you to ruin the family name and destroy Cecelia's future. I'll throw myself in front of your horse if I have to!"

"Do not tempt me, Aunt."

"She's made you mad! Can you not see?"

"You want me to go after her, you just don't know it yet."

"She's bewitched you." She shook her head and grasped his coat sleeves more tightly. "I won't let you ruin us all—"

"My dear aunt," he said, forcing himself to speak calmly, "Miss Colbrook is secretly the wealthiest heiress in Somerset."

Lady Carlton stilled. She held her breath, staring at him in disbelief.

"She is worth over one hundred thousand pounds. Now unhand me, or I swear I'll toss you in the pond on my way out."

"Over one hundred thousand?" she whispered, releasing his sleeves. "Miss Colbrook?"

"Yes."

Lady Carlton turned a deep red shade, something he'd never seen before, and her mouth all but disappeared in an angry pucker.

Adrian turned and strode into the foyer. Seconds later, his aunt caught up to him and rushed alongside him, waving her arms frantically as Smith swung open the front door. "Do not let Sir Neville marry her—ride your horse to death if you must, but go. Go."

Adrian rode his horse as fast as he dared without risking exhausting the animal.

He had to stop them. The idea of Anna married to someone else was—unbearable.

After just over an hour's ride, Adrian almost didn't believe it when he spotted Sir Neville's carriage stopped in front of the first inn he came to in Hepton. He'd assumed that if he had any chance of catching up with them, it wouldn't be so soon. They must have taken a long break for some reason.

But now Neville's driver was climbing atop the carriage as if they were about to leave…

Adrian leapt from his horse, calling out to the driver to wait. Then he strode to the carriage. The curtains were drawn so he could not see inside the coach. He grabbed the handle and yanked the door open.

Inside, on the left, was Sir Neville. And opposite him, her eyes wide with shock, was Madeline.

CHAPTER TWENTY-THREE

A FEW SECONDS PASSED BEFORE ADRIAN could believe the sight before him. Relief at not finding Anna with Sir Neville was quickly replaced with fury at her stepsister. And at Sir Neville.

"What on earth are you doing?" Adrian said, finally finding his voice. "Madeline, get out of the carriage."

Madeline stared at him for a few seconds before she took his hand. Adrian practically dragged her out of the coach. Her fingers trembled in his grip.

Sir Neville stepped out after her and motioned for his driver to step down. The driver discreetly exited on the other side of the coach and disappeared from view.

Adrian tried to draw Madeline farther away, but she tugged her hand free and moved to Sir Neville's side.

Adrian cursed under his breath and glared at Sir Neville. "What happened?" he said quietly, looking back at Madeline. "Did he coerce you?"

"No," Madeline said. "He did not." She met Adrian's gaze. "I…deceived him."

"What?" Adrian said.

"I sent him an urgent message to meet me here," she said, "but I did not say why. And when I asked him to run away to Scotland, he said no. He convinced me not to act so imprudently." She looked up at Sir Neville, smiling foolishly. "He is too honorable." Sir Neville gazed down at her with an equally foolish grin.

"Why?" Adrian resisted the urge to tear her away from Sir Neville. He could tell that she spoke the truth; he simply didn't wish to believe it. "Why would you do such a thing?"

She turned and met his gaze. "I did it so you and Anna could marry as soon as possible."

"Madeline—"

"I heard you argue yesterday." She flushed. "I did not intend to eavesdrop, but I was in the garden and..." She curled her hands into fists. "I know I am the reason she has been unable to marry all these years, and I am the reason she will not marry you now. But you must marry, and not just because..." She blushed again. Evidently, she'd heard enough to realize that Anna had been fully compromised. "I cannot bear to keep her from happiness again."

Adrian shook his head. "She would not want you to marry for this reason."

"Why not? I am fond of Sir Neville." She glanced at him again, smiling. "And Anna made it clear that she would never have him."

Had she? Adrian pushed aside the pleasure he felt at that news. He could still barely believe what Madeline had almost done.

He would decide how to resolve this situation later. As if he didn't already have enough to contend with at the moment. Like Anna.

Would she be home when he returned? Her maid believed that Anna had left the manor early that morning. If not with Sir Neville, where had she gone?

"Madeline," Adrian said, "where is Anna?"

"She told me last night," Madeline said, looking nervous, "but made me promise not to say until she was gone."

"She has been gone for hours," Adrian said.

"Yes, well since it concerns you both..." She glanced at Sir Neville before meeting Adrian's gaze again. "I may as well tell you now. She went to see Miss Howe."

Miss Howe? Of course. To ask her about Edmund, presumably.

Sir Neville's eyes widened, but he seemed to quickly

compose himself.

"But she refused to tell me why," Madeline added. She glanced between Adrian and Sir Neville, clearly hoping one of them might provide an answer.

Adrian had no wish to discuss Miss Howe with Sir Neville, let alone speak of the matter in front of Madeline.

"We are going home this instant," Adrian said. "Come, Madeline."

Madeline nodded. She turned to Sir Neville, leaned close, and whispered something. He smiled. He lifted her hand and placed a kiss on her gloved fingers.

"Now, Madeline," Adrian growled.

Sir Neville might have behaved with honor by refusing to elope with her, but the way he looked at Madeline now suggested his affections had switched from one sister to the other rather abruptly. The day had been full of too many surprises, and it was enough to make Adrian's head spin. He would have to sort this all out later. At this moment he just wanted to take Madeline home and then find Anna.

"You should take her in my carriage," Sir Neville said, glancing toward Adrian's horse. "I will ride your mare back if you like."

Gracious, as usual.

Still, Adrian wanted to refuse. But it made sense. Arranging for a hired coach could take some time. The sooner they were back home, the better.

Their journey back to Wareton was almost entirely silent for the first hour.

Adrian studied Madeline across the carriage. He'd liked his cousin from the moment he came to Wareton, but her actions today made him see her in an entirely new light. Beneath her sweet, gentle exterior, there was a tenacity that surprised him. And what she'd been willing to do for Anna amazed him. He'd thought Madeline was the sweet, biddable one, but she was turning out to be nearly as much trouble as her stepsister.

"I am sorry for all the trouble I caused," Madeline said abruptly, as if she sensed his thoughts. "But I was only trying to make things right. So much of this is my fault."

"It is not," he said.

"It is. I know my grandfather was cruel in what he did, but... Years ago, when I learned Anna had found a gentleman who might make her happy and would take her away from me, I was frightened. I told my grandfather that I didn't want her to leave, and that is why he trapped her with me."

"You were only a child." He understood now why Anna had been so reluctant to tell Madeline the truth.

"I was twelve," she said, "old enough to not be so selfish."

"You are too hard on yourself. The old earl would have probably done the same no matter how you behaved."

"Anna has spent nearly half her life caring for me," she said, her voice cracking, "and she has already lost six years she never should have, and a man she cared about, and now she will not marry you because of it."

"That may not be why," he said softly.

Madeline shook her head. "She said because of the settlement, and now I understand why. I went to see the solicitor yesterday and persuaded him to share the details with me. I wanted to be certain before I acted.

"Of course, she would wish to wait for such a fortune," she continued. "And since that is what stands in your way, there are two alternatives." She sat up straight and folded her hands in her lap. "Either I marry right away, or else you can accept my word that once I am married I will return the money to her. To you both."

Adrian smiled. "You cannot make such a promise, Madeline. Your husband might not agree to it."

"I shall not marry anyone who won't," she said, lifting her head higher. "I'll not take Anna's money in addition to everything else I've taken from her."

"It is not your fault," he said. "None of it. And no matter what you heard her say, her refusal is not really about the money."

Madeline frowned, her green eyes wide. "But then why?"

"Because she wants to marry for love."

"Then that must mean..." She leaned forward. "But you must marry her now, even if she doesn't w—" She flushed and glanced down at her hands. *Even if she doesn't want to marry you,* she'd likely been about to say.

Adrian's gut tightened. He'd been trying not to think about the possibility that no matter what, Anna might simply not want to be his wife.

CHAPTER TWENTY-FOUR

ANNA STARED OUT AT THE countryside, her gaze following the stone wall that edged the road. Her stomach churned with each bump and rattle of the carriage.

She'd barely eaten anything yesterday and nothing this morning. The hackney she'd paid a neighbor to quietly arrange for had been waiting at the end of the main road to the manor at dawn, just as she'd asked. The driver had hesitated when he realized she was traveling alone, but when she promised him extra payment, he'd snapped his mouth shut and helped her into the closed carriage.

Hopefully Madeline had kept her word not to tell anyone where she was headed until she was well on her way. She had no doubt that Adrian would be furious if he knew. But she must learn the truth from Julia Howe. If she could prove that Mr. Sinclair was innocent, the brothers could reconcile. Perhaps then Adrian might also begin to forgive himself for his past.

Her heart ached every time she thought of how they'd argued yesterday. When she'd refused him, he'd seemed so upset that she'd almost believed she'd hurt more than his ego and sense of honor by refusing him, that she'd actually affected his heart.

Foolish, wishful thinking. His anxiety over the match, and his wanting to marry without even telling the family, proved his true feelings. He wanted to marry her out of duty, not love.

The carriage slowed when they reached the village of Easton, where Adrian had said Julia resided. The driver soon learned from a helpful shopkeeper that Mrs. Jameson lived a short ride from the center of town.

The closer Anna drew to Julia's, the better she felt. Julia might be lonely, isolated from her old friends and living under a false name. She might be pleased to see Anna and relieved to speak the truth to someone. Perhaps Julia would even confirm Mr. Sinclair's innocence.

One question gnawed at Anna. But if Mr. Sinclair wasn't guilty, why had Julia accused him? Perhaps because of his reputation, knowing she'd be believed, and he would likely be forced to care for her? Still, it seemed an odd coincidence that of all the gentlemen in London, Julia blamed a man connected to her neighbor's family. Then again, life was full of such strange happenings.

At the end of a road bordered by pastures, the carriage turned down a long drive. Anna peered out the window, startled by the size of Julia's home. It was larger than she'd expected, looking more like a home an earl would provide for a favored mistress than for an illegitimate niece.

The carriage came to a stop before a wide stairway that led up to the front doors. She paid the driver and made her way up the stairs. Once inside, she gave her name to a maid, who quickly returned to say Mrs. Jameson was not well enough to accept callers.

Anna didn't believe it for an instant.

"Tell Mrs. Jameson that I will not leave until I have spoken with her."

A few minutes later she was escorted not to a sitting room, but to a small flower garden behind the house. She did not have to wait long for Julia to appear. Julia stepped out through a doorway and stopped several paces away. Her arms were crossed at her chest, wrapped in a dark green shawl that perfectly matched her fashionable muslin gown.

"You should not have come, Miss Colbrook." She looked plumper than when Anna had last seen her over a year ago, and her chestnut hair was more elegantly styled.

Anna took a step towards her then paused. "Did you receive my letter?"

Julia nodded, her face grave.

"Why did you not reply?"

Julia opened her mouth to answer and then hesitated. Finally, she said quietly, "I had nothing to say to you. Nothing I should say at any rate." She glanced towards the house. "I must ask you to leave."

"No," Anna said. "Not until we have spoken about Edmund Sinclair."

Julia's eyes widened, and then narrowed. She stared at Anna for a moment as if deciding whether she meant it.

"Not here," Julia finally said, glancing at the open windows. "Will you walk with me?"

Anna nodded.

Without another word, Julia led her along a path through the garden and down a gentle hillside towards the woods below.

They walked briskly in silence for several minutes. As the trail entered the woods, the air turned damp. Ash and elm trees gave way to birch and aspen, with thick ferns concealing their bases.

Julia slowed her pace to a stroll. "No one will hear us out here. What is it you wished to speak to me about?"

"Tell me what happened in London last year."

"Why should I?" Julia said, walking faster again. "What business is it of yours?"

"What happened to you is disrupting my life," Anna said, "and the lives of my family. Your child isn't Mr. Sinclair's, is she?"

Julia abruptly stopped walking.

"Why did you lie?" Anna said.

For a few seconds Julia looked like a startled animal ready to flee. Then her shoulders slumped, and she drew her shawl across her chest. With a mix of anxiety and excitement on her face, Julia glanced from the ground to Anna and back to the ground again.

She wanted to tell the truth.

Likely she'd never been able to speak it to anyone. Anna knew all too well what a terrible burden a secret could be. And Julia had more than just a secret. Her whole identity, her entire past, was all a concealment. When was the last time she'd even been called by her real name?

Julia looked at Anna and shook her head. "You of all people," she said softly.

Anna frowned. What did that mean?

"Why did you lie?" Anna repeated.

"Why?" Julia's eyes narrowed. Her gaze drifted from Anna to somewhere behind her. "I was angry and upset, and I wanted to punish the scoundrel for what he did to me. And, well, I wasn't thinking clearly." Anger flashed in her eyes. "Although if I'd been cleverer about it, it could have worked."

"But why name Mr. Sinclair?"

Julia straightened and met Anna's gaze again. "I chose Mr. Sinclair because he is your cousin." Her voice was ragged, her eyes shining. "I wanted to create a scandal between Sir Neville and your family. I wanted him to have to challenge Mr. Sinclair to save face. So Sir Neville would never get what he wanted, the reason he abandoned me. You."

CHAPTER TWENTY-FIVE

SHORTLY AFTER THEY RETURNED HOME, Adrian went in search of Edmund. As he neared the drawing room, he heard words that stopped him cold. He froze, standing just before the doorway, unable to see in.

"I cannot believe you nearly married Sir Neville. True, he is a respectable gentleman and his heroics have raised him above his birth, but he's still beneath you, Madeline. You are granddaughter and cousin to an earl, you can marry far better."

The words were verbatim to ones he'd heard Lady Carlton speak a dozen times, but the voice wasn't. It was higher pitched, softer.

It was Cecelia's voice.

Adrian leaned one arm against the wall. He felt ill.

"If I shall marry a duke," Cecelia continued, "you can at the least snare a viscount or an earl."

Madeline sighed. "If I should be fortunate enough to form an attachment to a viscount or—"

"Form an attachment?" Cecelia laughed softly, but the hint of a scoff had crept into her voice. "That is unimportant. Indeed, it is probably unwise."

"I disagree," Madeline said. "In fact, I worry for you, Cecelia. Do you care for the duke?"

"A foolish question," Cecelia said quickly. But her tone had cracked, the haughty imitation of Lady Carlton fading. At least Adrian desperately hoped it was still only an imitation.

He envisioned Cecelia years from now if she married the Duke of Dulverton. He'd only focused on the status of

such a match before and never fully considered the woman
she might become as Duchess of Dulverton. The image
his mind presented was sad and frightening, even more
disturbing than what he heard now.

Then he thought of her if she married a man she cared
for instead, imagined the sweet girl she still was in many
ways and the happy woman she could become if she
married for love.

Married for love.

Once again, Anna was right. About Cecelia, and maybe
about Edmund as well.

The duty that drove him, the way he tried to do what
was best for his family was suddenly, horribly, all wrong.

"Besides, it is my duty." Cecelia's voice was her own now,
but heavy, sad. Adrian's chest felt tight. "And it will please
everyone," she added.

"Everyone?" Madeline asked gently.

There was a long pause. God love his cousin. She was a
caring, sweet girl, and if her influence could help Cecelia—

"It will please me," Cecelia said quickly. "To be a duchess.
What could be better?" The words echoed what he'd said
to Cecelia several times.

Damn it, he was no better than Lady Carlton.

"I only meant—"

"You are jealous," Cecelia said, "because the duke prefers
me!"

"That is not true," Madeline said.

"My aunt says that—"

Adrian had heard enough. He pushed away from the wall.
As he strode into the room, Cecelia and Madeline looked
up from the sofa, startled. Madeline appeared weary, but
Cecelia's face brightened.

"Adrian, there you are!" Cecelia said, suddenly looking
happy. Happier than she ever did in the duke's company,
he realized.

"Cecelia," he said, forcing himself to speak calmly.

"What is it?" Cecelia asked, her smile fading. "You look pale."

"Will you do me a favor?" he said gently.

"Of course." She leaned towards him. "Anything, Adrian. What is it?"

"Should the duke make you an offer, please refuse him."

She frowned. "Refuse him?"

"Yes. Refuse him. And anyone else Lady Carlton tells you to accept. Unless you also have affection for the gentleman. Strong affection."

"Strong...affection?" Cecelia stared at him, her mouth falling open. Madeline smiled, suddenly looking less tired.

"Yes," he said. "We can discuss it further later, but right now there is something I must do."

"Very well," Cecelia said softly, her eyes wide.

"Where is Edmund?" he asked.

"Outside," Cecelia said. "On the west lawn, last I saw him."

Adrian found Edmund alone beneath a huge oak tree, lounging at a table with a cloud of smoke hovering around him and a full glass of port beside him.

Edmund puffed on a cheroot as he watched Adrian approach. When Adrian stopped beside the table, Edmund exhaled, sending a perfectly round smoke ring wafting towards him.

"Enjoying my cheroots, I see." Adrian waved his hand to dissipate the smoke.

"I heard you returned with the wrong cousin," Edmund said.

"Madeline was ready to marry him." Adrian shook his head. "She's more headstrong than I'd believed."

Edmund nodded. "Just like her stepsister. Where is the lovely Miss Colbrook, by the way? It was she you went to fetch, was it not?"

"She has gone to see Miss Howe."

"Indeed? How fascinating." Edmund sounded not the least bit surprised.

"She believes you are innocent."

"I told you she was mentally unbalanced." Edmund leaned back in the chair and blew a smoke ring straight up in the air; it drifted into the branches of the oak.

"She says I have been wrong to believe you guilty all this time. Now tell me, why would Miss Howe name you if it weren't true?"

"Of course, it's true." Edmund straightened. "Why should you doubt it? Aren't I the most lecherous, misbegotten wastrel in England? The man who cannot pass a fortnight without losing a fortune at cards or ruining some young lady's reputation? Do you not always say so? And you could never be wrong—"

"Stop it, Edmund."

"Stop what?" Edmund rose, turned his back to him, and strolled closer to the tree.

Adrian followed him. "Did you ruin Miss Howe, or not?"

Edmund turned and glared at him, his fingers clenched around the smoldering cheroot.

"Did you?" Adrian repeated.

Edmund's voice and face suddenly softened. "No."

In the quiet that followed that one word, Adrian let out a long breath. His head began to ache, and his chest tightened. "But...you were still considering telling Sir Neville that you did and risk his challenge? Why?"

The fury returned to Edmund's face. Abruptly, he hurled the cigar to the ground.

"Because I'm tired," Edmund said, staring at the wisps of smoke drifting up from the cheroot, all the sarcasm drained from his voice. "Bloody tired of living like this. One way or the other I'd be free from...this damned nonsense." He stepped forward and crushed the cheroot into the ground until the smoke stopped.

"I'm sorry," Adrian said. "But you must understand why I believed you did it, after Miss Carpenter—" No, that was only an excuse. He should have listened to Edmund better from the start. He shouldn't have assumed him guilty despite his past. "No, I am simply sorry. I should have listened to you in the beginning."

"I do not bloody believe it," Edmund whispered, staring at him. "You actually are sorry." Edmund stepped back and looked at the flattened stub of cigar for a moment. Then he attacked it, swiping at it with his boot until all that remained were shreds of muddy paper and tobacco.

"Edmund." Adrian reached out to grasp Edmund's shoulder but hesitated. He let his arm drop.

Edmund cursed louder and gave the ground another powerful kick.

Adrian said, "If you want to take a swing at me for what I've done—"

"You bet I do!" Edmund spun around. "For months now, I've been planning my revenge, waiting for the right moment to tell Sir Neville it was me just to spite you, and you have to go and ruin it—"

Edmund punched him straight on the jaw. Hard.

Adrian stumbled back. Pain exploded in his face, but he forced himself to speak. "You want another?"

"Yes!" Edmund raised his fists again. "No." He frowned and lowered them. "It's Miss Colbrook." Edmund jabbed a finger at him. "She's done this to you. You've changed." Edmund sounded almost upset that Adrian finally believed him.

Adrian frowned. "Are you not glad that—"

"Yes. Well, no, I..." Edmund sighed. "All my plans are ruined. What the hell am I supposed to do now?" Edmund turned and marched away from the manor, down the slope towards the duck pond.

"Why did Miss Howe accuse you?" Adrian asked as he followed him. "Have you any idea?"

"Because she knew with my reputation that you'd believe it and take care of her?" Edmund scowled. "How the hell would I know why? I hardly knew her. Spoke to her a few times in London after we were introduced by a mutual acquaintance. Danced with her once at a ball, and that was it. Nothing about our interaction was especially memorable, frankly. I was more shocked than anyone when she accused me."

Adrian sighed. "I must speak with Sir Neville."

"Well you can't right now," Edmund said.

Adrian frowned. "Why not?"

"Because on my way back here, he nearly ran me off the road. I don't think he even recognized me. He was riding north like a madman."

A chill rushed through Adrian. "*What* did you say?"

"I said I saw Sir Neville riding north…" Edmund frowned. "Why? What is it?"

Sir Neville had understandably appeared startled when Madeline first said that Anna had gone to see Julia. But he'd seemed completely composed by the time they'd said goodbye. So why in blazes would he be racing north?

Unless he was desperate to stop Anna from speaking to Julia.

Adrian let out a long, loud string of curses.

"It's him," Adrian said. "Sir Neville's the one responsible."

"What?" Edmund frowned. "Sir Neville? No…"

Adrian's mind raced. He thought back to that day when Miss Howe had come to his townhouse. She was hysterical and had seemed to *want* Sir Neville to have to challenge Edmund. Clearly, she had also been angry that Sir Neville was sending her away, but Adrian had assumed what she wanted most was revenge on Edmund for ruining her life. But what if Edmund wasn't her real target?

"Maybe…" Adrian said. "Maybe she accused you because of who your cousins are."

Edmund frowned. "My cousins?"

"Anna," Adrian said. "Maybe Miss Howe knew that Sir Neville wanted to marry Anna, and she wanted to try to ruin it for him. To create a scandal between our families."

Adrian thought back to that night when he'd gone to see Sir Neville. Sir Neville's initial shock and anger, and his wanting nothing to do with Miss Howe, all made sense considering what Adrian thought had happened. But the man's anger might not have been for the reasons Adrian had assumed. He might have been enraged at Miss Howe for running off and accusing Edmund out of revenge.

Edmund suddenly paled. "If it was Sir Neville, then that would also mean he knew all along that neither of us touched her."

"He let us take the blame," Adrian growled.

"That evil bastard," Edmund whispered, almost sounding impressed.

"Yes," Adrian said. He knew, in his gut, it was Sir Neville.

Adrian had gone to Sir Neville's townhouse that night to save Edmund, having no idea he was giving Sir Neville the perfect cover for his own crime. And all this time while Adrian had been worried that Sir Neville would challenge Edmund, Sir Neville had played on Adrian's fear shamelessly, even telling Anna that he'd ruined Julia, betting that Adrian wouldn't dare refute it.

Could the man really be so devious, so lacking in the tiniest shred of decency?

Yes. And a man capable of that was likely capable of anything.

"When it gets out that he ruined his own ward," Edmund said, shaking his head, "the scandal will destroy his reputation, his life. He's finished."

"And he knows it," Adrian muttered.

Anna and Miss Howe might be in grave danger.

Adrian turned and ran towards the stables, with Edmund on his heels.

For the second time that day, Adrian yelled for a horse. This time, he also called for his pistols.

CHAPTER TWENTY-SIX

ANNA STARED AT JULIA, DUMBFOUNDED. "You and Sir Neville?"

Julia's eyes widened. "I thought you already knew."

"I didn't think it was Sir Neville..." Anna trailed off, feeling foolish and overwhelmed. He'd been with Julia while his wife lay dying?

"He accused me of trying to trap him into marriage," Julia said, "of trying to ruin his future." She snorted. "As if I'd held a gun to his head and forced him into a dalliance." Julia began walking again. "When he announced he was sending me away, I decided to punish him for what he'd done." Her voice cracked, and she paused to regain her composure. "I knew he wished to marry you after he was widowed. I thought if I accused Mr. Sinclair, the scandal between our families would ruin his plans."

Anna frowned. Sir Neville didn't know her well at that time, as they hadn't yet become close friends. It made no sense. Was Julia lying? She seemed sincere, but Anna wasn't certain. And she was clearly capable of deception.

"But he was still tending to Lady Mary," Anna said. "He seemed so grief-stricken—"

Julia laughed dryly. "His *grief* did not keep him from my bed. But I understand your shock. I felt the same when Lady Mary first told me about his true character." Julia's expression grew somber. "At first, I thought she was lying because she sensed my feelings for him. I didn't wish to believe what she said. I was fooled by him, just like nearly everyone else.

"He is heavily in debt, you know," Julia continued. She

kept her gaze on the winding path as she strolled, carefully navigating around the increasing number of muddy spots. "They lived far better than they could afford. Lady Mary also told me that when he rescued the carriage from the robbers, two were shot in the back. A detail left out of the 'heroic' tale."

Anna's head pounded. Could Sir Neville, the seemingly noble gentleman she thought she knew well, in truth be so dishonorable?

A terrible suspicion began to form in her mind.

"Sir Neville told you before Lady Mary died that he wished to marry me?"

"No. And he never actually told me. When he was making arrangements to send me away, I was listening at the door to his study. I overheard him tell Mr. Roland."

Mr. Roland?

Mr. Roland was one of the men Sir Neville had rescued from the robbers. He had been Lord Harwick's solicitor and was riding in his coach with him when it was attacked. But Mr. Roland was not Sir Neville's solicitor. He had been the old earl's.

And he was hers.

She stopped walking. She was such a fool.

Julia paused and looked back. "What is it?"

"I believe you," Anna said. "I know why Sir Neville wished to marry me." And why he was so patient, and why he hadn't argued with her about waiting for Madeline to wed first. What he'd told her about promising his wife to wait longer before he remarried was such a clever story, and so well acted that she hadn't doubted it for an instant. But if he'd planned to pursue her before his wife even died, before they'd ever become friends, there could be only one reason.

She swallowed against the lump in her throat. "He knows I am wealthy."

"Oh." Julia nodded, relief softening her face. "Of course.

I knew it had to be something like that…" She sighed. "I just couldn't believe he loved you."

Julia still loved Sir Neville, the poor fool.

But she was a fool too. She'd trusted her solicitor, and she'd never considered Sir Neville or anyone else might know her secret.

He'd been plotting all along to marry her for her money. Even worse, he'd ruined his own ward, tossed her aside, and let another take the blame for his debauchery.

"You must tell Lord Wareton the truth," Anna said.

Julia laughed. "Never."

"Does it not trouble you to live such a lie?"

Julia flinched. She had a conscience then, in spite of everything.

"Did you not see how generously Lord Wareton provides for us?" Julia said. "Do you think he would do all this if he knew Emily wasn't his niece?"

"Lord Wareton would continue to help you no matter what," Anna said. "He is too good a man to abandon you and the baby."

Julia shook her head. "I would be a fool to trust any man. Even him."

Anna touched Julia's arm. "Please. Come back with me and tell him the truth."

Julia pulled away. "Lord Wareton will be furious. He might very well put us out on the street. And what of Sir Neville? His reputation is everything to him. The scandal would ruin him. Once I wanted that but…" She shook her head. "Now I am wiser."

Sir Neville had hurt so many people with his lies that he deserved to be unmasked for what he was. The heroic status and honorable reputation that was so precious to him would be lost, yet he deserved no less for what he'd done.

"Come back with me now," Anna said. "Tell the truth. You will be protected."

"I cannot risk it."

"Do you not wish to punish Sir Neville for what he's done?"

Julia grimaced, looking as if she were fighting tears. "I do, but...now that you know the truth, you will never marry him. That is revenge enough."

What could she say to convince her?

"Lord Wareton and his brother are close to killing each other because of this. Meanwhile, Sir Neville lives with none of the consequences. Is this truly what you wish?"

Julia shook her head. "No." She twisted her shawl around her hands. "But I am afraid. Sir Neville can be terribly cruel if someone crosses him. And he is so clever, he always finds a way to get what he wants."

"Not this time," Anna said. "Please, come with me."

They turned to follow the path back. They'd gone only a few steps when they heard footfalls ahead on the trail, growing louder.

Julia frowned. "I told the servants not to disturb us."

Through a break in the trees they glimpsed a man. A well-dressed man walking swiftly, leaning heavily on a walking stick. His coat bulged oddly at the sides, as if—

Anna stifled a gasp and grabbed Julia's arm. Julia's arm shook beneath Anna's fingers. Julia pressed her hand to her mouth, her eyes wide, terrified.

"What do we do?" Julia whispered.

Anna whispered back, "We run."

CHAPTER TWENTY-SEVEN

JULIA AND ANNA HIKED UP their skirts and rushed deeper into the woods. The trail grew rougher as it climbed to drier, rockier ground and then descended again. The muddy path sucked at their half boots, and brush and thickets clawed at their skirts as they ran.

Though Anna could hear no sound of pursuit over their footfalls, she had no doubt if she stopped long enough to listen, she would.

The path narrowed, forcing them to slow even more, then seemed to disappear completely. They stumbled to a halt, breathless, scanning the trees and thickets all around.

"It does go on," Julia whispered, peering to the northwest. "Wait, I think I see it—"

Anna clutched her arm to silence her.

Not far behind them, a twig snapped, and something crunched against leaves.

Anna pushed Julia in the direction where she had said the path restarted. Let the noise only be a deer, she willed silently.

A shot rang out. The ball smashed into a moss-covered tree trunk only a few yards from them.

They ran. They ran as fast as they could, stumbling back onto the trail, which was now much narrower. Anna's heart pounded. Her chest ached. Tears threatened to spill from her eyes.

How could this be happening? How could Sir Neville be so different from the man she thought she knew?

Behind her, she heard Julia stumble. She stopped and spun back. Julia rose shakily, grimaced, and quickly shifted her weight to her left leg.

Anna rushed back to her.

"My ankle," Julia whispered. She took a step and gasped.

Anna slid an arm around her. "Lean on me," she whispered. They started forward again, as quickly as they could with Julia hobbling.

"It is no use," Julia whispered after a moment, panting. "He'll catch us for certain this way. You should leave me. It's my fault. I'll face him alone."

"No," Anna whispered. She couldn't abandon Julia. Any hope that Sir Neville might not wish them harm was gone.

Nothing she'd believed of him was true. She thought of the strange look that sometimes shone on his face when he spoke of killing the bandits. Suddenly, in her memory, it seemed disturbing, as if he'd enjoyed it. And now that his reputation—his entire future—was at stake, he would apparently preserve it at all costs.

She forced back tears. She had to focus on escape. She scanned to the west of the path and chose a spot where the ground was rocky for a dozen or so yards before ferns and bushes covered it again. She helped Julia across the dry ground and through the brush beyond. Anna kept glancing back to check the path. Once she was certain it was well out of view, she stopped.

"Hide here," she whispered, "I'll draw him away."

"You mustn't risk yourself." Julia was wide-eyed but she lowered herself to the ground.

"This way we both have a chance," Anna murmured. She turned and hurried back towards the path as quietly and as quickly as she could.

She paused to check that they hadn't left a conspicuous trail into the brush. Then she sped forward again, deliberately making deep impressions in the mud with her half boots. She ran noisily along the winding path for a few moments. When she spotted a rocky rise off to the west, she left the trail and forged her way up the brush-covered slope. Atop the hill, she hiked up her skirt and clambered on top of the largest boulder. She peered out from the cover of trees, back towards the path, catching her breath.

She spotted Sir Neville in the distance, his dark hat bobbing among the brush as he followed the trail. He seemed to be close to where Julia was hidden when he suddenly disappeared from view behind some trees.

Anna held her breath, waiting for him to reappear. She thought of Julia's twisted ankle, and how she'd be utterly helpless against him. She thought of Julia's baby.

She took a few deep breaths and pushed aside all her instincts telling her to remain silent, to slip away into the woods and save herself. Instead, trembling, her stomach in knots, she shouted, "Help! Help!"

Silence followed. She stared at the spot where Sir Neville had disappeared.

Follow the path. Please follow the path.

After a moment, Sir Neville reappeared, hurrying through the trees, headed along the path. After her.

Adrian and Edmund rode at a gallop as far as the horses could take it. Adrian's side ached from the pistol jostling inside his coat, and his fingers were sore from gripping the reins too tightly.

They were forced to stop in Stanbury. Adrian paced in front of the inn as they waited for fresh horses to be brought around.

Sir Neville had left hours before, and with a bit of luck he might have found Miss Howe's home in little time—

"He might have stopped to switch horses. And he must have been delayed trying to learn where Miss Howe lived." Edmund spoke quietly, apparently thinking the same thing. "He likely does not even know her new name. He may yet be searching for the house."

"He knows to search for Anna." Adrian said. "She would

have likely drawn attention. A young lady riding alone in the countryside in a hired hack? A few questions would be all it would take."

"They might have left Miss Howe's. They might have—"

"Enough," Adrian said. He knew Edmund meant well, but nothing he could say would do any good. Not until Anna was safe with him.

Sir Neville had ruined his own ward. He'd lied and let an innocent man take the blame to hide his crime. Adrian thought of the steeliness that shone in Sir Neville's eyes, and the cold, calculated way he'd manipulated him and Edmund.

And the way he'd seemed so honorable, refusing to elope with Madeline, looked entirely different now. Anna had made it clear that she'd never marry him, so he'd turned his charms to Madeline. Sir Neville knew Madeline was an heiress, and after this morning he likely knew she stood to be an even greater one if Anna married first.

Until Sir Neville learned Anna was going to see Julia. There was only one reason for Sir Neville to rush north: to try and stop the truth from coming out.

But how far would he go to protect it? Was he so ruthless as to harm two women, even to protect his reputation?

Adrian looked to Edmund. "Once we reach the crossroad to Easton, you ride to get the constable."

Edmund shook his head. "We'll send a messenger. I'm staying with you."

Adrian hesitated a moment then nodded. "What in damnation is taking so long with the horses?"

Five minutes later they were riding north again, having sent a message to the constable. It seemed an eternity to Adrian before they reached Easton. Adrian knew back roads, shortcuts Sir Neville wasn't likely familiar with, yet all he could think of was how long a head start Sir Neville had. And what could have happened in that time, what could be happening even now.

He loved her.

Anna had given him so much. The care she showed the estate was just the beginning. She'd given him Edmund back. Helped him to see Cecelia as he should have all along. And she'd given him herself, without expecting anything in return. Perhaps, it pained him to admit, without wanting anything in return.

He wouldn't think on that now. He must ensure that she was safe and afterwards... Afterwards he would try and convince her to be his wife.

He gently nudged his horse once more, willing every ounce of strength from the animal. Trees and hedgerows and stone walls raced by in a blur. He forced himself not to imagine the worst should Sir Neville arrive at Julia's first.

Surely he wasn't so ruthless as to harm them?

Though Adrian was loath to accept it, his instincts told him the answer might very well be yes.

As Adrian had feared, Sir Neville had reached Julia's house before they did. A saddled horse, looking like it had been at rest for some time, grazed outside the home. The elderly butler could only tell them that his mistress had gone walking with a female caller, and that soon after a gentleman had also called, asked after them, and said he would join them on their stroll.

Adrian and Edmund started down the path at a run, pausing where footprints marked the soft ground. Two sets were women's boot prints, narrow at the toes, with small square impressions from the heels. A set of larger and wider prints, with a small hole every few feet from a walking stick, overlapped the women's footprints.

Adrian and Edmund ran on, the air growing damper and the path muddier. Suddenly the prints changed, the women's becoming more widely spaced.

"They were running," Adrian said. "They must have seen

Sir Neville coming." His heart lifted.

"They can outrun him," Edmund said. "His leg."

Yes, but for how long?

Just then a gunshot rang out in the distance, from deeper in the woods.

Adrian's throat went dry. He tried not to imagine what could have just happened.

They raced ahead. The path narrowed, brush and leaves slapping at Adrian's face and shoulders as he ran. Every few minutes they paused to listen, but they heard only the sounds of birds.

Adrian realized they now followed only two sets of prints: Sir Neville's and one woman's. Likely Anna's, from the larger size of the boot print.

"They split up," Adrian said, stopping. "You should go back and find the other trail."

"Yes." Edmund nodded and then added, "Be careful, Adrian." He disappeared down the path.

Adrian strode forward again and then abruptly stopped. He was tired of stumbling around in the trees while the devil knew what was happening nearby.

He left the trail and pushed through the brush towards a stand of tall trees. One stood apart from the shorter trees around it, affording a relatively unobstructed view to the north and west. If he climbed it and Sir Neville happened to be looking his way, he'd make an easy target, but it was worth the risk if he could learn what was happening.

He grabbed a thick branch and hoisted himself up. It had been a long time since he'd climbed a tree, and it was more difficult than he remembered. After several scrapes and much shredded bark, he stopped, braced himself on a stout limb, and pushed aside a thick branch to peer out at the woods around him.

Almost immediately, he spotted Sir Neville. He was moving north, his dark hat and coat visible through a stretch of thin trees. He appeared to be alone.

Adrian scanned the landscape ahead of Sir Neville and at first saw nothing. Then, to the northwest, he thought he glimpsed something yellow. Or perhaps he'd only imagined it. A moment later, the yellow reappeared.

Anna's bonnet. Only a few hundred yards from Sir Neville, who appeared to be slowly gaining on her.

Were Adrian to follow the winding trail, even at a run, it might take too long, but if he were to cut northwest through where the woods became marsh, with some luck he might reach Anna first.

On the other hand, the bog would almost certainly slow him down. He decided it was worth the risk.

He leapt from the tree and pushed into the marsh.

His boots were quickly coated with mud. Where the ground was too soft for his weight, the bog sucked at his feet, forcing him to slow. Pools of stagnant water and mire that appeared dangerously deep required him to detour.

When his path was suddenly blocked by a weedy pond stretching hundreds of yards before him, he splashed straight into it, relieved when it never became deeper than his shins. He passed across a stretch of drier land, then came to another stagnant pond. He waded through the foul water, avoiding rotting logs and clutching weeds as he swatted away the dragonflies that lunged at his face.

At the end of the pond he spied a cluster of boulders. The first few that he tried offered limited views to the north, but finally he stood on one and was able to see across the last stretch of mire before the trees took over again. He quickly spotted Sir Neville paused on a hillock. Looking directly back at him.

As the shot rang out, Adrian dove from the boulder. He landed in a thick slog of mud, its stinky weight sucking at his arms and legs, plastering his chin, and oozing into the neck of his shirt. The ball crashed harmlessly into the brush behind him.

At least Anna should be alerted to Sir Neville's location.

And he had one less shot for his pistol. Would he come after him now, rather than Anna? Not likely.

Adrian tried to rise to his hands and knees. The mud was so thick that the ground sunk beneath his limbs.

He had to get to Anna. Now.

He shoved forward, his knees and elbows squishing into the sludge. He strained his neck to keep his mouth free of mud as he labored to reach drier ground.

His left boot was slipping, the muck threatening to pull it off, when his elbows finally met more solid earth. He dragged himself out of the mire, curling his toes to keep from losing his boot.

Stumbling to his feet, he stomped to shove the boot back on. Sir Neville could be practically upon Anna by now. Maybe close enough to get a shot.

He stepped forward and stopped. Like the rest of his clothes, his waistcoat should feel heavier now, with the mud caking it, but it didn't. He patted his side.

His pistol was gone.

He spun around. The tracks in the mud where he'd dragged himself were already filling with water. Nowhere along the vanishing trail was the gleam of metal. He could slosh back in and search for the pistol, but the muck had likely ruined it anyway. Meanwhile, Sir Neville could be closing on Anna.

Cursing, he turned away and hurried north. At least he was well camouflaged now.

Too well, apparently. He scrambled through a thicket and into a small clearing. He ducked as a moss-covered log swung at his face.

Anna stood over him, her blue eyes narrowed, her hands shaking as she prepared to swing the log at him again.

"Anna." He fought to keep his voice a whisper.

Her eyes widened and her mouth fell open. She lowered the log.

She took a step towards him. "You found us—"

He grabbed the log from her, tossed it away, and crushed her into his arms. She felt so strong, so vital and warm, so slender and fragile at the same time. Even now, mud-spattered and perspiring, she smelled good. Felt good. His heart pounded as he let out a long, deep breath.

"You aren't hurt?" he whispered, his mouth pressed against her bonnet.

"No, I—"

"I must take you to safety," he whispered. He released her and she stepped back. Their embrace had left smears of mud on her dress.

"Sir Neville is close," she said softly, gesturing north. "The trail is just over there."

He nodded and whispered, "I am unarmed."

Should he try and draw Sir Neville back through the marsh, where it would be more difficult for him to move and shoot? It might even the odds more, but it could also put them at greater risk. Or should they press ahead to the west and hope to outrun him before he could get a clear shot at them?

He took her hand and she knitted her fingers with his, clutching him tightly. The warm press of her hand energized him, fueling his determination.

He would protect her. No matter what, he would see her safely out of this horror.

The shot came without warning. A bang followed by a rush of air close by and the sharp scent of powder all too familiar to him.

He dragged Anna to the ground, rolling her into the shelter of the trees. He held her close, silently waiting for the sound of approaching footsteps.

There were none.

He brushed a damp leaf from his face and slowly, quietly, lifted himself off her, just enough to peek above the brush and scan for Sir Neville. He kept her sheltered beneath him.

The shot had been close, very close, but fortunately—

He smelled blood. The sharp, coppery scent had become commonplace in his life not long ago but now seemed as strange and startling as if it were the first time he'd ever smelled it.

He touched something sticky and warm on his sleeve.

Had he been hit after all? He felt nothing other than the sting of where the ground had burned him as he fell.

He rose to his knees and glanced down at the dark spatter on his coat. He frowned.

It wasn't his blood.

His gaze flew to Anna. She stared up at him, her face pale, one hand pressed to her side. Beneath her fingers, her yellow dress was rapidly turning dark brown.

CHAPTER TWENTY-EIGHT

"NO," ADRIAN WHISPERED. ALL THE breath left his body. A lump formed in his throat, as if he'd swallowed a stone.

Bushes rustled nearby. He turned to see Sir Neville step into the small clearing, his walking stick gone and his pistol ready.

As Sir Neville limped rapidly towards them, Adrian looked down at Anna. Her arms had fallen to her sides, and her eyes were closed. The dark stain had spread across her stomach and up to the bodice of her gown. Adrian tore off his cravat, bunched it, and pressed the cloth against her wound, willing the blood to stop.

At least she wouldn't have to see what was about to happen.

Adrian lifted his gaze to meet Sir Neville's. "If you let me help her now, she may yet live. It could save your neck."

"My neck is not in danger." Sir Neville stopped several paces away and lowered the barrel at Adrian's head.

"You would think to hide all this?" Somehow, Adrian kept his voice calm. "When so many have seen you here?"

"Seen is one thing," Sir Neville said, "proof quite another." His dark eyes were unblinking, never leaving Adrian, and his hands gripped the pistol without the slightest tremor. "And these bogs have hidden bodies before, no doubt. The land will hold a few more."

Calm, reasoned evil.

Adrian doubted he could antagonize the man into delaying or making a mistake. He was too far away to make a grab for the pistol, and even if he did, a misfire might kill

Anna for certain.

"You will not find Julia," Adrian said quickly. "You cannot conceal what happened."

"Yes, I can. I'll not let that whore, or anyone else, ruin my life. One little mistake shouldn't cost me all I've worked so hard for." Sir Neville's voice was eerily calm. "Now stand up. With her."

Keeping the gun aimed at him, Sir Neville lurched across the edge of clearing. His limp was pronounced, but he still moved quickly. He glanced to the side, checking out the steep slope.

Still pointing the pistol at Adrian, Sir Neville stepped back from the edge. "Move, Lord Wareton," he said impatiently.

Adrian slowly rose, cradling Anna in his arms.

"Over there." Sir Neville jerked his head towards the slope. "Move!"

Adrian moved slowly towards the slope, his eyes on the stagnant pool of water below. If he tried to leap ahead of Sir Neville's shot, the fall might kill Anna. And once at the bottom, there was no cover close enough that they could likely escape Sir Neville's aim anyway. His mind raced through options and found almost nothing; all he could do was try and cover her, making it difficult for Sir Neville to hurt her further. If he did that, perhaps he could buy some time and Edmund might find them—

A branch snapped in the trees across the clearing. Adrian's heart leapt.

Sir Neville spun in the direction of the sound. He drew a second pistol from his waistcoat and pointed it towards the trees, all the while keeping the other gun steadily aimed at Adrian.

A shot came from the woods. Adrian fell to the ground, holding Anna beneath him. He saw Sir Neville dive backward, and heard the ball zing through the trees.

Damn.

Adrian lifted his gaze. Sir Neville bent low as he hurried

into the cover of woods, rustling branches and pounding earth as he vanished. He was smart enough to know his best chance of success was to slink off and shoot from cover—just as he had when he'd first made a name for himself.

Trees rustled on the other side of the clearing. A moment later Edmund appeared, peering out from behind a thick tree trunk. He spotted Adrian, crouched, and dashed across the clearing, following Adrian to the shelter of a cluster of boulders several yards away.

Adrian checked Anna's wound. Thankfully the bleeding seemed to have stopped, but her eyes remained closed and her face ashen.

"How is she?" Edmund whispered.

"She needs a doctor right away." Adrian looked up. "Sir Neville has two pistols," he whispered.

Edmund nodded. "I found Miss Howe and carried her partway back. A servant who heard the gunfire met me and took her to the house."

"Sir Neville will circle around and try to get us," Adrian whispered.

Edmund nodded. He began to reload his pistol, glanced at Adrian, and frowned. "Your gun?"

"The mud took it."

"You must take Anna for help." Edmund rose slightly to peer through the trees. "I shall draw him away, try and get him to empty his gun."

"At this point he'll not likely shoot without a good chance of striking."

"True." Edmund crouched and rechecked his pistol. His fingers trembled.

"I should go after him," Adrian said. "You take Anna to safety." Sir Neville was a skilled marksman, and Adrian was almost certainly a better shot than his brother, no matter what Anna had said of Edmund's practicing.

"No." Edmund brushed back his hair, slick with sweat,

leaving a streak of mud across his forehead. "We shall stay together until we know where he is. Then I will deal with him while you help her."

"No." Even if Edmund were lucky enough to fire a shot at Sir Neville, he could still be killed. Adrian would lose him.

He had to protect his younger brother, as he always had.

"Adrian." It was Anna's voice, barely a whisper. Adrian's gaze snapped to her face. Her eyelids lifted slightly. She slowly raised one hand, just high enough to grasp at his sleeve. "He can shoot rocks off a tree…let him…" Her voice fell to an unintelligible murmur.

Rocks off a tree? She was delirious.

"You've been ordered," Edmund whispered, a nervous smile flashing across his face. "Besides which, I have the gun."

"Edmund…" Adrian shook his head. For Edmund to insist, terrified as he was, was amazing.

Edmund met Adrian's gaze. Despite the tremors in his hand, Edmund's blue eyes shone with determination.

"Ever since I let you take the blame for me," Edmund whispered, "I've barely been able to live with myself for being such a coward…I've realized I've nothing to be proud of. Not like you."

A man needed something…a man needed something or eventually all the drink and rowdiness in the world could no longer hide the emptiness of his soul. Adrian understood that too well. Knew what it was to live in such misery that even love seemed an impossible dream.

But to let Edmund die—

Branches rustled behind Adrian. Edmund dropped to the ground and crawled towards the noise, holding his pistol ready between the rocks. He paused and turned to mouth at Adrian, *Go. Now.*

Anna stirred in his arms. Her eyes opened slightly, and her fingers brushed his sleeve.

Adrian gathered her in his arms and rose. Trying to stay low, and keeping himself curled over her as best he could, he hurried in the opposite direction, into the cover of trees.

After a dozen strides he heard a blast. He staggered, his gait slowing. Behind him it was quiet.

Now Edmund could also be shot.

But Anna needed him.

He couldn't likely save them both.

Anna moaned in his arms. Moving her seemed to have restarted the bleeding; a new, circle of brown was growing on her dress. Yet he had to move her. He had to get her out of here, now.

He pressed his bloodied cravat more tightly against the wound and rushed forward again.

When a moment later a pistol shot cracked the air behind him, he prayed to the heavens it was Edmund firing again. Holding Anna as tightly as he dared without risking hurting her more, he kept running.

CHAPTER TWENTY-NINE

ANNA WAS CERTAIN SHE MUST be dead. Dead, and her sins had brought her to purgatory—if not worse—for when she opened her eyes, Lady Carlton was leaning over her, her weight slanting the bed precariously, the scent of her face powder strong in Anna's nostrils. Most frightening of all, Lady Carlton was smiling at her.

"At last, my dear," Lady Carlton said softly. "We have feared for you so, missed you so." She grasped Anna's hand in her own, pressing tightly.

"I am dead," Anna said hoarsely.

Familiar male laughter came from somewhere beyond Lady Carlton, from past the filmy curtain at the bottom of the bed.

"She thinks herself in hell, Aunt."

His voice.

Adrian moved into view.

He looked awful—unshaven, with deep shadows under his eyes, and his shirt rumpled as if he'd slept a week in it—but he was the most handsome sight she'd ever seen.

Lady Carlton scowled. "Really, Adrian, how can you jest at a time like this?" She rose, still clutching Anna's hand. With the other hand she pulled Adrian forward. "Three days she's been at death's door, and this is your response?" Lady Carlton jammed their hands together. "Sit with her. It is you she called for all this time."

"Get well, my dear," Lady Carlton added. "May I call you Anna now, dearest? We are family, after all. Now I shall go tell Madeline and Cecelia the good news." She paused on her way to the door. "Do not exhaust her," she said, frowning at Adrian. "She may still be in danger. I shall see the doctor is informed that she is awake." Lady Carlton marched out the door, and her steps echoed down the hallway.

Anna quickly released Adrian's hand and looked away from his intense gaze. She touched the sheer curtain hanging at the other side of the bed, and she glanced around the enormous room, strange and so familiar at the same time.

"I am...in my mother's bedroom," she said.

"My aunt insisted." He pulled a chair close to her, sat down, and clasped his hands in his lap. "She said you belonged in the countess's chamber."

She sighed. "She knows of my inheritance."

"I am afraid so." He smiled.

"My own room would be fine." And her own worn, blue counterpane was far softer than the fancy striped satin one bunched around her.

"I doubt you have the strength to win that argument now," he said.

"I have been asleep for how many days?"

"Three." His smile faltered. "Three very long days. Your fever finally broke last night."

"I have been sick?"

"Sick?" He frowned and leaned closer to her. "You were shot. Do you not remember?"

Shot? That explained the strange pain in her side. Through her nightgown, she felt the soft linen of bandages.

"What happened?" She tried to sit up and suddenly remembered everything. "Julia is well? Is everyone well?"

"Lie back." He pushed her gently against the pillows. "Yes, everyone is well, everyone but Sir Neville."

"Is he...?"

"Recovering from his wounds in prison."

"Oh."

"Edmund shot him."

"Did he?" She looked into Adrian's eyes and saw something new there. Pride in his brother. And forgiveness.

"Edmund is reveling in the attention of being a hero." He sighed. "Perhaps a bit too much. I am already weary of it." But there was genuine happiness in his voice.

She smiled. "It was good of you to let him be the hero."

He stared into her eyes. "I am indebted to you, Anna." He spoke her name softly, his tone similar to the one after they'd made love. The memory made her feel suddenly warm.

"For what?" she said quickly.

"For helping my brother. And me. If you hadn't interfered, heaven knows what might have happened." His expression grew even more somber. "I...regret what I said to you before you left." He actually sounded apprehensive.

"I understand why you refused me," he continued. "But I want you to know that I still wish to marry you. And I would wish it even if...we had never been together."

Hope made her pulse quicken. She looked into his eyes, faintly reflecting the square light of the window behind her. Worried eyes that had clearly rested little the past several days.

"And if I must wait until Madeline marries first to make you my wife," he added, "I will. I will wait as long as you wish."

Her throat tightened as her hope evaporated. He would wait as long as she wished? Of course, he would wait, now that he knew of her fortune. And that was undoubtedly why he no longer seemed anxious about marrying her. Now that it was known she was wealthy, while her birth would likely keep her from ever being fully embraced by the ton, she would at least be grudgingly accepted.

"I was pleased to learn the old earl was generous with you," he added. "After how he treated you, it was the least he could do."

"The least he could do? It was a horrid, hateful gift."

She shook her head. "I tried everything to be rid of it. The terms would not allow me to give it away, only invest it, so I choose the riskiest investments possible. But I only kept earning more money!"

He gazed at her as if she were mad. "You *tried* to lose it?"

She sighed. "Do you not understand? Four thousand pounds was perfect, just enough money that a gentleman could afford to marry me if he wished, but not so much that anyone would likely marry me only for the money. But fourteen thousand. That changed everything."

He frowned. "Then why did you not try to marry anyway, with no inheritance?"

"As the money only grew and time passed," she said, "I began to think about how much good could be done with such a fortune. I decided I did want it after all. But...I never imagined Mr. Roland would betray my confidence."

Adrian nodded. "Miss Howe told us. You can be sure that everyone will hear of what he did. He'll not find work again."

"He knew I didn't want anyone to know."

"You didn't wish to end up like your mother," he said quietly.

"Yes."

She looked past him, staring at the green and gold wallpaper. She could even smell the faint scent of her mother's perfume. The bottles still sat on the chestnut dressing table, faithfully dusted these past fourteen years. She turned her gaze back to the bed curtains beside her. The bed she now lay in had been a lonely place for her mother after the first few months of marriage. She had died where Anna lay now.

"I should not have allowed you to be brought to this room," he said, gazing down at her, his brow furrowed. "It was foolish of me—"

"No." She shook her head. "It is all right." She drew herself straighter against the pillows and clasped her hands.

"But I cannot marry you," she said quietly, not meeting his gaze.

The chair creaked as he leaned forward. "Anna, my wanting to marry you has nothing to do with your fortune. Nothing."

She stared at the bedclothes. How she wished to believe him.

She was no martyr, sacrificing her personal happiness solely for the good of the family. A marriage between them would still be looked down upon by society, even with her inheritance, but that was not her reason for denying him. No, it was far more selfish than that. And it was cowardice as well. She feared the misery her own mother had suffered, feared a life of pathetic sorrow where too much of her happiness depended on one man's love and fidelity.

He tried to grasp her hand, but she drew it away, tucking both hands beneath the bedclothes.

"Anna—"

"I'm sorry," she said, fighting to keep her voice from breaking. "I cannot."

"Anna." Madeline burst into the room. Adrian stood to give Madeline the chair but she ignored it, falling onto the bed beside Anna.

Anna forced back tears and tried to compose herself.

"I am not hurting you, am I?" Madeline said. "I am so glad you are awake."

"You are not hurting me." Anna managed to smile. Madeline looked sleepy but happy, her dark curls pulled back in a simple topknot.

"I am so sorry that I ever encouraged you to marry that, that odious man. To think I almost married him myself."

Anna gasped. "You what?"

"Oh." Madeline looked sheepish. She glanced at Adrian. "You did not tell her?"

He shook his head.

"Well, never mind that now," Madeline said, turning

back to her. "But I am sorry, for I learned why you hadn't married all these years."

Adrian stepped away and slipped out the door.

"It wasn't your fault," Anna said.

"Yes, it was." Madeline glanced after Adrian and turned back to her. "Now I understand why…why you behaved as you did at times." Pain shone in her eyes.

"I should have told you long ago," Anna said.

"Yes, you should have." Madeline smiled again. "But I am so pleased you are rich. How delightful. You should hear the way Lady Carlton has been speaking about you now." Madeline lowered her voice. "Horrid woman."

"You've missed so much these past few days," Madeline added. "And the most surprising news of all…" Madeline drew a letter from the pocket of her gown and handed it to Anna.

"What's this?" It was on fine paper, written in an elegant hand.

"An invitation." Madeline shifted on the bed. "Or rather, a promise of an invitation. Read it."

Anna opened the letter, creased as if it had been unfolded and refolded dozens of times already. She sat up higher, and Madeline rearranged the pillows behind her.

"Who is this from?" Anna asked. "I do not recognize the hand."

"Read." Madeline bounced up and down, making the bed tremble.

"Very well."

My dear Lord Wareton,

I am writing to request the honor of hosting a grand fete at Carbridge House in Mayfair during the upcoming season to launch the new Countess of Wareton…

"Carbridge House?" That was Duke of Dulverton's London home. Anna dropped her gaze to the bottom of the page, to the signature.

Jane Dulverton

"What?" Anna sat up straighter. "Lady Stratford married the duke?"

"Eloped with him to Gretna Green. Infuriated his mother and half the family too. Is it not tremendous?"

"But what of Cecelia?"

"She put up a bit of a fuss at first, but in truth I think she's relieved." Madeline smiled. "Lady Carlton ranted about it for a day or two but forgave Lady Stratford—I mean, the duchess—when she sent the letter."

Anna stared at the page a moment longer, shaking her head. Then she began to laugh. She stopped when a sharp pain suddenly shot out from her side and across her stomach.

"The poor duke," Anna said, lying back against the pillows. "I almost feel sorry for him." She handed the letter back to Madeline, who was frowning at her.

"Is that all you have to say?" Madeline said. "Did you not see who the ball is to be for?"

"For Cecelia?"

Madeline scowled. "The Countess of Wareton!"

Anna frowned. "The Countess of Wareton?"

"One would think you were shot in the head, not the side," Madeline said. "She means you, silly."

"Me? Oh… No." Anna dragged the counterpane higher and began pulling at the flounced border.

"Oh yes, you will." Madeline leaned closer. "I know what happened," she whispered, "and you had best marry him. You'd be a fool not to. He's spent the last three nights pacing a rut in the floor for you." Madeline straightened. "And once I am married I will return your inheritance to you, so that need not stop you—"

"You cannot promise that. Besides, it is not that simple."

"What else could possibly keep you from marrying him? I know you love him. Do not pretend you don't."

That was all the more reason why she couldn't marry him. How could she explain to Madeline how scared she was?

Madeline barely recalled when their parents had married each other, and she didn't remember how miserable they were. Madeline was so idealistic and so optimistic about marriage. But no matter what Adrian had said, Anna feared he'd still only be marrying her out of duty, duty made easier by the fortune he now knew she had. Money was no cure for eventual resentment, however; she knew that all too well.

Madeline stood, shaking the letter at her. "You think about how foolish you are being. I am sending him back in."

"No, please, I am tired."

Madeline spun around and marched out the door. A moment later Adrian's heavy footfalls sounded in the hall. The door creaked open, and he filled the doorway with his broad form, his face in shadow.

"Madeline said you asked for me?"

"No." She saw his back go rigid. Guilt washed over her. "Come in," she added softly. She owed him an explanation at least. "Close the door, please."

The door clicked shut and he turned toward her, his hands clasped behind his back.

"I must explain why I cannot marry you," she said.

He stared at her, waiting.

"You said yourself," she continued, "to marry me is to lose a chance at far better connections for you and the family—"

"I was an idiot. Spouting nonsense."

"A match with me will be looked at as unfortunate for you. Even with my inheritance, society will not welcome me—"

"I do not give a damn. And even so, few will dare snub you with the Duchess of Dulverton as an ally."

It was true. He was not making this easy for her. Damn him.

"You might eventually regret such a choice," she said.

"You might grow to resent me—"

"Resent you?" He looked at her as if she were mad. "For what?"

"For lost opportunities. For my birth—"

"The devil I would. What do I care who your father was?" He strode to the side of the bed and gazed down at her. "Who is better for Wareton than the woman who has been her true mistress these past years?"

She shook her head. "You care for the estate as well as I have." Perhaps even better, but she refused to admit that to him. Ever.

"Perhaps," he said, smiling faintly, "but who will save me from myself the next time I am too stubborn to see what is right in front of me?"

"You have saved yourself before—"

"Only partly. I was reformed, but my heart was not healed. I couldn't see what I had done to my own brother, and I couldn't forgive..." He leaned closer and reached out to her.

"Look at me, Anna," he whispered, cradling her cheek with one strong hand. "I want you to be my wife. Not because you are rich, not because I have compromised you, but because the past few days have been, quite frankly, the worst of my entire life. The thought of losing you..."

He took her face in both hands, leaned down, and kissed her tenderly.

Everything he said, the tone of his voice, the softness in his eyes, and the press of his lips told her that her dearest wish had come true and yet... Her distrustful heart still doubted, weighed down by the fear of how more than one hundred thousand pounds could make a man behave.

Adrian kissed her gently, then not so gently. Then he stopped abruptly. Damn it, he was a fool, he might be hurting her.

"I shall say it again," he said. "I ask you to marry me. And if you doubt my reasons, I have a solution."

"A solution?" She gazed up at him, her lips swollen and pink from their kisses. A mix of hope and worry clouded her eyes.

"I said that I'd wait to marry you if that is your wish. And I would, I would wait an eternity if I have to." He could see doubt flicker in her eyes. "But if I had my way, I'd not wait one hour past when you're well enough to ride to the church."

Her eyes widened.

"I understand you don't wish to give up your fortune," he continued, "and the plans you had for it. So my solution is I shall sell Eastgate and give you the funds." Her eyes widened even further. "In the end, it will not be as much as your inheritance, but I shall give you full legal control of it. I can have the papers drawn up before we marry, and then once sold, you can give the money to the Forlorn Females Fund or do whatever you like with it. Whatever it takes for you to know my motives are honest."

"Sell Eastgate?" she whispered. "You would do that?"

"Yes." To hell with Eastgate. Wareton was his real home now, ever since he'd come here and fallen in love with its mistress. For that was who she was, and who she would continue to be if he had anything to say in the matter.

"You would forfeit my inheritance *and* pay me a fortune to marry you now?" she said, her voice cracking.

"Yes," he said.

She flung herself into his arms.

"You will hurt yourself." He tried to pry her away but she clung to him, trembling.

At first, he thought she was crying, but no, it was laughter, her mouth muffled against his chest. He cradled her against him, reveling in her sweet warmth and the softness of her hair against his cheek.

God how he loved her. He would marry her no matter

whose child she was, no matter how little money she had, and no matter what other people thought, just so long as he could hold her like this whenever he wished. She was forever a part of him, of his soul.

She turned her face towards him. "You do love me." She was radiant, her eyes bright. He reached out and touched a lock of her hair, smoothing it back from her eyes.

"Of course I love you," he whispered. "How could I not?" He paused to stare at her a moment. "You will be my wife?"

She nodded, smiling.

"As soon as possible?"

"Yes. I too would gladly forfeit the money rather than wait." She blushed delightfully. "I am happy for Madeline to have it. And I shall not allow you to sell Eastgate either. Not on my account. But…" She entwined her fingers with his. "I would ask you for a much smaller amount of money."

"Anything you want," he said. "What do you need it for?"

"Well…" She smiled at him, her eyes sparkling. "There are some updates to Wareton that I've wanted to arrange for."

He laughed. "Of course there are." He realized again one of the many reasons he loved her—her practical nature.

He drew her closer, until her lips were inches from his. "And were you going to share these plans with me ahead of time?"

"Not at all," she whispered.

And her difficult nature as well. He smiled and began kissing her.

He'd desire her no other way.

ABOUT THE AUTHOR

Elizabeth Rue lives in Massachusetts with her high school sweetheart husband and two children. She was a finalist in Romance Writers of America Golden Heart® Contest in 2016 and 2017. *Undone by the Earl* is her debut novel.

www.elizabethrue.com

CPSIA information can be obtained
at www.ICGtesting.com
Printed in the USA
BVHW031203061020
590417BV00001B/44